A NOVEL

DARLENE: A NOVEL
ISBN 978-1-989559-26-0

First Edition. December 2020

Written by J.T. Marsh
Published by J.T. Marsh

This novel is dedicated to victims of domestic

violence and abuse

Chapter One

1

When Darlene Bernier told her husband Marcel she was leaving him, he threatened to kill himself. He said she was making a mistake, and he accused her of having been brainwashed by 'lesbian feminists' and by 'cruel bitches.' After all she'd been through over the last fifteen years, it seemed to her as though this was the last moment she'd have to finally break free. But at the time, in the darkness of the night, she felt so alone, so afraid. Her hands quivered and her heart slammed at a rapid pace. Darlene didn't know it, couldn't know it, but in the darkness of the night there was something stalking her, something unseen but acutely felt there along with what she could see, something unfelt along with what she could feel. "I don't care what you're going to say about it," she said, firmly but awkwardly standing her ground. "You can't do this to me," he said, "and you can't do this to us." This she ignored, and kept on calmly—as calmly as she could—laying out her case, what she planned to do, even still caught up in the act.

"You're destroying our life," he said, "you're destroying our children. How can you do this?" At that moment, Darlene felt as though something was coming, that Marcel might call over his brother to make her change her mind. This wasn't something she'd considered lightly, but had taken to considering, in fits and spurts, whenever spare moments had presented themselves over the past

.T. Marsh

several months. The decision to go ahead and finally leave her husband of more than ten years had, itself, come about only recently, very recently, as if she couldn't remember even the very moment that it'd come to her but only the general sensibility that it must've been recently. Actually, it didn't matter. None of that mattered. All that mattered to her at that very moment, as she faced down the monster that her husband had become, was escaping with her life and the lives of her children, the three sons she'd had with her soon to be ex-husband.

"You're going to kill me if you do this," he said. "All I'm doing is leaving you," she said. "If you do that I'll die," he said, "we'll all die. You're killing our family." But she knew this had already happened over the past fifteen years. The house's inner spaces, the halls and the bedrooms and the foyer all seemed to Darlene so much more cavernous and threatening, ominous, full of an awful presence, the same awful presence Darlene had come to imagine filling every aspect of her life. Although Darlene had hoped she'd have been able to spend the night at their home before leaving in the morning, to have broken the news to Marcel that she was leaving him from the safety of a motel room an hour or two away, it wasn't to have been. "I can't stay here," she'd said, "I'm, I'm leaving you, and I'm taking the boys with m-me."

Even as she'd spoken, she saw and felt things she'd never have thought she'd have seen or felt, things that were impossible, things that were unreal. There was more yelling, more screaming, more threatening of this and that. As had become his habit, he threatened only to harm himself, never her, even as he towered over her and seemed to turn into the snarling, sniveling monster he'd so often taken to becoming. "You can't do this," he said, "you can't do this to me."

But Marcel's insistence, far from intimidating her into surrender, only stiffened her resolve. "It's done," she said. "After everything I've done for you," he said, "you're killing me. You're going to kill me. And you're going to kill our sons. They're going to die because of you." But Darlene didn't, couldn't take this threat seriously, fearful as she was rather of something happening, anything at all that could cause the deaths of her three sons and then herself. She didn't think he would kill them or her, not deliberately, but rather that he might do something that could kill any or all of them; she was still rationalizing, still justifying, still excusing the terror imposed on her by her husband, by the father of her children, by the deranged illness that caused him to believe he was something that he wasn't, to act as though he was something other than what he was.

When she went to leave with their three young sons, he stood in the door. "You're not going anywhere," he said, seeming to growl, a throaty, rumbling growl that suddenly make him look much taller than he was. He towered over her, his lanky figure more ominous and threatening, as if he'd been possessed by some inanimate force. His eyes burned, their whites straining red, the blueness of their irises disappeared into an awful blackness. It was as though his teeth, his teeth had stained some kind of translucent yellow, slick as they were with drool that flung from his lips with every word he hurled at her. And then there was the breath, the foul-smelling breath, the sharp stench of booze mixed with the noxious odour of the perfume he'd used. It was dark, too dark, and in the darkness of the middle of the night it seemed to Darlene as though any hope she'd had of quickly and quietly escaping into the night had been dashed, in the time it'd taken Marcel to put his arm in front of her and block the way forward her hopes for a relatively quick and easy exit thrown. She wouldn't call the police; she knew full well she couldn't call the police, because the police would do nothing to help her, could do nothing to help her. As she'd been taught by so many years of painful experience, she was in this all by herself. Although she could've escaped at any of a number of earlier occasions, it'd taken this long for her to turn against, to rise against the evil that'd come to seize her family in its grips. Even then, should she have paused the moment and looked down on herself, her husband, and her two young sons, she might've seen a woman paralyzed, frightened, yet determined to free herself at last from a relentless terror and horror she'd been living under for nearly twenty years.

But it was the dress, the dress that'd come to frighten her most of all. This was the first time he'd worn the dress in front of the boys. The significance of this, even in the heat of the moment, wasn't lost on Darlene. Whether she made it out of their home that night seemed a foregone conclusion, with only the screaming and the shouting and the banging against walls to be worked through like any other crisis, like any of the many other crises that'd emerged, that were yet to emerge throughout her life. Darlene was so small, so thin and short, her slender figure contrasted so markedly against the hulking mass of Marcel's masculine body. He seemed to sway slightly, even in the briefest of moments seeming to Darlene to be someone other than who he was. His grip on the doorframe seemed to tighten and loosen in time with the throbbing of veins against his forehead, his whole face coloured an almost beet red. But she stood her ground. There was something inside her that compelled her to stand her ground, for the brief moment that she needed to some unknown reserve of strength to survive. Even still there was that familiar wick of fear licking up from somewhere inside her, a kind of waking paralysis that'd seized her long ago and wouldn't give her up without a fight.

What'd begun as a small part of her life, of her husband's life had years earlier begun to totally take over either and increasingly come to blur the line between both. It was as though Darlene was becoming erased, as though she was ceasing to exist. She'd felt this way for years, but'd only recently begun to realize the ability to do anything about it, to avert her own demise at the hands of the ogre of a man she'd once fallen in love with. Even then, she'd been a different person, a woman younger and more naïve than the battered and bruised but not broken mother of two she was to have eventually become. As she stumbled through a grave confrontation with her cross-dressing, gender-confused husband, she felt as though she'd

13

already made some mistake, some kind of mistake, the doubt within her welling up even as she'd reached out to do what she believed she should've done a long time before.

But there was more to it than that, as there'd always been more to it than that, as there always must've been more to it than that. A pulse-pounding middle of the night could have no clear ending, no real climax, only a petering out of tensions and emotions. Some time, a few days after breaking the news to her husband, Darlene left, taking her sons with her as she drove away. She left almost everything behind that night, fleeing not to safety but to a kind of hardship a little different but no less difficult than what she'd been through until then. But even this wouldn't happen right away, wouldn't happen so easily, the few days that were to pass before she could leave seeing her emerge from a different kind of hell.

2

A little over fifteen years earlier, Darlene Bernier was still Darlene Thompson, the young, unmarried, recent university graduate living in the city of Vancouver, looking for a life for herself. The city of Vancouver, back around the turn of the century, was a different place than it was to become, after twenty years of sometimes-rapid change. The city was as rainy and morose back then as it'd always been, as it'd always be, only then stuck in an awkward transition from the sleepy, provincial backwater it'd been to the urbane, cosmopolitan global city it was never to have

14

become. The gleaming, glass and steel towers that'd come to be littered here and there, around every neighbourhood, were flanked by older apartment blocks, the stout, squat concrete shells that'd been thrown up in a hurry nearly a century before. After arriving, Darlene found herself alone, but eager to make friends. It was on one night out, one night out at a pub with some of her would-be friends she'd met through work that she found herself unexpectedly having a good time. The bar was something that purported to model itself on an Irish pub, but lacked anything other than a strategically-placed Irish flag and the odd clover-leaf decoration here and there. The beer flowed freely, soon after the conversation following. Darlene was there with a group of five others, two her co-workers, the other two their friends. She thought it was too loud and crowded, not only their table but the whole bar, but she played along anyways, smiling and chatting, making herself seem to the others as though she was genuinely enjoying the moment. She'd been invited to the bar tonight by one of her co-workers. It'd always occurred to her that she could've just declined to go altogether, but she was too good-natured and good-humoured to decline. Although she was single and in her mid-twenties, Darlene would've just as well stayed at home to work her way through a good book. But she was worried, she knew she didn't want to be alone in the world forever. So she went along with it.

The pub was crowded, too crowded, the voices of dozens of customers and staff blending together. At once, it made Darlene acutely uncomfortable, as she sat in her seat with some of her new, would-be friends she unable to keep herself from fidgeting in place a little. It was then that she looked across the pub and saw a young man looking at her, only momentarily, their eyes locked for only the briefest of moments before they both looked away, first she then he averting their eyes. After excusing herself from her group of friends to use the restroom, Darlene felt the man's eyes tracking her across the room. But this, this didn't bother her, instead making her feel a little lighter in her step. After arriving at the bathroom's door, she turned and cast a look back at the young man's spot, finding him still there, looking no longer at her but paying attention to someone else in the bar. Actually, this made her feel a little disappointed, as she entered the bathroom and stood in line the thought occurring to her that she might've missed one opportunity or another. But the music played loud and long in the bar, bleeding into the bathroom, the sound of dozens of voices lingering too. Darlene had never been much of a bar-hopper or partier when she was younger, and sometimes being surrounded by so many people made her uncomfortable, as if she could've seized up at any moment and spent the night staring off into space while avoiding all conversation. Her limited experience taught her her that this would only further isolate her, and her goal in having moved to a strange city was to make friends and be happy.

But loneliness wasn't young Darlene's only problem. The part of the city she lived in had long been a working class neighbourhood, filled with mostly white Canadians who worked in the shipyards and mills, on the docks that loaded and unloaded container ships and the warehouses they sent their containers to. This wasn't the case anymore, and hadn't been for twenty or thirty years, nearly all of the Canadian workers displaced by waves of new immigrants from Asia, first China and then India. Darlene wasn't like them, not exactly, as she'd come to Vancouver to work as a medical stenographer, having recently graduated from nursing school at the University of British Columbia. She'd taken a job with the Vancouver Coastal Health authority, to work as a psychiatric nurse at the city's main general purpose hospital, Vancouver General. Having studied nursing through university, this was her chosen profession, the chance to work in one of the province's biggest and busiest hospitals a draw to her. Her first few shifts at the hospital came and went without incident; although psychiatric nursing was difficult, it wasn't as though every single shift saw pain and suffering. Even still, over the years she was to work at Vancouver General Hospital she'd have to abandon all her preconceived notions of nursing, only to have those notions snatched away from her seemingly as quickly as she'd learned them. The pain and suffering she saw every shift reminded her of the things she'd seen throughout her life, as far back as she could remember; she wanted to help the people who were like her. It really was that simple. Despite all she'd been through in the first twenty years of her life, she was still so naïve as to cling to these notions, notions she wouldn't become disabused of until much, much later.

After leaving the pub's restroom, Darlene didn't head back for her group of friends right away, instead heading for the bar. At the time, she didn't really know what she was doing, so young as she was that her limited experience offered her no real help. "Haven't seen you around here before," he said. "I'm new in town," she said, casually leaning back against the bar. "Maybe I can show you around sometime," he said. "Maybe you can," she said. "My name's Marcel," he said. She told him her name. They got to talking. After she was about finished the drink she ordered, Marcel turned to the bar and ordered her another, then another, then another. She was soon drunk, the bar slurring into a warm haze. But she wasn't so drunk as to lose control of her own faculties, only enough for her inhibitions to have fallen a little bit, then a little more, her ability to focus on things other than the thing right in front of her gone. Marcel, already a tall and handsome young man, suddenly seemed to her like the most charming and attractive man she'd ever met. And so it was that they kept on chatting, kept on flirting, at the bar, at the pool table, until it seemed as though the good times that night and in her life would never end. She felt charmed by him; she found herself laughing and nervously fidgeting with her drink, her hair a little bit, nervously but confidently. "I don't even know what I'm doing here," she said at one point, after finishing one drink but before ordering another. "A beautiful woman like this has every place to be here," he said, smiling before taking a drink of his own. She couldn't help but giggle nervously on hearing this. She looked away and blushed slightly, blushed slightly above her cheeks already-reddened from the drinking.

The neighbourhood Darlene had come to live in, it was dominated by short, squat, grey and white apartment blocks, the kind thrown up in the middle of the twentieth century at minimal cost, probably never designed to last as long as they had been made to. On her first night living in the new apartment, she heard people shouting in the unit over, occasionally their shouting interspersed with banging and crashing of one thing or another. She hadn't asked much about the building or the neighbourhood when looking at the unit, her viewing conducted by the building's manager, a gruff, grey-haired man with liver spots under his eyes and who stood and walked with his back hunched over. Even still, she'd taken the apartment out of expediency; she needed a place to live after moving out of student housing, and fast. This was one of the many decisions made in haste that was to have consequences she'd only realize later, after lengthy reflection. It was a small apartment, too small for any more than a single person to have lived in. Yet, the building was full of identical apartments occupied by elderly couples, single mothers, even the occasional university student determined to return to school and complete a degree if not this fall then surely the next. Living in that building Darlene never really felt at home, but neither did she feel like a stranger. She'd never get to know anyone else living in that building, except to learn the little moments here and there when people could be heard fighting, when glass could be heard breaking, when moans and gasps of those

19

who could be heard fucking even into the early morning and late into the mid-afternoon. But none of this bothered Darlene. She slept through the nights all the same, never minding the noise or the smells, the smell of marijuana that sometimes wafted in through her bedroom's open window, a window that had to be left open through the summer or she she'd have overheated in an apartment without air conditioning.

At the pub that night, Darlene was soon drunk enough to find him the most attractive man she'd ever seen. But she was still in control of her faculties, or so she thought, able to stand and walk, just a lot chattier and friendlier than anyone had seen her. "What's a place like you doing in a girl like this?" Marcel asked. Although Darlene didn't notice, he was drunk, too, though no more than she was. "I was told there were some men here," she said, giggling as she spoke. She asked, "do you see any men here?" She raised a flat hand above her eyes and made as if to scan the room, looking everywhere but at her new friend. Then, before he could say anything, she laughed. Her friends looked for her, but she didn't see them, not yet. "I like you," he said. "I like me too," she said. He laughed. She laughed. Somehow, he managed to talk her back to his apartment not that first night, not right after they'd met, but after they'd met up a couple more times. She wouldn't have ordinarily wanted to sleep with a young man she'd met at the pub so quickly, having had only one sexual partner in her life before this. They both undressed quickly, him a little quicker, then he laid her back down on his bed while whispering into her ear. He was inside her quicker than she'd expected, causing her to gasp a little, soon the lewd slap of skin against skin filling the bedroom. There was little kissing; she held him as he moved against her, as he moved inside her, the end coming as quickly as it'd started. She felt a little unsatisfied, but enjoyed it anyways, looking forward as she was to the next time, thinking she'd surely enjoy it more.

That first apartment was located in a neighbourhood not unlike the working-class neighbourhoods Darlene had been familiar with growing up. A few nights, maybe a week or two after she moved in, she began to notice men coming and going frequently into the unit on the other side of hers, not the one that hosted the frequent violence but the other. She might've noticed these strange men coming and going earlier if not for her work schedule that kept her out of the apartment four nights a week. That night she noticed because she was up late, at home but unable to sleep. It was raining that night, an early-fall storm having lashed the city with the hardest rainfall in months. She wound up staying up a couple of hours extra, losing herself in the pages of a book she'd been working on for a week. Marcel was to come over not that night but the next, the two of them to watch a movie and have dinner at home. She was a little apprehensive about having him into her apartment. This wasn't because she was afraid of him, but because it was difficult for her to let someone, anyone into her home, into her sanctuary. She'd put aside these apprehensions because she genuinely liked Marcel and wanted to keep on seeing him, wanted to have a real *relationship* with him, something that couldn't be done by nights out to the pub. That first night he was to come over to her place, she'd spent extra time cleaning, making sure there was no dirty laundry in the hamper, that the floors in the kitchen had been scrubbed, even that the dressers in her bedroom had been dusted and the bedspread washed. Still she was nervous, a nervousness that wasn't to let up until he'd come over and sat with her on the living room couch. "I'm glad you made it," she said, after they'd curled up, after she'd nestled her head on his shoulder. "Why wouldn't I have?" he asked, his hand finding hers. "Oh, it's nothing," she said. And he didn't press the matter.

What Darlene didn't know, couldn't have known while she was still just dating Marcel was that even he was consumed in *something*, something he didn't understand or appreciate. While she sat on the living room couch, he went to the washroom, then to the kitchen to get them each a drink. A little while later, after he returned from the kitchen with a couple of glasses of wine, she said to him, "it's nice to have met someone as sweet as you." He paused for a moment, then said, "thank you for that." Even these early dates, sometimes the kind of quiet, intimate dates Darlene would've preferred, it seemed to her as though he was someone other than who he might've been. And then there were the nights out, the nights at the pub, the nights on the town, the nights Darlene would've had some misgivings about but found herself enjoying anyways. Soon she was falling in love with him. Whether it was the sweet nothings he whispered in her ear on their quiet nights in or the wild times he showed her on their nights out, or the little gifts like flowers and stuffed animals he bought for her at random intervals, she felt special when she was with him back then. She didn't know, couldn't have known what was coming as she fell in love with him, but then neither could he. Even then, Marcel was only in the very early stages of becoming the man he was to become. Even then, she wouldn't have known what to do if he'd have shown the deeply disturbed man he was to become over the next ten to fifteen years. Even then, she didn't know, couldn't have known the urges he might've been wrestling with on the inside. It might not've mattered if she had known; she might've still wound up doing all the same things, in all the same places.

Darlene's night at the pub, that first night when they'd met, ended soon after, she taken home by one of her almost-friends. She kept Marcel's number in her phone for a while before mustering the courage to actually call him, without so much alcohol in her Darlene reverting to the shy, mild-mannered young woman she was. That was how they met, that was how they met, but it wasn't to be the real beginning of what was to become their relationship, something Darlene never would've expected. After Darlene had seen Marcel a few more times, that first night they'd slept together saw her still quietly look ahead to what might've come to be. Although their sex hadn't been the soft and sensual lovemaking Darlene would've liked, there was a part of her that felt thrilled in the taboo of becoming introduced to a whole new world. And when he'd finished, he collapsed in bed to her side, allowing her to turn on her side to face him. They slept that night together, in the morning him getting up and leaving after giving her a goodbye kiss. He winked on his way out the door, as if to suggest to her they'd be seeing each other again soon. If she'd known then what was to come, she wouldn't have seen him again; but then, sometimes you can't tell what someone will become from these early times, when all seemed well. In truth, even Marcel didn't know what he was to become. The thing that'd come to consume them both was there, lingering in the background, about to appear in front of them suddenly. By the time Darlene saw it, it would be too late to save her a lot of pain.

3

It was hard for Darlene, carving out a life for herself, again, after returning to Vancouver and finding it completely different from when she'd left. It wasn't only that the city had become dramatically more expensive even in those ten years, although that was enough to cause her much stress. Some of the same steel and glass towers thrust at the sky, only to have been surrounded by clusters of yet more steel and glass, some newly-built, some still under construction when she arrived. After having left Marcel without a job waiting for her in Vancouver, she had practically nothing. She looked for an apartment in the same neighbourhood as the one she'd lived in when she lived in the city the first time, and found rents much higher than they'd been. Of course, she needed two bedrooms at least, having taken her three sons with her. All this passed, though, seemingly in a fully-visible blur, Darlene managing to find a place barely big enough for the three of them, a small place in a bad neighbourhood with cigarette butts and beer bottles strewn across the sidewalks and weeds sprouting between fractures along the roads. Actually, it was a lot poorer than she'd remembered this part of the city when last she'd lived there. In between blocks of ordinary, squat apartment blocks that'd been there for decades were brand new towers of glass and steel, the former rented to capacity, the latter almost completely unoccupied. All Darlene could think to do, all she could do was try to make it work in the few spare moments that presented themselves, however rare those spare moments were. Even as she moved herself and her two young sons into that little apartment somewhere on the city's east side, she focused her energies only on surviving the imminent crisis, still fresh in her mind were the recent extreme hardships.

A few years after moving back to Vancouver, all seemed well, at least as well as Darlene could've expected or hoped for. After some difficulty, she'd found work as a registered psychiatric nurse again, only at St. Paul's hospital in downtown Vancouver rather than Vancouver General Hospital further from the city centre. St. Paul's was one of a network of hospitals run by Providence Health Care, a Catholic health provider and one of the only such hospitals in British Columbia. Although Darlene wasn't Catholic, and hadn't been at any point in her life, they required nothing but good work and good workers, offering salaries that weren't really enough to afford a decent life for a single mother with two boys but better than the poverty she'd lived through as a child. Charity wasn't the easiest way to live; if Darlene had a daughter at any point in her life, she'd have named her Charity. From her first day at St. Paul's hospital, she found the staff there kind and patient, the patients challenging and diverse. Those admitted to inpatient psychiatry tended to be those who were either completely destitute or otherwise on the street, those who had strained or non-existent relationships with families. Even Darlene had to put on the mask of the dispassionate professional when tending to patients, although sometimes she felt sympathetic to their difficulties. She realized psychiatry wasn't like many other medical professions, in that every case was unique and there were no magic bullets, no easy solutions to complex problems that never manifested in front of her and the other nurses and doctors until someone had come from a very long and winding path through to the crisis point.

Although Darlene would've liked to have known some of the patients a little better, this was impossible. Most of the patients spent a few days, at most, on the ward, preventing her from getting to know any of them, furthering her isolation. Many of her fellow nurses were older, and came across as rather jaded if not uncommitted to their jobs. This became abundantly clear to Darlene as the months turned into years. Even as she dispensed medication, supervised patients, and tended to crises in the inpatient psychiatry ward at

Darlene

St. Paul's, there were always those moments when she felt, herself, only one bad day or one angry patient from a breakdown. Marcel, her now-estranged husband, continued to harass her, principally through the internet but also through phone calls. The latter frequently came in the middle of the night, calls sometimes to her cell phone directly, calls that came sometimes from blocked numbers, calls that amounted to little more than him repeating the same slurs over and over again. Even after she'd made the decision to strike out on her own, still her estranged husband had seemingly determined to keep an iron grip on her, to insert himself into her life through whatever means necessary. It all seemed too much for even Darlene to handle, sometimes. This was how, one day, she collapsed in the middle of the psychiatric ward at St. Paul's hospital, even in the middle of her shift collapsing at only the slightest provocation. It came so suddenly, after she'd thought herself toughened against crisis, toughened by so many years of relentless experience.

Then, some time passed, a few years. She and Marcel divorced. They divorced only after they'd separated, and their divorce had been less than amicable. After Darlene had finally reconnected with her best friend, Cherise, the two of them had taken to meeting for coffee every now and then. When they met up, shortly before events in Darlene's life were about to take another turn, it wasn't anywhere else but at Darlene's home for coffee. Both her sons had moved out by this time, and Darlene had begun to feel lonely. She and Cherise had known each other nearly as long as

Darlene had known Marcel, but hadn't always been in each other's lives throughout that time. This wasn't either of their choosing, though. There was a little bit of lingering resentment between them, hidden behind so many smiles. But then it was gone, as soon as it'd appeared. "How have you been?" Cherise asked. It was the same question she asked almost every time they'd seen each other, almost every time they'd spoken on the phone since Darlene had returned to Vancouver. "As well as could be expected," said Darlene, giving the same answer she'd given almost every time she'd been asked. But Cherise seemed to know better. "Are you sure?" asked Darlene's friend. But Darlene only took a sip of coffee and then shrugged slightly. There was no resentment between them, none at all, only a quiet but not entirely unspoken understanding between them. Cherise had been frustrated at her inability overcome her own loneliness; Darlene knew this but wouldn't say anything about it, having come to rely on Cherise in more ways than one.

"How have the boys been?" asked Cherise. Although she worried about how things might've looked generally, Cherise was one of her oldest friends, someone she could rely on to keep her confidence. "The same as always," Darlene said, "Stuart's on the straight and narrow, but Stephen…" She let her voice trail off, before changing the subject. Even the city itself seemed to have changed so much, not only in the years that Darlene had been away but in the few months she'd been back. For her part, Darlene never knew what influence their father's habits had had on them. She worried, from time to time, that they might grow up to imitate his habits. But even this, by this time, had manifested to be not entirely true, Darlene having watched as her oldest son had grown up, had made it through high school, on to employment, and somewhere in there having enrolled in a technical school, all the while stumbling from one dysfunctional relationship to the next. All through this time Darlene had tried to offer guidance, only managing to steady her own course and providing a good example for her oldest son, as well as a place to come home to whenever he had it particularly rough. Darlene liked to spend time with her friend Cherise because she never had to conceal from Cherise any of her wounds or insecurities, things she never could've brought herself to bare even to her own family. "I like the coffee here," said Darlene. "It's not the worst coffee in the world," said Cherise, pausing to take a sip. Darlene had always taken her coffee black, while Cherise put in sugar and cream. "It's been so long since we've been able to talk like this," said Darlene, for the moment managing to let herself relax just a bit.

"It's not all that good," said Cherise, "my parents aren't doing so well, and Chuck, well, Chuck's in the distance." She was referring latterly to her brother, with whom she'd had a strained relationship over the years. "You've still got a good friendship with him," said Darlene. She tried to divert the conversation and her thoughts to another topic besides her own sons, but couldn't think of anything else. "Yes," said Cherise, "until he moved to Winnipeg." Darlene said, "not a lot of people move *to* Winnipeg," before the two of them shared a nervous laugh. "I'm glad we still get together," said Cherise. "Me too," said Darlene. But when Darlene had struck out on her own with both sons, she thought she had a chance to turn them both in the right direction. She came to believe that if she could help her oldest son have something resembling a normal, healthy social life, then he'd be fine. Over the years, he took in with a group of friends that spent a lot of time at her apartment after school, taking advantage of the twelve-hour shifts that kept her away from home and left him mostly unsupervised. The younger son was still too young to really process what was going on, Darlene thought, leaving only the older, Stephen, to pose a significant *risk*. They were both *at risk*, she knew, but she had a lot less road ahead of Stephen to make good on her efforts. It was hard for Darlene to imagine just how wrong she was. "I hope you know what you're doing," said Cherise, the last thing she said to Darlene before leaving after their coffee was over. "Me too," said Darlene, "me too."

But after she called him one Saturday afternoon, suddenly the truth behind his behaviour was made clear to her. "It's good to hear from you," she said, "I've been missing you." But he wouldn't take it. "I've got something to tell you," he said, "something important." His voice seemed almost to be cracking and creaking like that of an uncertain and awkward teenager as he spoke. "Whatever you have to say, I'll always love you," she said, trying to reassure herself as much as her oldest son. But then it came. He declared himself to be a woman. What followed was a lengthy conversation, one-sided and angry, ending only when her oldest son hung up on her. In the time it'd taken for that phone call to begin and end, everything had changed. Seemingly so soon after she'd put her life back together again, arduously and painfully, it'd been upended, a single phone call all that it took to bring about crisis again. There were a sequence of events that took place between her arrival back in Vancouver with her two young sons and her oldest son turning on her, a sequence of events that even Darlene couldn't quite understand.

Chapter Two

2

This is a story about woman who would wind up falling in love with a man, a man who dressed in miniskirts and fuck-me pumps, in cheap lingerie and women's wigs, as part of a deranged sexual desire to force his wife to act out every degenerate fantasy that crossed his mind. A few weeks had passed since Darlene and Marcel met for the first time in that pub, and they began dating. At first, Darlene was smitten with Marcel, their relationship progressing rapidly enough that she thought she'd found a sweet and sensitive man, yet one masculine and strong. As they were both in their twenties, their dates amounted to more nights out at bars, even to nightclubs, as well as not-infrequent outings with other couples to barbeques, beach days, and dinner parties, among other things. All this was sometimes too much for Darlene, leading to her preferring to spend many weekend nights curled up on the couch with a good book and a glass of wine, sometimes a lit cigarette dangling from her lips if she read outside on a lazy summer evening. But then she'd hear from Marcel, interrupting her moments of tranquility. It'd be hard even for Darlene herself to explain just why she persisted in her relationship, in dating and then moving in with Marcel while the dark side of him presented itself in early moments, in early occasions. It wasn't as though Darlene was a passive victim, reacting, only reacting to the things that were done to her or around her; no, she actively pursued the course of action to which she found herself committed, stepping down a path fully conscious of where it might've led her. Even still, sometimes she'd spend those lazy summer weekend nights reading, sipping wine, and smoking a cigarette, pausing only every now and then to think about Marcel, about the man who would come to be much more. Although she had so many things on her mind, so many different things that couldn't have made anything seem like the man she'd eventually come to see him for.

The first time she saw him in a wig and skirt, it took her by surprise. It was in the apartment they shared together, not the night after they'd moved in with each other but a few weeks later. She'd come home from work after a lengthy shift at Vancouver General; he'd been home from his office job for some time. "I wasn't expecting you home so soon," he said, looking her over as she walked in through their apartment's front door. "I'm home at the same time I always come home," she said, unsure what else to say. She stood in their apartment's little foyer, looking down the main room, still holding her keys and bag as he looked right back. There was a wry little smile on his face, and his eyes were thin slits. He'd planned this. He'd planned this. But something else struck her just the wrong way. "I'll go change then," he said, before turning and heading into the bedroom, shutting the door only halfway. She took a step into the apartment, out of the foyer, and found herself standing in a spot where she could look through the half-way open, half-way shut bedroom door. She watched as Marcel stood in the bedroom, in front of the large mirror on top of the dresser, as he took off the wig and the dress, seeming to slowly slink out of the dress, shaking his hips slightly all the while. It all seemed so odd to Darlene, so odd that she couldn't have known what to do next. After Marcel had changed out of the wig and dress, he emerged from the bedroom, with Darlene still carrying the grocery bags she'd brought into the apartment. A little later in the evening, Marcel seemed more open to talking about it, and they sat down on the living room couch to do just that. Darlene was shocked by what she saw, but she was also in love. Even though Darlene was in her mid-twenties, she fell under the influence of a feeling that would lead her stray. Following that night, Marcel wouldn't dress in women's clothes for some time, a few months at least, reverting to the attentive and caring lover he'd proven himself to be so early in their relationship.

But nothing seemed right from then on. A few nights after Darlene saw Marcel in a dress and wig for the first time, they sat down to talk about it. Actually, he seemed suspiciously eager to talk about it with her, like he'd meant to do so for a while but had chosen not to. She'd thought having seen Marcel in a dress and wig would've been not the beginning but the end of something strange, but there was something inside her that strangely compelled her to listen on. He began to relate a story about a particular incident from his youth, when he was only eight years old and had tried to run away from home. He left home in the middle of the day, he said, and made it a few blocks before coming across a house with linens and things hung out to dry in the backyard. "When I saw the women's panties on the line," he said, "something changed. It was like I was turned on to a part of me I never knew about but it was always there." Darlene and Marcel sat at their little apartment's kitchen table, each of them nursing cups of coffee as they spoke. Some of the books she'd been reading were scattered here and there, a small pile always on top of the kitchen table, there to be between them as they spoke. By the time she worked up the courage to tell someone about what she'd seen, more than a month had passed, and she'd already come to terms with what she'd seen in Marcel that night. But this was only the beginning. Despite Darlene's misgivings, she was willing to see another side, another good side to the sweet and sensitive young man she'd fallen in love with.

Marcel grew up in the Saguenay region of Quebec, not far from the capital Quebec City. This she'd learned while they were dating, long before they moved in with each other. They'd moved into a new place together as soon as the one year lease on her first apartment in Vancouver had expired. She was eager to get out of that roach and rat infested apartment and into the slightly bigger place she and Marcel would share for the rest of their time in the city. The first night they spent together in their new apartment, Darlene was too exhausted from the move to do anything but collapse into bed. It wasn't that night but a few nights later that they'd have sex for the first time in that new apartment, their sex this time as quick and seemingly perfunctory as it'd been, yet satisfying Marcel more than Darlene. When it was over, Marcel fell asleep almost right away, as he usually did, leaving Darlene to think in the darkness of their bedroom at night. Although she'd thought extensively on the things he'd told her, the things he'd told her about his experiences as a youth dabbling in cross-dressing, she still saw it as only one part of him. She was right, but in ways she couldn't have known. They'd talked a few more times, here and there, each time Marcel disclosing something but seeming only to disclose bits and pieces before turning and asking her to tell him something about her own upbringing, probing her own insecurities. By the time she'd fallen asleep, the night had almost passed, and sunrise was only a couple of hours away. When she woke up, Marcel was already up, making breakfast for her, wearing his woman's wig as he cooked and served her bacon and eggs. "I like cooking," he said, inviting her to pull up a chair at the kitchen table. She was still unsure of the night's revelations. "You don't like it?" he asked. He seemed to pout slightly, yet confused as ever. To placate him, she said, "no, it's delicious," although they both seemed uncomfortable with it. He really wanted to cook, at least then, and she wanted to make him feel good about himself.

But still Darlene saw the good in him, or so she told herself. In fact, these sorts of shocking revelations only deepened her love for him; it seemed to her as though she began to think about him every moment of every day, like she was a teenager on her first crush again. In these early times, when things had seemed so much easier, the possibilities were infinite and the boundaries limitless for Darlene, something she'd later in life come to see as part of the personal foolishness and impetuousness of her youth. She was still determined to become a new person, and becoming a new person meant to young Darlene acceptance. But that night, those few nights later, Darlene and Marcel stopped talking about his early childhood experiences in cross-dressing, instead Marcel seeming intent on instead deepening their relationship by asking her to open up to him. As those early months wore on, she began to feel more comfortable in telling him about the troubles in being raised by a single father, her mother having been in psychiatric care for as long as she could remember. This he seemed particularly interested in, asking about many little details of being raised by her father, by the time she would realize what was really going on it would've proven to be too late.

3

After Darlene's oldest son, Stephen, had declared to her in a phone call that he was really a woman, nothing seemed right. That phone call when he'd declared himself a woman, that phone call she'll always remember with frightful clarity and detail, every last breath, every brief pause, every angry shout and every insulting accusation, it changed everything. "You're to never use my dead name again," Stephen said, "not even when I'm not around. And you have to tell me you believe I'm a woman." She tried to gently express her concerns. She said, "are you sure this is the real you?" But this only enraged him. "If you don't accept who I am, then I'll kill myself," he said. "Don't say that," she said, "You're a vile, manipulative person," he said, "you abused me and belittled me as a child. You wouldn't ever accept who I was. You never could do that. You made me worse than I could be. It's because of you that I can't deal with the reality of who I am or my struggle with gender dysphoria." Even these statements sounded to Darlene as though they were being read from a script, as though they were rehearsed. "This isn't you," she said, "this isn't my son." But this only enraged him still. He proceeded to recount a litany of incidents from his childhood in which he claimed he was abused, if not by her then by teachers, other students at school, even by other members of the community like a police officer or a counselor. He accused her of failing to protect him from virtually everyone in his life, except his father, Marcel, who was spared any accusations. Even though she hadn't been involved in any of these supposed incidents, he declared she was responsible through her failure or through her refusal to protect him. When she meekly protested she'd never heard of any of these incidents, that she'd known him to be a happy-go-lucky child at least until adolescence, he shouted over her again, repeating the same accusations, stinging at Darlene like a whip.

"I don't remember you ever saying you felt you were a girl," she said. But this only enraged him further. "You don't know me," he said, "you never knew me. And you don't own me either. You're just trying to make yourself out to be some kind of angel. You're just a transphobic terf who doesn't know anything about me or anyone else." Darlene began to feel a sadness well up from within her. Almost instantaneously, she began to cry, softly at first, then sobbing into the phone. "Please don't do this," she said. "You're just trying to manipulate me like you've always done," said Stephen. "I'm not," she said, "I'm not. I love—" "You don't love me," he said, "you don't know me at all. I don't love you anymore. You're not even a friend to me." "Please stop this," she said. "If you want to have any kind of relationship with me in the future you're going to have to accept me for who I am," he said, "you have to accept that I'm a woman and you've got a daughter and not a son." He paused for a moment, seemingly to catch his breath. "But it's probably too late for that," he said. There was another pause. "You're such a horrible person," he said, "you make me want to kill myself. I'll have nothing more to do with you." And then he hung up, leaving Darlene clutching the phone, rocking back and forth slightly as she sat on the edge of the couch, still sobbing quietly, hardly able to think, her breaths sharp and shallow, her whole body shaking and shuddering. That night would pass with Darlene mostly continuing to sit on the couch, hardly able to do anything at all, until she finally managed to pull herself up and make her way to her bedroom. She fell into bed, then lay there in her clothes, on top of the sheets. At some point in the evening, she'd get a call from a friend,

from her old friend Cherise. But she didn't answer.
She didn't answer.

All throughout the conversation, Darlene was
struck by the fact that he seemed much angrier
even than she'd seen him at his angriest. "I don't
know what to say," said Darlene. "You have to say
you'll support me," said Stephen. There was a
pause. "You have to say you'll respect me," he said.
After all her oldest son had seemed to have
accomplished over the last few years of his life, all
had come undone. She would learn a lot more
about him, about what he'd been through, about
what he'd come to do over the next few months,
although little of it would mean anything to her
beyond the plain and simple truth that everything
had seemed to have gone wrong again. Her next
few calls to Stephen went ignored, as did her texts.
A little while later, she returned Cherise's call. After
that night had gone through, her friend Cherise
came over in the morning and spent the whole day
with her, affording her a kind of support she'd
never had elsewhere, not during her time living on
the other side of the country with Marcel. It was
during those years when they were apart, apart not
because of the vast distance between them but
because of Marcel's declaration to Darlene that she
should have no contact with Cherise.

The feminine name Stephen had decided on
for himself was Stephanie. Darlene remembered
him at various times in his life asking to be called
different nicknames, from Sonic to Robin, but
never asking to be referred to by a girl's name.
He'd sometimes concoct entire personalities to go
along with these various nicknames, something

which Darlene didn't think anything of at the time; she thought it was normal for children to 'try on' certain roles, treating the young Stephen's trying as like children playing house. But an entire sequence of events in her oldest son's life had led up to this sudden and altogether shocking declaration. Some of the events in this sequence Darlene was familiar with. Others she knew nothing about. As with everything else in life, the prospect of having to fill in the gaps in order to make any sense at all of what was happening. "If you support me then we can have a relationship," said Stephen, on that phone call when she'd found out he'd intended to become a woman. "I'll support you in everything you do," said Darlene, "I always have and I always will." But Stephen bitterly replied, "you haven't always." And Darlene thought about if before saying, "I'm doing that now." She stopped short of acknowledging him as a woman, knowing as she did that was one thing she could never have done. By the time this phone call was through Darlene took more verbal abuse, some of the open insults exactly the kind that she'd once received from her husband, Marcel.

Even through this time, her work at the St. Paul's hospital in downtown Vancouver took up most of her time. There was no relief in having worked there for many years now; the opioid crisis continued to produce new casualties in the form of the dead and dying. Sometimes patients would come to inpatient psychiatry after having been brought into the emergency room in the midst of an overdose, those Darlene saw in inpatient psychiatry a subset of the larger number of patients, the survivors of the dead. And then there were the boozers. Some of those brought in weren't any harder into the booze than Darlene had been at various points in her life, than she remembered being. Even still, when there was one particular woman brought in with injuries not unlike those sustained by Darlene at the hands of her husband, it took Darlene a moment to adjust herself. Suddenly it was later, much later, Darlene having gone through a couple of hours on the ward, conducting her job exactly as she should've but without any recollection of having done so. She'd been in full control of her body the whole time, but had been seemingly transported forward in time, like the kind of hypnosis that sometimes overtakes drivers on long and lonely highways. She completed her shift that night and went home, went home shaken by the sudden realization that she hadn't the slightest clue what to do. She drank that night, enough to dull the pain by immersing herself in the warm haze only drinking could provide. In the morning (she had the following two days off) she woke up to find a series of texts sent to Stephen, sent without reply, sent without any memory of having sent them.

Eventually, she meant to visit her oldest son at the basement suite he lived in, but a drive there and a knock on the door revealed he'd moved out and hadn't left a forwarding address. Uncertain what else to do, she asked her younger son, Stuart, if he knew anything at all about what Stephen had been going through. But Stuart knew nothing. even that was an awkward and uncertain conversation, one which made Darlene feel self-conscious and guilty to not know the answer to these questions, to have to resort to asking her one son about the other. She went through that weekend paralyzed with fear, thinking about where Stephen could've gone, where he could've been, the things he could've been doing to compensate for the hurt he'd been nursing all his life. By the time she'd made it through the weekend and back into work to start the next week, she felt as though she'd accomplished nothing except to drive herself crazier.

It fell to her, to accept that Stephen was to live his own life. She still thought of him as a young man, a troubled young man but still a man. As she'd done many years earlier when adjusting to his father's increasingly bizarre and violent behaviour, she took to drinking, having learned to use alcohol as an escape route. But this time, this time the booze didn't do it. This time, the drinking didn't help her escape.

1

What followed Darlene's decision to take her two young sons and leave Marcel once and for all was a night of terror. Her old friend Cherise still lived in Vancouver, having never left the city in the years Darlene had been away; their friendship picked back up as though they'd never been apart, and became the source of support instantaneously. But what'd happened that night, that night when she'd announced her decision to leave her husband of almost ten years, it'd been something she'd prepared for, the kind of thing someone hopes to try and prepare for but can't, just can't. Even after she'd taken her young sons and struck out on her own, that night, that night seemed to loom large in her memory, keeping her fixated on that moment when Marcel had loomed large over him, his burly figure seeming so much bigger as he stood in her way. The dress he'd worn, Darlene wasn't sure when he'd bought it, only that he'd only taken to wearing it around the house over the last six months before that night. This wasn't the first dress he'd worn, of course. Although Darlene had been careful who to say it around, inwardly she was broken-hearted every time she saw him in some new piece of women's clothing, whether a dress, underwear, jewellery, or even one of the wigs he'd come to have owned. The cost of other things had been so steadily rising, year over year, every year since she'd moved with her husband and two sons out to Quebec from Vancouver, that financial hardship was only one of the reasons to finally make the decision to leave him. "You can't do this to me," he'd said, not only that night but many nights before. "I don't know what you're talking about," she'd said, each time he'd accused her. "You're trying to destroy me," he'd sometimes said, "you're trying to destroy our whole family." But she'd said, "please don't say things like that." These things would always be said in the context of her reluctance to indulge in one sexual fantasy of his or another, even sometimes when she'd agreed but not as quickly or enthusiastically as he'd have liked.

Although Marcel had threatened to commit suicide, Darlene hadn't been moved by this threat.

She'd feared for her own life too many times over the course of the last ten years to take him seriously. But there was more to it than that. He'd threatened to kill himself before, just as he'd worn a dress before, only never in front of the sons. As the benefit of the doubt was something Darlene had never had trouble giving anyone, not even the man who would come to inflict horrendous cruelty and sexual abuse on her. After he'd escalated his deranged and neurotic behaviour to attacking her, it'd seemed there was little left for Darlene to endure. She knew she'd come to be at her wit's end. After having hung by the loosest of threads, it'd seemed to her as though there was nothing left to endure, no further escalation possible in the cruel and violent abuse to which she'd been subject. As the nights had passed and the days had come to grow, Darlene lived in that little house still fearful that Marcel would kill her and her sons. She'd woken up in the morning, every morning, sleeping in until after Marcel had left for work; on the rare occasion that she woke up before him, or less rarely after he'd gotten up but before he'd left for work, she stayed in bed and pretended to be asleep until she heard him leave out the front door, even usually waiting until she heard his car start up and drive away before getting up. Often the boys were up before she was. But that was then, only after her life had worsened over many, many years. "You're planning to turn against me," Marcel had said to her, once, not long before she would end up leaving him. "I'm not planning anything," she said, pleading for mercy even in front of their sons. "I don't believe you," he said. "What can I do to prove it to you?" she asked. But later she'd regret asking that question.

The confrontation with Marcel that night, that night when she'd told him she was going to leave him, it continued even long after it'd ended. The look of her husband, her soon-to-be ex-husband breathing fire had seemed to have slowed time to a crawl. It was as though Darlene had badly miscalculated his response, something she shouldn't have done, something she'd come to firmly believe she shouldn't have done, given the way he'd forcibly raped her not a few days earlier. "You've been brainwashed," he'd said, "by feminists and lesbians and cruel bitches." He sometimes tended to revert back to his native language when angry, and in between insulting her in the most cruel and profane terms imaginable he lapsed into French, using terms Darlene couldn't recognize, speaking so quickly it all blended into a series of snarls. Although she wound up leaving nearly everything behind that night, she wasn't to leave for Vancouver right then as she'd originally planned. The city of Vancouver was entirely unlike the provincial Quebec towns she'd lived in with Marcel and their sons for years. But neither was it any like the city she'd lived in as a young adult. The city had changed in the years she'd been away, true, but not nearly as much as she'd imagined, not nearly as much as she believed it had by the time she was to have returned. But enough of that, for now. "You don't know anything about what you're doing," he said, "you think you know everything but you don't know shit." Then he lapsed into French, swearing at her, calling her all kinds of deeply disturbing things she couldn't understand, not even after having lived for years in the province with him. Every time he'd lapsed into French, every time since that climactic night that'd convinced her finally to leave him, she was shaken by the sudden, instantaneous recollection of that night when he'd forced himself on her.

After he'd blocked her way forward and growled at her, she didn't know what to do. "You're not going anywhere," he'd said, growling, with one large, masculine hand placed on the doorframe. "If you don't move, I'll scream," she said. But even she must've been aware how feeble this sounded. Still he towered over her, his bulk seeming to have darkened. "No one will hear you," he said. It'd only been a few nights earlier that she'd last told him she loved him. Actually, Darlene hadn't planned on leaving Marcel at that exact moment. It was only an impromptu decision, one made in light of a steadily worsening pain. Marcel had a brother, Guy, who Darlene had met before moving with her husband to Quebec but hardly knew at all. The same could've been said about the rest of Marcel's family, who nearly all lived in the Quebec. "Get out of my way," she said, her pulse pounding and her heart lodged in her throat. But Marcel's hand seemed only to tighten, the veins in his arm seeming to harden, as if to pop slightly for all the hate surging through his body. "It's my house," he said, "and neither of us are going to go anywhere." He took a step towards her, causing Darlene to take a step back. At that moment, time seemed to slow to a crawl, each moment passing but permitting Darlene an extended look at every one. It was one of those times when she seemed to leave her own body and then look down on herself, even as that's not what happened at all. "Now you get in here and get on the bed," said Marcel. He reached to grab for her.

The rest of the confrontation that night continued, despite Darlene's best efforts to bring it to a close. She was frightened, yet her resolve was steeled against the moment in a way she'd never expected nor planned for. The darkness of the night left little in the way of doubt. But after Marcel had stood in front of her, blocking her way, she'd relented, turning back into their home's kitchen, unable to think of what to do but certain to do it anyways. In a state of mind where she was thinking yet not thinking at the same time, she reached into a kitchen drawer and pulled out a can of Lysol spray before turning back to face Marcel, raising the can to his face, and spraying him in the eyes. She only managed a second or so of spray before he crumpled back, reeling, clutching his eyes as he fell to the floor. Obstacle removed, Darlene dropped the can and took her sons' hands in hers, leading them out quickly past Marcel, through the front door, and into the front yard. But then, as she was about to back out into the street, a car pulled across the driveway, blocking her. She slammed on the brakes and stopped just in time. As she stopped, a siren blared briefly and red blue lights flashed. From there, there was the sound of doors opening and slamming shut, of voices shouting commands, and of crying, more crying, always crying. Even though the blackness of the night had impressed itself upon the city, upon the little city in which Darlene and her family had come to live, she was fixated on the desperate feeling that'd grown inside her, that'd been growing inside her even since before she'd met the man who would turn out to be her husband. Although Marcel's obsession with the thought of himself as a woman had come to dominate her life and the lives of their two young sons, she hadn't known whether the threats he'd made over the past few years were serious or just melodramatic.

But it wasn't always this way. Darlene's first memory was of her sitting in the back of a car. The car was driven by her mother. It was a Hyundai sedan, coloured inside and out some light brown, tan sort of colour that might've been common at the time. Her mother's name was Marilyn, and she'd stopped the car on the side of the road somewhere in one of Vancouver's suburbs, which one Darlene wouldn't remember. Marilyn was crying, had started crying suddenly, seemingly unprompted, unknown to Darlene prompted by a runaway train of thoughts that'd led Marilyn to a dark place. This was a common memory of Darlene's from her early childhood, that of her mother in tears, each and every time Darlene too young to know what was happening. Even during those earliest years of her life, her father and mother were still together. Her father's name was Wayne. Later in life she could remember from those very early years that her father and mother never, never fought, not even during these early moments when her mother was perpetually on the brink of crisis. But then there were the positive memories, like the whole family on Christmas Day,

Wayne and Marilyn watching as she excitedly tore open presents like any other kid. Even these early memories for Darlene were that odd mix of happy and surreal. Children, children are resilient, capable of adapting to circumstances in their own way, even Darlene as a young child understanding the need to be between her parents, even when they weren't fighting. But as she tried to flee her home, two young sons in the back of her car, she was stopped by the sudden arrival of two cars, from out of those cars emerging people whose figures were cloaked in dark blue clothes that rendered them almost invisible against the darkness of the night. The flashing of lights and the wailing of sirens all blended together, trapping her in the worst moment of her life.

It was the police. They separated Darlene and Marcel, but spoke to her, at first, only in French. They always spoke only French in this part of the province. The police would've found Marcel inside, still in his dress, his wig somewhere on the floor. By the time the night was through, Darlene would leave with the sons, only not heading out of town as she'd originally hoped. That night kept going on and on, seeming to last forever, for Darlene the consequence of so many nights spent unslept, so many arguments left unfinished all coming to a head. By the time this night was through, she'd escape, but wouldn't make it very far. Her escape would come at a cost, a cost she couldn't have predicted but would come to believe she should've. By then, even Marcel would make his own decisions, leaving Darlene to fend for herself.

Chapter Three

2

After Darlene had first seen Marcel in a dress, in that first little apartment they shared in Vancouver, even after he'd confessed to her that first occasion he'd worn women's clothes as a child, there was still one secret she'd had left to tell him. But that was to come later. Eventually she became used to him dressing in women's clothes around the apartment, although he made her promise not to tell anyone. He was still coming to terms with that part of his life, he told her, and he didn't want anyone else to know until he was ready. So early in their relationship it was that Darlene felt it was the least she could do, even though she was unsure what to think about his habit of cross-dressing. Much of her adult life had been spent in the company of more liberal-minded friends, colleagues, and classmates, those who would've purported to accept Marcel's cross-dressing habits. A few of them might've even thought it a sign he wasn't a man, but a 'trans-woman,' a man with the 'gender identity' of a woman. But she never told any of them. As Marcel had asked her to keep his secret, she'd complied. It wasn't something so simple as just opening up and telling someone, not even someone like Marcel, who she was beginning to trust despite all her misgivings. The summer after they'd moved in with each other was unusually hot and humid, and it was followed by an unusually cold and snowy winter, cold and snowy by Vancouver's moderate standards. Although they both worked, they also spent enough time together having fun to reassure Darlene that Marcel was more or less *normal*. She was confused, yes, but also turned on by his displays, in the back of her mind some malformed circuit seemingly completed by the electric touch of his kinks, his habits, or so she thought. By the time she was to have realized what was really going on, that she wasn't attracted to these kinks, it was to have been too late.

Eventually, maybe a few months after he first showed himself wearing a dress in the apartment, she finally broke down and confessed her own secret to him. There wasn't any particular reason for it, nor any particular occasion that precipitated it. They were at home on a Saturday night, a rare night when they both had the night off. (Marcel worked in IT at a local college, and had something resembling a normal, nine-to-five schedule). This is how it happened. "I was abused as a child," she said, "by a man who worked at the daycare I went to." They were both drinking a little, nursing little glasses of vodka and coke. "When I grew up I was so confused," she said, "as a teenager I couldn't ever trust any man, not even my own father." It wasn't true, not exactly, but that didn't matter to her. She paused to reflect on the things she'd said, the things she'd wanted to say. "My father wasn't responsible for it," she said, "he was a good man and a good father. But I couldn't trust any man, not yet. I blamed him in particular for letting it happen to me, even though he never knew anything about it." She paused again, this time to take a drink before looking Marcel right in the eye. "I never told anyone," she said, "until now." He wasn't wearing women's clothes while they spoke. Even this wasn't beyond him, back then. She felt a little relieved from the act of telling him, as though some kind of weight had been lifted from her shoulders, as though she could've walked upright again for the first time in years. She went on to tell him that after she'd come to terms with what'd happened to her, she was able to rely on her father more often than she'd been as a younger teenager. This wasn't all that long ago; around ten years. When he asked where her mother had been through this time, she began to feel the urge to withdraw again, choosing instead to tell him. "She was in psychiatric care a lot of this time," said Darlene, "and when she wasn't, she was living apart from us. She wasn't really in my life at all." And Marcel, Marcel didn't say anything, from Darlene's point of view seeming to choose to say nothing, the silence compelling Darlene to keep on talking, to keep on telling him the most intimate and embarrassing details about her childhood.

He seemed to listen intently, one of the few times in their long and convoluted relationship that he'd done so. He wasn't a good listener, normally. But now he was hanging off her every word. She'd later decide this was only because he was driven by the subconscious compulsion to record her secrets for future use against her, but at the time she only thought it was that he was letting her in, that she was coming to know him intimately. "You don't have to say that," he said, seeming to have momentarily snapped back into reality. "No," she said, "it's true." And for a moment his own lucidity seemed to sharpen, as if by some force of nature

his attention focusing on her. The catharsis that
went along with telling someone, anyone at all
about what she'd gone through, it was unlike
anything she'd ever experienced. It was like a drug,
like a rush of exhilaration flowing through her
veins with every slamming of her heart against her
ribs. Although Marcel hadn't yet taken to his
worst—that wouldn't come until much, much later
in their relationship—she was still surprised by his
acceptance. She'd been drilled into the expectation
that no one, anywhere, at any time, would accept
her for who she was, for what she'd been through,
so to be seemingly proven wrong was an amazing
experience for her. It'd only be later—much, much
later—that he'd use this against her, in ways even
she never could've expected. "You make me feel
like I can talk to you about anything," Darlene said,
although even then she didn't believe it. "You
can," said Marcel, "there are a lot of people you
can't trust with these things, but you can always
trust me." Even he didn't realize what he was
saying, nor did Darlene when she replied, "I'm
lucky to have a guy like you." He nodded and
smiled. She sometimes withdrew into the books
she'd read, not into fantasies romantic or sexual
but stories about people traveling to new places
and new experiences. Even in these early times, she
found herself withdrawing into books as often as
she could, justifying it as she did by assuring herself
that reading was the taking up of an old hobby.

But things quickly turned for Darlene. The
charming young man she'd become so smitten with
changed as his habit of dressing like a woman
became more common, gradually taking over his

life, and hers, too. He said he wore women's clothes to relax, because it helped him in his battle with depression and anxiety. At times, this seemed believable to Darlene, from the way she could see him become someone completely different, someone completely new just by putting on an oversized blond wig or a pair of high heels. They came to an understanding that his experimentation was to be confined to the home, that she wasn't to object too strenuously, for reasons even she didn't understand at the time. While they went through the act of building a life together, there were always those little moments when it seemed to Darlene as though something uncertain was in their future, something uncertain but definitely there. From her upbringing Darlene had fallen in love with the idea of finding someone to build a life with, someone she could have something worth having with. And when she came home to find him dressed as he'd begun to dress at home, she became more confused than upset. This was the critical moment, the time at which she could've extricated herself from what'd come. This was the moment she'd look back on, later, and wonder why she chose not to, why she chose to continue to cling to notions of life and love. Marcel seemed just as confused as she was. "You're the only one who can help me explore myself," he said, one night. Darlene thought he seemed to fully believe it. She didn't know exactly what he meant, but she was still fully in love with him. She said, "I'll do whatever I can to help you." Even then, it seemed to her the right thing to say.

When he first insisted they have sex while he was dressed as a woman, she complained. But he only told her that her own experiments with her sexuality when she was in college meant she should've had no objection. They were in their apartment, late at night, after she'd come home from a lengthy shift at Vancouver General Hospital. She'd come home to find him wearing women's lingerie; not hers, as hers were far too small for his grotesque proportions. "It's late," she said, "and I'm tired." She'd hoped this minimal objection would not raise his anger too much. "Eat your dinner," he said, "and then meet me in the bed." Without waiting for a response, he turned around and walked slowly into the bedroom, leaving her at the kitchen table. By the time she made it into the bedroom, only some minutes later, Marcel was standing at the foot of the bed, and invited her to dress appropriately. He said he wanted her to push him forcibly onto the bed and then slap and punch him while calling him all sorts of lewd and disturbing names. The act would culminate in them switching roles, with him slapping and punching her while calling her the very lewd names he'd wanted to be called. It was the very first time he'd brought these tendencies, these ideas into the bedroom with her, and even she didn't know what to make of it. Neither of them seemed to know what they were doing. She very gently and lightly slapped him at first, while he simultaneously begged her to stop and demanded her to go harder. "Please mistress, punish me," he'd say, only to then say, "no, you're not doing it right, you've got to hit me harder." Darlene would say, "I'm sorry, I'm trying to do what you want." But this would only annoy him, as he stopped her to show her exactly what he wanted. After she'd resumed, hitting him a few more times while he purported to beg for mercy, he suddenly stood and grabbed her, then pushed her to the bed. They'd switched roles; he rapidly entered her and in a matter of moments finished inside her. In the aftermath it was awkward, with both Darlene and Marcel uncertain about what'd happened. She didn't know what to say. He wound up saying, "thank you." Before she replied, he fell asleep.

It was at these early times that she tried to remember the way she'd felt when he'd opened up to her, but in particular when she'd opened up to him. In the end, that night she wound up following Marcel into the bedroom, finding him already in bed, still wearing the lingerie and wig, ready and waiting for her. She wound up doing things that night that she'd never done before, not before she'd met Marcel at least, things that made her deeply uncomfortable with herself. And he knew it, he knew it. Marcel would later apologize for what he'd done, for what he'd asked her to do that night, claiming that it'd made even him feel uncomfortable to ask her to do those things. It was the next day, a Saturday, one they both had off. As she sipped on a cup of coffee, she told him it was fine, that he'd done nothing wrong. She was still in love with him. She still felt the pull of the catharsis from having unburdened some of her most intimate secrets to him. This would last long enough to see her betrayed by her own body. After that first night of roleplay, Darlene wasn't at all comfortable with what'd happened. But she chose to believe that this might've been the limit of his ideas, of his fantasies, that it'd get this bad and no worse. She was wrong. She still loved him, though, and love compromised her judgment and clouded her senses just as it does for anyone else. Still young, Darlene didn't know any better. Still young, Darlene couldn't have known what the future held.

1

But the police who'd arrived that night during Darlene's escape from Marcel wouldn't just let her go. In French, they ordered her out of the car, an order she couldn't understand; she complied after they gestured for her to come out. She began to speak hurriedly and haggardly directing the police to go inside. She spoke in English interspersed with the limited, broken French she'd learned over the past few years, begging for the policemen to let her leave. When they wouldn't or couldn't, she begged them to take her away, so long as they took her young sons as well. The truth was that all those years she'd feared losing her sons to their father if she should leave him, and that it'd be the police— not necessarily the police, but the courts who would have taken them from her. At the minimum, the police would've been there to enforce one court order or another, if she had been so inclined as to dispute them, which would've put her squarely in the firing line, so to speak. Although these facts may not have been true, may not have been facts so much as vaguely powerful and altogether visceral feelings, they were real, very real possibilities, threats that made her reluctant to do what she'd needed to do all along. Now, as she stood in the driveway outside their home in the small Quebec town where they'd come to live, pleading with the police who couldn't understand her to let her go, she felt a rising fear for herself and her two young sons.

The police, she knew then, would've thought their fight just another domestic disturbance, to be smoothed over with a few words and maybe a card handed out for the local mental health authority. They didn't want to be there, they didn't want to become involved in a fight like this, she thought, she would've thought. Yet, she also would've thought the police determined to uphold the law. Had he been drinking then the police might've smelled alcohol on his breath, might've taken the smell of alcohol on his breath as a sign that some small part of what she would've said was true. But this wasn't even possible, the language barrier standing between her and them. At once, she felt a surge of fear, a new surge of fear with every moment that passed, with every agonizingly long moment that scrawled past. As the two policemen on the scene stopped to look at her, to try and say something to her in a language she couldn't understand, a number of thoughts and feelings ran through her mind uncontrollably. Marcel could speak French. Marcel's first language was French. He could talk to the police and say whatever he wanted, whatever he needed to get whatever outcome it was that he wanted. And as soon as the police left, she thought, he might very well have killed her. These facts dominated her thoughts, in the rapid, frenetic way they did, even as the police separated her from her husband and kept her children at her side. Although Darlene's perception was that this all seemed to be happening slowly, very slowly, in fact it'd been only an hour since she'd confronted Marcel, only an hour since she'd bravely confronted him. She might've thought that time in moments like this would've passed quickly, quicker than she could've noticed, but would've been wrong.

The two police first on the scene held Darlene outside, and she saw one of them call for something on their radio. The police officer who called on the radio, saying something in a coded, rapidly-spoken French that she couldn't understand, soon but not soon enough more police arriving in two cars. It was a flurry of activity that seemed to pass quickly, Darlene suddenly surrounded by police. Parked cruisers sat alongside the road, some with their lights still flashing. If Darlene hadn't been so caught up in the terror and the anxiety of the moment, she might've seen some of her neighbours coming out of their houses to look on the scene, to gawk at her and her family like tourists watching monkeys at the zoo. Even Darlene could remember those moments when she was young, when she was a small child, moments not when her parents were fighting but when her mother was in the midst of a breakdown. Her mother, Marilyn, had recently been fired from her job after an outburst. Darlene, still a young child, didn't know them. It wasn't the first job Marilyn had been fired from for similar reasons. What Darlene would remember most about this particular breakdown was the way her mother cried on the phone with Wayne, her father, who shortly arrived and embraced her and her mother at the same time. They went to the nearby Royal Jubilee Hospital, where Marilyn was admitted to inpatient psychiatry. What Darlene would remember most clearly about that day was the way her mother looked at them as she and her father left after her mother's admission, the look on her mother's face of total defeat and sadness, the redness around her eyes and the wetness on her cheeks. But this wasn't the end, wasn't the point beyond which Marilyn would get better. The following intervention in Marilyn's life—and by extension Darlene's life, too—would breed distrust in Darlene for those who would purport to offer her help. But it wasn't so simple as that.

Outside her home in Quebec, the police had arrived, but then they separated her from her sons. This, this was why she never went to the police in the first place, despite the years of steadily escalating abuse and sexual violence. This was why she'd planned her escape to take place in the dead of night. She couldn't have guaranteed getting away without the interference from police officers she couldn't understand who were inclined only to see the night in a particular way, from a particular point of view. It was hard for her to imagine the terror and the anxiety of having been separated from her own sons. She wanted to find them, take them by the hand, and run as far away as she could, as fast as she could, without stopping until there was no one left chasing them, no one around them. In her panicked state, it would've been the only

J.T. Marsh

way to make sure they were safe. There might've been a lot of reasons not to try something like that; the threat of arrest, a threat backed up by all the training, physical strength, and weapons the police had to enforce compliance. But none of those reasons were in Darlene's thoughts at the moment, at the moment only a sheer terror running through her whole body. Even as this scene played out over the course of an hour or two, it seemed to Darlene as though time had stopped. It was like she'd become someone other than who she was, as though someone entirely unlike her had come to be in the place where she'd been all her life. By the time the police went inside, Marcel had taken his women's clothes off and put on a shirt and a pair of shorts. He'd also removed the wig, leaving his short, balding hair. As he hadn't been wearing any makeup that night, he looked, to the police, like a man, like any other boring, middle-aged man. Although Darlene was too wound up, too panicked to think clearly, she must've known what he was telling the police, whether he was telling them things she couldn't understand. The police might've seen nothing more than an ordinary home, with ordinary people living inside, and knew nothing of what'd gone on in that home for the years Darlene and her family had been living there.

Some time passed, not much, maybe an hour or two. The police seemed determined to hold everything and everyone in place, as if to freeze the situation at exactly the moment of terror and anxiety that Darlene had found herself trapped in. The sights and the sounds were overwhelming to her, and she seemed to be in a perpetual state of

64

waking fear. But the whole city's police can't have turned out for a domestic disturbance. After about an hour or two, more police arrived, two officers pulling up in another car. These officers, a middle-aged man and a somewhat younger woman, approached her, the woman beginning to speak to her in English. They were attempting to persuade her to go back inside. It was all going horribly wrong for Darlene, all contrary to the plan she'd come up with but never particularly thought out. She'd determined to flee, somehow, someway, but little else. But then things took a turn for the worse. The policewoman came back to her, approaching her side, and said, "the children might be better staying at home." This caused Darlene's insides to turn ice-cold. She couldn't say anything. She looked nervously past the police, checking the front door, all the while clutching her sons hands tight. "He says you are trying to abduct them," said the policewoman. "No," said Darlene, "no, no, no!" It was all she could think to say. She started crying, the first time that night she cried. But her cries weren't sobs, weren't gasps for air, instead tears running down her cheeks as she struggled to say anything at all. The policewoman seemed to try and console her, sort of. "Are you having trouble in the house?" asked the policewoman. But even the policewoman must've realized the question. "It's just—" Darlene began, before saying, "he's lying!" It took every ounce of strength she had just to push the words across her lips. "Then why are you running?" asked the policewoman.

Finally she broke. "He's going to kill me," she said, "he's going to kill me!" The policewoman seemed unimpressed and unmoved, continuing to speak to Darlene in the same calm, dispassionate, almost bored tone. "Has he threatened to kill you?" asked the policewoman. "No," said Darlene, "but you have to believe me!" Still the policewoman's attitude remained unsympathetic, her voice seeming forced and flat. "What has he done to hurt you?" asked the policewoman. But Darlene couldn't, couldn't even begin to bring herself to describe the unrelenting sexual torture and terror she'd been subject to over the last few years at Marcel's hands. It was impossible to distill the moments of raw terror and agonizing fear into a few things to say to the police. "Do you have anywhere you can go?" asked the policewoman. "Yes," said Darlene, "that's what I was trying to do!"

But it wasn't that simple, as it couldn't have ever been so simple. In the end, it was to be had, that she could've left right away. The police stayed at the house for a little while longer, seeming to make a vague attempt at interviewing Marcel again. She couldn't tell what they were saying, speaking as they were in French. There was some part of her that imagined they were assuring him, that one of the policemen was saying something to the effect of, "we have to tell her we're going to help her," from the way Marcel seemed to have relaxed a little bit, from the way Marcel made no effort to continue the attack on her. In the end, she wasn't to have been forced to remain at home, but neither was she to be allowed to leave, not exactly. While the police tried feebly to coax her back into her own home, Darlene tried just as feebly to keep herself grounded. The night went on.

3

After having escaped her husband Marcel's clutches and fled clear across the country back to Vancouver, her two young sons provided her with the only reason she ever found to keep on living. She hit the bottle around this time, having to keep her drinking low-key enough to be worked in around the twelve-hour shifts, the relentless errands and work around the home, along with the dousing of one crisis or another involving the sons. The drinking she'd taken to as a means of coping with stresses, it never amounted to getting drunk but a slow and steady habit that helped take the edge off just a little bit. There were plenty of situations where she might've been found out, but was always able to escape detection. She wasn't proud of her habit, but relied on it all the same. She never drank at work, nor did she ever work under the influence of alcohol. Even as these were these the things she said to herself to rationalize her own behaviour, she'd come to rely on these behaviours to get through the day. Sometimes, sometimes she'd get yelled at by patients, or by family and friends of patients on the ward. But even during these times, she tried, she tried her best to work through each day, making it home late at night and getting out of bed early in the morning, yet always seeming stuck in place, never moving forward. It didn't bode well for the future, she thought, that throughout this time she could've hardly lived without a drink in the fridge at home, waiting for her to come home, but neither did she know how to do anything else, neither did she know how to reach out for and kind of help. Every time she thought to do so, there was something that inevitably happened, some new crisis emerged. Her life was a series of crises.

After leaving Quebec for Vancouver, Darlene eventually filed for divorce, unwilling or unable as she was to prove the most serious abuse Marcel had inflicted on her during their years together. During those early years back in Vancouver, Darlene thought the best way to help her oldest son was to ensure he had an active social life. This seemed easy enough, when he formed a group of friends in middle school, the six or seven of them frequently hanging out at Darlene's after school whenever she was working. She was happy that he'd found friends, although she didn't know any of them, and suspected at least some of them might've been no good. It didn't matter. It was a confusing and disjointed time for Darlene, when a good day was one where she avoided having some recollection of all things she'd been through. These times, these times when Darlene felt as though her grip on independence was hanging by the most tenuous of grips, they seemed at the time to her like a dream, passing so quickly yet stretched out over a long time. It'd seemed to Darlene, though she never could've put it as such, that this condition had emerged out of nowhere, like a light being flicked on in the middle of the darkest night. She wasn't able even to think about looking for work, not right away, relying instead on the help of others as well as the available balance on her credit cards. She found temporary work at a few private nursing homes; the pay was lousy, but it served her for a few months until she was able to get a proper nursing job at the St. Paul's Hospital, the job that would sustain her for over a decade.

But even then, something seemed amiss to Darlene. As far as she could tell, Stephen spent too much time playing video games, and too much time surfing internet sites associated with video gaming. She could see this when she came home after a lengthy shift at the hospital to find him still up, still on the computer, dirty dishes in the sink that hadn't been there when she'd left. But still she let him be, choosing instead to focus what little energy she had to spare on her younger son. Stuart was coming up well, earning good grades, and was in good health. Sometimes Stephen and Stuart had fought when they were younger, but by this time they both seemed to learn to avoid pushing each other's buttons. Stuart was her favourite; she tried to hide this as best she could, but she thought they both knew it. They both knew it. Even Darlene could understand that children are capable of figuring these things out, in the way they are. There were arguments, fights even, when Stephen would openly accuse her of favouring Stuart. All Darlene could think to do during these arguments, the only response she could think of was to deny it. But whenever there were fights between Stephen and Stuart—not fights, exactly, but dust ups—she felt as though there was nothing she could do to avoid Stephen accusing her of favouring Stuart. And she would deny it, as always, but as always she would know it was true. "Don't you remember anything?" Stephen asked. "I'm trying to remember," she said. "Are you really drunk all the time?" Stephen asked. And Darlene said, "I'm sorry about that." But even these little conversations were only part of a much larger whole. Nothing about this made sense to Darlene. Everything made complete sense, at the time and in retrospect to her. "I'm so sorry," she said.

Still, there was nothing she could do, nothing she could think to do, consumed as she was in the task of keeping everything at home running as smoothly as possible. On a nurse's pay, the cost of a two-bedroom apartment in the city of Vancouver was astronomical, driven much higher than anything she could've ever recalled from the last time she'd lived there. Apartments were available for a little less in the farther-out cities of Surrey, Langley, or Maple Ridge, but even these were too distant from work. So she let it be, she let it be, giving Stephen the space she thought she needed. After that phone call when he told her he wanted to be a woman, that he thought he was a woman, that he really, truly, honestly was a woman, she began to go over these little moments, these moments when she'd noticed something amiss but'd done nothing about it or done something but not enough, never enough. Most people never have the chance to look back on what might've been and blame themselves for all kinds of pain and suffering, she would've thought. "I'll never love you again," Stephen had said, not during that climactic conversation when he announced himself a woman but in one of the few phone calls they'd shared since. "Please don't say that," she said. "I've never loved you at all," he said. "Please stop doing this to me," she said. "See?" he asked. "See what?" she asked. "You're only concerned with yourself," he said, "that's why I never loved you." Even to hear him say that broke her heart. But then she said something she'd almost immediately regret. Darlene said, "then why are you still talking to me?" This prompted a flurry of obscenities from Stephen, leaving Darlene to wonder what'd prompted her to say that.

All this had happened in the years after she'd left Marcel in that little Quebec town and moved back to Vancouver, seeking as fresh a start as she could manage. In the end, whether her son was to continue speaking with her or not was something she couldn't control. But he wasn't a woman. She believed he wasn't a woman, and nothing she could say or do would ever change that very fundamental belief. As she browsed articles on the internet she found nearly every source took the issue as ideological or political, one way or the other, a stance she found utterly distasteful. She just wanted her son back as a son, not as the daughter he'd declared himself to be. But there were those who would've made her feel guilty even for this simple longing. Even she wasn't immune from all the changes in the world, made as she was to feel guilty for not wanting to entertain Stephen's notions of his own supposed femininity. That wasn't even the first argument they'd had over Stephen's gender, just the first when he'd told her he thought— believed?—he was a woman, that he'd been a woman all along. "The fact that you don't even get

71

it proves everything," Stephen had said, "because this is the reason everything's so fucked up in my life. It's your fault for raising me to be a man instead of the woman I am that's caused all my problems." It was the passion and the sincerity with which he'd seemed to believe it that stuck with Darlene, that lingered in her recollections as she tried to get on with her life. "Please don't say things like that," Darlene said. "Why shouldn't I?" asked Stephen. He said, "they're true. They're the truth." But Darlene could only say, "please…" She was overcome by uncontrollable flashbacks to the arguments and to the abuse that'd been heaped on her by Marcel barely more than ten years earlier.

It was around this time that Darlene began returning to the source of some of these ideas, began looking for support in the most surreptitious way she could've thought of. She began searching the internet for communities, finding too much for any one person to wade through. Except for her long-time friend, Cherise, Darlene was still simply unable to talk to anyone at all about what Stephen was going through. Even with Cherise, Darlene was unable to say exactly what'd happened, exactly what'd been said and done, only to refer to Stephen's decision in the vaguest, most general of terms. When they went for coffee on a rare evening out, she ordered her usual, two crème and two sugar, and proceeded to nervously talk about it. At first, she didn't know how to broach the issue. But even this was bound to lead her astray, the result of her search a confusing mess of mutually contradictory information. Everyone seemed to have an opinion, but no one seemed to know what they were talking about. Her friend Cherise, unknown to her, had seen the same things taking place in the world, and had much the same opinions. But that wasn't all there was to it. Even Darlene feeling guilty over not being willing to see her son as her daughter was only the very beginning of a long and winding journey. The city itself, it seemed to seethe with every day that passed, seemed to ooze a toxic energy that Darlene hadn't seen before, hadn't seen when she'd last lived in Vancouver. "I haven't got the slightest clue what I'm doing," Darlene would say when next meeting her long-time best friend, able to admit that weakness to one person. "Neither do I," said Cherise. "But you always seem like you've—" Darlene began, but stopped herself short. She then said, "I'm sorry," before looking down and shaking her head a bit. "It's okay," said Cherise, "sometimes I wonder myself." More was said. They parted ways, not to see each other for a little while.

Eventually, her feeble attempts to remain in good standing with her oldest son would prove to be her undoing. After having quit drinking some years earlier, when both her sons were entering adolescence, she took up the habit again. One night, a few nights after having tried for the last time in a while to get in contact with Stephen, Darlene stopped at a liquor store on the way home from work, buying only a bottle of vodka, the same bottle of vodka she'd once bought regularly, even going so far as to groan a little bit when seeing the price was noticeably higher than it'd been. The clerk at the liquor store was a different clerk, this one a little older. When she'd been drinking before, she'd memorized the locations of various liquor stores that were reasonably on the way home from work, making sure to stop at a different one each time so that she wouldn't, couldn't be seen at the same liquor store more than once a week. It was an indeterminate time in her life, and by extension the lives of her children, her friends, and her coworkers. She wouldn't hear from Stephen for a while. That she could've guessed. She kept on with her life, feeling exactly as lonely and close to crisis as ever.

Chapter Four

1

The police wouldn't let her take the car, because it was registered in Marcel's name. Instead, they *took* her away, along with her sons Stephen and Stuart driving her to a battered women's shelter, the only battered women's shelter in the area, where she could stay with her sons for as long as she needed. That night, that night, it wasn't until into the morning hours that she finally managed to fall asleep, until then sitting on the edge of the bed in the room. The sons were asleep already, having fallen asleep almost the moment they laid down on the cot in the room Darlene had been shown to after arrival. It was dark, although the night's sky visible through nearby windows had only just begun to brighten, the blackness having turned a very deep navy blue. The stars had begun to fade, at first one by one, then many at once, the sky brightening as morning came. In the middle of the summer, daylight began to approach early in the morning, even by four o'clock half-bright. Darlene hadn't been sure what she'd been planning, exactly, when she'd confronted Marcel and announced her intent to leave him. Although she might've thought to leave and drive somewhere, anywhere at all where she could've spent the night before continuing to drive the following morning, even that plan had been only vaguely-formed, existing as it had only in her own mind. There were a lot of reasons why she hadn't reached out, why she hadn't stepped outside herself and asked for help, reasons even she couldn't have begun to appreciate yet.

But many of the things that'd been said at that confrontation would stay with her for a long time, that's a given. What she remembered most, what continued to trouble her for months, even years after escaping to the church and beyond, was the way Marcel had become a completely different person after the police had arrived. It wasn't the way he'd slipped out of the dress and wig, putting on men's clothes for his interactions with the police, although that was certainly part of it. No, it was the look on his face, the passive, placid, entirely docile look that seemed coldly calculated to make the police see him as no threat to anyone at all. Although he'd remained inside for a little while, after emerging into the front yard he'd shoot her a sharp frown for a moment before talking to the police. Except when speaking specifically to her and her alone, the police kept on speaking in French, among themselves and with Marcel, not even bothering to conceal from her their preference. It made her feel as though they were hiding something, as though these police were the very police she'd feared going to for so many years, even from the very first time Marcel had done things to her that she hadn't wanted done, that she'd asked not to be done. Even then, the little French she'd picked up after having lived in Quebec for a few years seemed to disappear, leaving her at their mercy. But above all, she clutched her sons hands, one of theirs in each of hers, after having been *allowed* by the police to be with them. Their front yard was ringed by sections of chain-link fence, with parts of the fence seeming to peel off the poles they were mounted on. The houses themselves were plain, single-story houses, coloured white, grey, and sometimes a very light brown.

Red and blue lights flashed across the front yard. Aside from the police speaking in French with each other and with Marcel, their radios crackled occasionally in broken, coded French. The police, they never wanted to be there. The police never wanted to be *involved* in that kind of thing. This was something Darlene had learned to expect from them. Even as they spoke in French, their voices seethed contempt, for Darlene even the notion of someone like them being there to help her impossible to grasp. The guns and tasers in holsters on the officers' hips, as well as the handcuffs drew Darlene's attention, in those confused and panicked moments the implicit threat of force seeming not so implicit. Questions were asked, some in French and some in broken English. "What are they doing?" asked Stuart, his hand still held firmly in hers. "They're, they're looking inside," said Darlene, "they're talking." Stephen looked quietly at her, and said nothing. "Are they going to take dad away?" asked Stuart. "I—I don't know," said Darlene. Even as she spoke, even as she tried feebly to reassure her own sons, she shook and shuddered, tears sliding down her cheeks.

There were only so many moments Darlene could've gone over again and again, only so many little looks half-remembered, only so many insults hurled or threats growled. She thought, she would've thought it unimportant exactly what'd led to this moment, unimportant to the police. That was part of the reason why she left out what'd happened in the days and weeks before that night. Later, after much reflection, she'd come to the determination that neither Stephen nor Stuart could process what was happening to them, could understand what they'd seen and heard, but neither could they have processed what'd been happening to them, what they'd seen and heard in the years that'd led up to that decisive moment, that decisive night. Over the years that'd led up to that decisive night, there'd been many moments when Darlene could've learned something new, could've reached out for someone, anyone at all to help her, but didn't. She'd learned this habit many years earlier, when she'd been only a child. After having seen her mother, Marilyn, into the psychiatric ward at Victoria's Royal Jubilee Hospital, all those years earlier, Darlene had become confused, confused in the way a young child can be. But her father, Wayne, and Marilyn weren't yet broken. She asked her father when her mother was coming home, still young as she was. But her father only shook his head and said her mother wasn't coming home. This only confused the young Darlene further when Marilyn returned home a few weeks after her discharge, having spent the intervening time convalescing at her mother's in the interior. By the time it was explained to her what was really going on, a lot had happened, very little of which Darlene would understand until much, much later in her life.

Darlene

The moment she'd been pondering for some time before working up the courage to leave her husband of some years, it came after she'd sprayed her husband in the face but before the police had arrived. The police would later record in their incident reports that Darlene was the only one who employed physical violence against another during the whole encounter, and that this was claimed by Marcel and admitted by Darlene. The police saw nothing, nothing of what'd led up to it, of the years of unrelenting sexual violence and psychological torture she'd been through at his hands. If she'd called the police and asked for help in escaping Marcel, she knew they'd have judged her on what they saw. She didn't show, couldn't have brought herself to show the physical scars that she'd accumulated over the years, and not only because those were all or nearly all concealed under her clothes. These were the scars she'd learned to conceal when she was much younger, when she'd been only a child. Living with a mother who was suffering from one mental illness or another at any given moment had never been easy for young Darlene. Sometimes she'd come home from school—she'd been allowed to walk home from school because her mother so frequently wouldn't or couldn't show up to pick her up, despite being off work more often than not—to find her mother, Marilyn, seemingly in a trance, sitting on the living room couch, crying while staring off into space. Darlene would come into the living room, but wouldn't draw her mother's stare, for the next few hours until her father came home from work her mother failing even to acknowledge her. Then, when Wayne came home, Darlene would rush to the door, wrapping her arms around her father, holding him tight. It was all so deeply confusing to the young Darlene, who didn't, couldn't know why it was happening.

That night, that night, after putting to bed in the shelter where she'd been offered, Darlene stayed awake long enough to realize something had changed even as nothing had changed at all. She was tormented by images forcing their way through her mind, images of her grotesque ogre of a husband towering over her, wearing a miniskirt and tank top, both stretched out until torn in places, leaving him with little more than strategically placed pieces of cloth. In these images, the room was always dark, obscuring his face but leaving his hulking silhouette to fill so much space. He always seemed to sway and stagger slightly, whether under the influence of alcohol or not. And then Darlene would snap back into reality, finding herself right there, in a dark room, her sons asleep while she had spent hours in a wakeful nightmare. It would've been hard for her even to have explained what it was like, that first night or any other night at the shelter, the vast complications having set themselves on her like an oppressive heat. When she was younger, Darlene sometimes saw her mother taking pills at various times of the day. She even saw her father asking her mother whether she'd remembered to take her morning pills or her evening pills. Most of the time the answer was yes. Sometimes there were tense, awkward reminders by Wayne on the importance of keeping up with doctor's orders. Occasionally these would escalate into full-blow arguments, with Marilyn yelling, throwing her dinner plate onto the floor or the TV remote against the wall before storming upstairs, leaving Wayne and Darlene in an awkward silence.

But there was nothing stopping Marcel from coming to the shelter, although he wouldn't have been able to get inside as the shelter allowed only women and children on the premises. The police had supposedly received his promise not to, until the matter had been settled, but she wouldn't trust them to ensure this. But he didn't come. He didn't come. It was pointless, she thought, to try and reason with anyone. She felt driven by an overwhelming fear, by a very primitive but very real fight-or-flight response to an all-powerful threat, and knew in the morning to keep on running, to never stop running, to never look back, to put as much physical distance between herself and her husband. And these police, they were forcing her to remain in place, compelling her by virtue of their authority to remain close to Marcel, for so long as it took for them to make their decision to let her be. That's all she wanted; to let be. In the darkness of the night, that night, Darlene felt herself suddenly overcome by a restless energy, something washing over her that she couldn't have understood. She continued to ruminate on the past. After one particularly bad outburst by her mother, her father, Wayne, sat her down to talk to her about it, seeming to try his best to explain things in a way Darlene, then only a child, could understand. "Your mother's very unwell," said Wayne, pausing before continuing. He said, "she's got a special kind of sickness. Her sickness is up here." He tapped a finger against the side of his head. "She's trying to get better," he said, "but it's really hard for her." Darlene only nodded. Even this she couldn't really process. They'd had these talks before, and they'd keep on having them, even long after they both knew these talks were unnecessary.

Even by this point Darlene hadn't decided whether to go back to Vancouver or try and make something work out east. Although she didn't speak French fluently, she'd thought it might've been possible to make something work in Montreal, a city with Anglophone neighbourhoods, an almost bilingual city. Although it'd been a few years since she'd worked, her nursing credentials were still valid, and she thought it possible to find work as a nurse at one of Montreal's many hospitals. Even this, though, was a fraud, an illusion, a dangerous fantasy, her only choice proving to have been to flee back to Vancouver. but even this choice was to have been fraught with danger, something she hadn't yet begun to appreciate.

3

Soon a teenaged Stephen began repeating things she'd never heard from him before, things she didn't know he'd picked up from certain internet message boards. He began displaying a fascination with war and the military, disturbing flashes of misogyny, and open derisiveness towards what he referred to as 'social justice warriors.' Although Darlene quickly surmised he must've been repeating things he'd learned elsewhere, she couldn't decide whether 'elsewhere' was his father, his friends, or the internet, or some combination of the three. When once Stephen went so far as to use a racial slur, Darlene upbraided him for it, only to be curtly told that it was just how people talked in 'the real world.' Even though Darlene was someone who rarely became angry, that evening she threatened to take away his phone or his internet access, only to be met with a storm of profanities and slurs against women. Too shocked to respond, Darlene said nothing as her oldest went to his room and threw the door shut, slamming it so hard the pictures on the wall seemed to rattle slightly. Stuart, the younger of her two sons, was still too young to be interested in any of the things Stephen had become drawn to. While Stephen was fifteen at this time, Stuart was only twelve, the younger brother only beginning to step into adolescence. Much to her later regret, Darlene let it be, saying nothing that night, instead going to bed like any other night, waking in the morning as though nothing had happened, as though nothing had been said. "I don't need anyone," he said, once, after coming home too late at night. He'd never displayed much interest in partying. "You may think that now," said Darlene, "but—" And then he cut her off, saying something that shocked her, before turning and making for his room.

At some point, Darlene began to try and counter the influence of these new ideas by talking to him, by giving him books and even films on things that would help him learn to accommodate different views. A few times she took books and magazines out of the library and then left them in

83

plain view on the kitchen table, hoping he'd see
them and at least give them a casual leaf through.
The topics of these books varied, from history to
space exploration to biographies of or memoirs by
famous or historical figures, things she thought he
might've been interested based on the things he'd
been interested in the past. It was no use. He'd
changed too much over the few years it'd been, in
ways Darlene had been sometimes horrified by.
The height of this came when he didn't come
home one night. It'd turn out that he spent the
night at a friend's place while that friend's parents
were out of town, a small party having taken place.
She imagined there must've been drinking and drug
use at the party, and wondered, feared Stephen
might've had sex with one person or another, long
before he was capable of understanding the
possible consequences of his actions. She didn't
even know how to broach the subject, and as she
waited for him to come home the following
morning she felt paralyzed with fear, the exact
same paralysis that'd seized her during those times
when she'd been married to Marcel. Even this
paralysis was enough to give her pause for thought.
But then there were those moments when Stephen
still seemed the soft-spoken and kind-hearted
young man she'd known him to be when he was
younger; moments when he'd let slip and show that
side. "What's for dinner?" he asked, one afternoon.
"I'm ordering Chinese," she said, "I thought it
would be a nice treat for us." He said, "thank you."
She said, "and I thought we could watch the
hockey game together." He said, "sure, that'd be
cool." He spoke with a softness that seemed to

belie his sometimes-angry demeanour. It was the little moments like these that sometimes tempted her to believe he was just dealing with a difficult time, that all she needed to do was *be there* for him.

But none of it worked. Nothing worked. Nothing Darlene could think of worked, although she was working too much to take much of an active role in shepherding her oldest son's development. It felt to her as though she was still powerless, even within her own home. The feeling of powerlessness, of helplessness to change something so close to her, to help someone so near to her, it paralyzed her in exactly the same way fear for her life and for the lives of both her sons had once so paralyzed her. Hearing Stephen repeat things he'd obviously picked up at school or on the internet, hurtful, hateful things broke Darlene's heart as they reminded her of the things Marcel had said to her. "Please make sure you're home after school," she said, "you have to watch over your brother." Darlene was to be working late that night, as with many other nights picking up an overtime shift at the hospital. "Why do I have to watch him?" he asked. "You know why," she said, "we've been over this before." It made her feel exasperated to even have this argument. "What if I don't come home?" asked Stephen. And this, this question caused Darlene to inwardly flinch. "He's old enough to look out for himself anyways," Stephen said. This was something Darlene had thought of herself, something she'd talked over not with Stephen or even Stuart but with her one and only real friend, Cherise. And this was something she'd keep on talking about, keep on arguing at least with herself about even after she'd stopped trying to get Stephen to look out for his younger brother. At the time, she knew they were both old enough to look out for themselves after school, at least to walk home alone. But she was stuck in a strange state of mind where she wanted to protect them but felt as though she was ultimately powerless to do anything more.

And then there was the drinking. Darlene thought she hid it well enough from her sons. The alcohol she kept at home was in a safe place, nowhere near the kitchen but in her bedroom, in a container in the back of the closet. Whenever she needed a drink at home, she'd start in the kitchen by dropping a few ice cubes into a glass, then head into her bedroom and close the door before pouring herself a drink. That's how it'd continued, anyways, after leaving Quebec and making her way back to Vancouver. Sometimes she was around her sons when under the influence of alcohol, and during these times she'd always preferred to imagine they couldn't tell, seeing as they were both children who knew nothing of addiction or alcoholism. But she didn't realize that children pick up on everything, in the ways that they do, processing what they see in the ways that they do. This was, of course, long before her oldest son had announced he was a woman, that he wasn't to be referred to as 'Stephen' but as 'Stephanie.' In those early years, it'd seemed to Darlene as though the most important thing was working to keep a roof over their heads, food on their tables, even as the spectre of Marcel reappearing in their lives was very real. their divorce had only been finalized some years earlier. Marcel took almost everything. It wasn't even clear to Darlene what Marcel was doing at the time, but she assumed he continued to teach at the CEGEP. She refused to have anything to do with him, beyond the minimum required to abide by the custody arrangement over Stephen and Stuart. Even she wouldn't talk on the phone with him, insisting on all communication being conducted through writing. It might've seemed extreme to the outside observer, had anyone been interested in her life, but this was a learned behaviour.

The sexual abuse and the psychological torture which she'd endured for over a decade seemed to have never truly ended, even as she'd accomplished at least part of the work in building a new life for herself. Even after she'd been there and back again, she felt as though she still had a long ways ago. She hadn't told her friend Cherise the exact extent of the problem, although Cherise she supposed could tell just by looking at her. But Cherise had her own problems; she was in the midst of her own struggle with loneliness and depression, having been single nearly her entire adult life. She rarely spoke of this with Darlene, their conversations over coffee instead about work, the rising cost of this and that, Darlene's sons of course, even the abysmal state of traffic in one of the most congested cities in the country. But Cherise, Cherise's loneliness was made manifest by the way she so often seemed braver than she really was. Even Cherise, always single, had reasons to complain. They sometimes commiserated over their shared loneliness. Cherise spoke of her difficulty in battling her own steadily-mounting depression, although she never came out and used that word. It seemed to both of them like the normal, default state of life, one that couldn't be overcome but could lapse at any moment into extreme and pain if not fought tooth and nail.

But then, after Stephen had begun his transition from man to woman, Darlene still faulted herself for having failed to prevent the worst of her own difficulties from impacting her sons. Long before this had begun, though, she'd re-established contact with Cherise, her old, long-time friend. "I wish my dad was still here," said Darlene, while having Cherise over for a cup of coffee one evening. "He'd help you so much," said Cherise. "It's not only that," said Darlene, "I never told him anything about what'd happened with Marcel." Even still, Darlene was acutely aware of her own limitations, of her own flaws, these evening coffees at home with Cherise an opportunity not to rely on drinking to deaden the nerves and pass the time. In truth, Darlene wasn't drinking so much as she'd used to, not nearly as much as she'd been drinking in those early months and years following her move back west with the boys. She'd tried twelve-stepping it at one point, while the boys were still in high school, but never found that particular approach very helpful. Darlene's drinking was the one thing Cherise never asked about. Cherise drank too, sometimes relying on a glass or two of wine at the end of the day to unwind, more often than she would've cared to admit. They had that much in common.

At some point in their conversation, Cherise said, "you know, your dad is still with you now, even if you can't see it." Darlene took a sip from her cup of coffee before saying, "I know that." She thought about it for a moment before asking, "are you suggesting I start going to church again?" Cherise said, "not exactly." Darlene asked, "what are you saying?" Cherise said, "you've got something." Darlene took another sip of coffee, and then said, "nobody really knows what they're doing. Some people are just better at faking it than others." Darlene had thought of these things before, but hadn't said anything. It was late at night, so late that there was nothing in the way of traffic outside. "Listen," said Darlene, "it's always one crisis or another. And he'd just tell me…" But she couldn't finish the thought. Instead, she decided to have a drink as soon as Cherise had left, something she was probably going to do anyways. A siren blared through the distance, louder and louder, passing right by them outside, then fading down the street in the other direction. It was too cold and wet for them to sit outside on Darlene's patio; even from inside, Darlene could tell the severity of the incident from the single siren heard, from the thrum of silence that soon pervaded in the distance of the night.

But Cherise wasn't to make any further probes, not on that night, leaving Darlene to guess her way through the next little while. If Darlene was to be fully honest with herself, she'd have had to take further steps on her own. The terror and the torture that'd begun so many years ago had never truly ended, even as Darlene worked herself through these problems. "I know what you mean," said Cherise. Darlene said, "I'll think about it."

They went on to talk about nothing at all, Darlene
fearful of the next time she might or might not
hear from her oldest son but willing to listen
anyways. This wasn't the kind of pain she'd been
used to, that she'd become used to over the many
years since leaving her husband behind and coming
into a new life, with her twin sons, back in
Vancouver again. But it was pain anyways, and pain
she knew well.

2

Soon, Marcel made demands on Darlene. He
began insisting on wearing women's clothes even
while they were having sex, and said she shouldn't
have a problem with this because of her self-
professed bisexuality. When she complained that
she hadn't exactly said she was bisexual, he
interrupted her and talked over her. One night, he
said, that she shouldn't think of herself as above
him. "We're both women," he said, as they were in
their little apartment's bedroom, "so you shouldn't
be such a hypocrite." Reluctantly, that night she
complied with his request, confused as she was by
her own mixed feelings. It was the first time they
had sex with him in the guise of the woman he
insisted he really was. Although Darlene had been
through some unpleasant experiences with men,
nothing had ever come close to this. It was the first
instance that she might've later considered sexual
torture. He forced her to participate in his sexual
fantasies, to help him in acting out the things he'd
thought up sometimes as recently as that day or the
day before. On that particular night, he produced a

small strap-on dildo and asked her to wear it while he penetrated her from behind. When she meekly pointed out that wearing the strap-on would make it impossible for her to take him inside her vaginally, he smiled that wry, wicked smile of his and said, "I won't be going in there." Sinister as his voice was, in that moment Darlene was struck by the insidious implication. By the time this particular episode was over, she'd be shivering and shuddering, crying quietly as Marcel undressed from his outfit, still in bed when he left the room. It wasn't until she heard the door to the bathroom open and shut that she began to look up, wasn't until she heard the rush of water from the shower that she got up.

Even as this was happening, they seemed like any other couple, continuing to go out with friends, attend parties, and host the odd dinner themselves. Despite all that was happening, despite Marcel's deepening descent into madness, Darlene still felt as though she loved him, still felt as though she was in love with him. She even felt as though she could still *salvage* him, still make him out to be the seemingly decent young man he'd been when they met. But it wasn't that simple. It couldn't have ever been that simple. Their one-bedroom apartment could only contain so much physical pain before all that pain transcended the physical boundaries imposed on it by the limitations of Darlene's own personal point of view. In the darkness of the night, that night, as he pressed himself into her quickly and firmly, he seemed altogether unaware of the pain he was causing her, even as she struggled not to cry out. The truth of it was that even the physical pain caused to her by his taking her in a way she didn't want to be taken was small compared to the anxiety Marcel's turn for the worst was causing her, by the knowledge that he could turn into a completely different person at any moment, without warning. She was able to conceal her anxiety, at least from him, by participating in the acting-out of his fantasies. Bent over as she was, the strap-on dildo she wore hung awkwardly from her, the harness chafing against her skin, until his violent movements against her pushed her prone on the bed, then the dildo forced up, pressing painfully into her abdomen. At one point she cried softly into the pillow, but only briefly before it was over, seemingly as quickly as it'd started. Even later, she wasn't sure if he heard her soft crying; he climaxed almost exactly at the moment she cried out, although neither of them could've known this. It wasn't always the case that sex had been this painful, this deeply uncomfortable for her. But even this was a small moment, only one against the many moments that made up their first few years together.

After she'd done the things he'd asked that night, he took off the women's clothes and put the sex toys away, then cuddled her while whispering sweet things into her ear. But for the still-lingering smell of the lubricant he'd used, it was the smell of sex that'd overpowered Darlene's senses. Years later, after she'd escaped, Darlene would realize she confused his grooming with love, real love, the kind of *true love* that only seemed possible to someone who was so young. After she was confident he was asleep, Darlene quietly got out of bed and slowly walked to the bedroom door, opening it without making a noise, then slinking into the bathroom. She examined herself in the mirror, the parts of her body that were visible above the counter. Her eyes were bloodshot. Her cheeks were covered in tears. Her whole face was reddened. Her hair was a matted mess. When she looked down at her lower body, she saw the marks left where the strap-on Marcel made her wear had pressed and pulled against her skin. It was deeply disturbing to her, even then, to be made to do this thing, this thing that was so far from the love she thought she'd wanted. "I'm sorry I hurt you," he said. She thought he seemed genuine in his concern and apology. "It's okay," she said. They spoke the following morning. "You're helping me explore myself," he said, "that's something only you can do." To Darlene he seemed to have changed so much in the time they'd been together. She remembered the way it felt to unburden herself of the troubled family life she'd had in the past, and this made her feel better. "I'm happy to help you," she said, fully meaning every word as she smiled warmly. Despite her pain, she was able to forget, for a moment, what he'd done to her and see the good person in Marcel, the good person she was sure was still there. And she, she was still happy to help him explore this confused side of himself, hopeful as she was that it'd all work itself out, sooner or later.

Even through this early period, both Darlene and Marcel continued to grow. He worked in the suburban city of Burnaby, not far from the main campus of BCIT, where he'd studied IT. "I love you," he said, seeming to have changed radically in the span of a few hours. It was frightening to Darlene how he could change so quickly, how he could become so radically different in the span of only a few years. "I love you too," she said. But then, she was still in love with him, still willing to believe that if she could only play along with his delusional and violent fantasies then she might've been able to win him over. It was hard for even her to articulate, but even at this early stage she thought the side to him she was seeing might've been only a small part of him. Even the disturbing and depraved sex acts he pressured her into only took place relatively rarely, she told herself, as she couldn't yet confront the truth about what was happening all around her. Even after she'd cleaned herself off, combed out her hair, and let the redness from her eyes fade, she still could hardly recognize herself. But she wasn't that far off, wasn't that far off from the young woman who'd fallen so hopelessly and helplessly in love with Marcel. Even in the meantime, though, she kept on piling their apartment high with books, books she'd never get around to reading but kept on buying anyways. Whether she'd get around to reading any given book, they always offered an escape.

A few months passed, with not-infrequent bouts of sexual torture and psychological games. Sometimes, in the midst of all this, Darlene and Marcel behaved like any other couple. They went out with other young couples, for dinner parties, nights at restaurants, even the odd concert or other show. Darlene's friends and co-workers knew nothing of the man Marcel was slowly becoming, the man that might've been there all along but might've only become emergent since he'd started seeing her. Her life continued to be otherwise made up of all the little things that make up day to day life; trips to the grocery store, maintenance on her car, talks of buying a townhouse if only they could afford one in the cripplingly expensive Vancouver market. At some point, she convinced Marcel to agree to adopt a cat, Darlene picking from the municipal animal shelter a male tabby cat said by the staff to be only three years old at the time. The cat came with the name Barney, a name she chose to keep because she thought it wouldn't have been right to change his name. Marcel wasn't interested in the cat, but agreed anyways. That cat soon came to be her best friend, bounding of his favourite hiding places to come and greet her when she came home at the end of the day. Still in that early time when she loved Marcel, the cat Barney was a valuable friend for her. Sometimes when they'd go out and spend time like any other couple, meeting friends for dinner or having a raucous night at the bar, Darlene would withdraw into herself, outwardly laughing and joking and chatting but inwardly craving the peace and quiet she'd sometimes had at home. She didn't know Marcel was acting, too, just in a different way, a horrifying way that'd only dawn on her after it was too late.

Even still, to the outside world they seemed like any other couple. Even Darlene's closest friend, Cherise, knew nothing of what Marcel did, of what Marcel liked to do in the bedroom. She didn't dare tell her father. She still didn't know where her mother was. She saw packages arrive at their apartment, packages addressed to him, but never summoned the courage to open them. If she had, she'd have found sex toys, or pieces of clothing meant to be worn during the sex act, things she'd have never been able to conceive of on her own. Inevitably, though, the person Marcel was slowly becoming would reappear, presenting in the form of a new sexual act Marcel wanted her to perform for him in the bedroom. He became increasingly obsessed with her taking the role of the dominant woman, asking her to use various instruments in inflicting pain and humiliation on him. But then he would always insist on switching roles for his climax, always insisting on inflicting whatever violence on her that he'd made her inflict on him. It was on one such evening, an evening after they'd both worked long through the day, that he dressed her up in an ill-fitting faux-leather outfit and asked her to penetrate him while he lay on his back in their bed. It was awkward and obscene to Darlene, and it made her feel uncomfortable even to hear him talk about it. But she did what he asked anyways. She did it anyways.

There were the moments afterwards, in the days to come, moments when Marcel brought her flowers and chocolates, took her on romantic dates, even cooked for her from time to time, although he wasn't very good at the latter. He promised to marry her and give her a family, to be with her forever, sometimes continuing to whisper these promises in the darkness of their bedroom after having made her do things she hadn't wanted to do. Although Darlene would come to look back on these moments and see them for the truth of

Darlene

what they were, back then she still fully believed in the good in Marcel, still fully believed in the inner turmoil she thought he must've been going through. All she needed to do, she thought, was nudge him in the right direction, something she resolved to do even as he subjected her to increasingly violent and disturbing acts. That night, as she built up a rhythm in pushing the apparatus she was wearing into him, he seemed to grow restless. "Faster," he said, "faster and harder." She complied reluctantly, firmly and quickly moving against him, driving the entire length of the solid strap-on attached to her harness into him. "Yes," he said, hissing as he spoke, "that's it." Finally, after a few minutes of this, he reached for her with both hands, pulled her on top of him, and shoved himself into her. Her vaginal opening was obstructed. He took her the other way. His sudden insertion caused her to experience searing pain, a pain that made her almost pass out. The next thing she knew, she was lying in bed next to him, staring at the ceiling as she gasped for breath. "That was wonderful," he said, the following morning. She mumbled something in response. "I can't wait until next time," he said. She looked at him. He was grinning wickedly. It all seemed to be happening so fast for Darlene, who hadn't come close yet to her breaking point. But she was getting closer.

Chapter Five

3

But Darlene's son, Stephen, continued to favour the opinions of his online friends over those of his friends at school or the views Darlene tried to introduce him to. At some point, she noticed that his friends from school had stopped coming over after school to play video games or watch TV, something she realized she must've noticed long after it'd happened. (She'd taken to working voluntary overtime shifts at St. Paul's, keeping her away from the home even more). But when she broached the issue with Stephen at first, he wouldn't say exactly what'd happened, insisting only that it wasn't his fault and that he knew how to handle it, that he knew what he was doing. Although he was still a teenager, still only sixteen, he seemed to think himself much older. Like in other occasions, Darlene decided the best thing to do was nothing at all, to let things be, in the vague hopes that he'd turn out right, that he'd make the right choices. Actually, that wasn't it, not quite. It wasn't that Darlene thought she knew best; in fact, she was aware of her own limitations as an outside observer. When he came home and threw his backpack over a chair in the kitchen before trundling into his room, Darlene felt powerless to do something, anything at all. When she left in the morning before work, he was usually still in bed. She justified this at the time by telling herself that boys needed lots of sleep to stay healthy, and supposed she'd rather have seen him sleep too much than too little. In the years since she came to recognize this as another lost opportunity to intervene.

One of Stephen's friends was dating a girl who identified as a trans boy, and it wasn't cool to be transphobic. In high schools at the time, gender non-conformity was a huge craze, with sometimes entire groups of friends experimenting in boys identifying as girls and girls as boys. All this was vaguely known to Darlene, who worried incessantly what schools were feeding young people, worried what kind of environment her young sons would have to develop in. With what'd happened to them only some years earlier, she wondered if Stephen might've picked up all kinds of ideas and habits from his father. There was nothing to be said, nothing to be said about any of that. It all came to a head one night when she came home from another lengthy shift at the hospital to find Stephen unexpectedly out, breaking the ten o'clock curfew she'd set for him. He came home just after midnight. When she angrily confronted him and demanded to know where he'd been, he only told her he'd been out with some of his 'new friends.' She asked, "what happened to your old friends?" Concern crept into her voice, prompting her tone to soften slightly, something she'd later consider Stephen might've mistook for weakness. After having lived around men and only men all her life, she'd only just begun to pick up on their habits, at great personal expense. "None of your business," he said, walking past her to get a can of coke from the fridge. "You live here and that makes it my business," she said, forcibly trying to maintain a level of composure she wasn't comfortable with.

Even still, Darlene didn't know what to do, couldn't have known what to do, besides always letting it be. Sometimes she thought about taking the boys and going back to church with them, but this never came to pass either. Mostly she privately, inwardly fretted at having lost her father, the only one she could've thought to speak with about Stephen's difficulties. But he was gone, he was gone, never to come back. It was her fault, she believed, for failing to live up to the example set by her own father, an example set when she'd been a child. That night, she'd been assaulted by a patient on the psychiatric ward, a patient who'd grabbed her by the throat with both hands and tried to strangle her. She wasn't injured all that badly; there was to be some bruising where he'd grabbed her, and some lingering pain from the ordeal, but it was the memories this had rekindled of the same injuries, the same assaults she'd sustained at the hands of her own husband just some years earlier. She took off work a few weeks while nursing he injured wrist, that time filled with difficulty, as she tried to sleep at night the discomfort of her injured wrist recalling the physical sensations of having been assaulted by Marcel. This kept her off work longer. In the darkness of her bedroom at night, she couldn't sleep, couldn't sleep with her injured wrist, too afraid as she was of the possibility of Marcel appearing out of the darkness to come after her again.

A few more months would pass before Darlene would learn the truth about what'd happened. Stephen had opposed the friend in his former group having begun dating a trans boy, which had resulted in Stephen's unceremonious expulsion from the group. When she tried to approach him to talk about what she'd learned, he refused to talk about it and stormed off to the room he shared with his younger brother. Again, she didn't pursue him, instead letting him have what she thought he needed, a moment to think about it. But inwardly she wondered what might've motivated him to make these decisions, whether he'd remembered all the little things Marcel had said and done when last they'd lived together, as a family, in Quebec. She wondered whether Marcel had been wearing women's clothes around the boys when she'd sent them off to see him following the breakup; this was something she thought about many times, but never summoned the courage to ask either of the boys about. All these things weighed on her mind as she worked through that early time following Stephen's declaration that he was really Stephanie, in her mind going over every moment, every little glance and every word uttered in excruciating detail, searching for the precise moment when she'd first started making mistakes. But she never could figure it out. Every time she thought she had that exact moment, she'd always think up an earlier moment. Every time she tempted herself to go further back, she might've thought about a later moment. Even sometimes there were those moments, those lonely moments in the darkness of her empty apartment, when she looked over photos of her sons when they were younger, when they were still small boys, taken at school when the whole family lived together in Quebec. The boys were smiling in those photos, they were smiling as they'd been instructed by the school photographer, their smiles coming as little as a few hours after they'd seen their father strike their mother, after they'd heard through thin walls the sounds of Marcel striking her, after they might've heard her crying as softly as possible in the night. It wouldn't work, it couldn't work.

That said, even Darlene thought it was normal and healthy for children, particularly teenagers, to have secrets. As long as he stayed in school, avoided drugs and alcohol, and achieved at least passable grades, then she thought not to upset him too much. Even though she'd tried to help point him in the right directions, she thought to avoid real confrontation. She felt a little guilty, as though she'd learned nothing at all from any of her many attempts to avoid confrontation during her marriage to Marcel before it was too late. But her evening coffees with her friend Cherise continued to be a source of reassurance and strength. Actually, she wouldn't have thought it that way, appreciating the comfort and routine that came along with things having stabilized. She never bothered with dating throughout this time, never even thought about trying to find someone for herself. "I don't know how long I can last like this," said Darlene. She tried to say it with a smile and a light tone of voice, as if to suggest she was making light of her own problems. "You're doing okay," said Cherise, "just keep doing what you're doing." But there was still a tension between them, Cherise's friendship valuable to Darlene even as the hint of resentment had grown. Cherise struggled with her own loneliness; this Darlene knew from many conversations but also just from looking at her friend. But it was as though something kept Cherise from ever bringing it up directly, still hurting as she must've been from her breakup with Chuck. It'd been some months by then, and Cherise secretly feared she'd never find anyone again. Even Darlene didn't know this, couldn't have known this, from the sometimes-awkward silence that took over whenever one or the other got too close to the subject.

"Have you heard from Marcel recently?" asked Cherise. "Thank God I haven't," said Darlene. "How do you know Stephen hasn't?" asked Cherise. "I'd rather imagine he hasn't," said Darlene. They'd been talking for about an hour, sipping coffee and snacking on a plate of veggies that Darlene had brought out, afterwards smoking cigarettes on the small patio. "You should quit," said Darlene. "So should you," said Cherise. They both laughed a little nervously. What more they talked about that evening wasn't altogether unlike the things they'd wanted to talk about, either of them. They wouldn't drink; they rarely drank together. By the time Cherise had left, Darlene's thoughts were racing, as if to suggest she'd contracted some kind of horrible disease by virtue of having been in close contact with someone she'd cared about, someone she'd loved. After Cherise had broken up with her old boyfriend, Chuck, Darlene noticed her best friend became a little more apprehensive about life generally, approaching certain topics a little more reluctantly whenever they got together. When Darlene asked if she'd heard from Chuck at all, Cherise hesitated before saying she had no reason to have heard from him. "We never married or had kids," said Cherise. And Darlene said, "that's true," before changing the subject. It was hard for Darlene, hard for both of them to relate to one another sometimes, even as they were more alike than they were different. Even these difficulties were minimal compared to the strength Darlene drew from having a friend, from having one friend in the entire world she could talk to about her family.

For the first time in the years since she'd broken free from Marcel's grasp, Darlene began to seriously consider that something might be wrong with one of her sons, that Stephen's problems might have come about, directly or indirectly, as a result of Marcel's influence. She'd always considered this possibility, but that night, after Cherise went home and left Darlene alone, she thought about it some more. She always thought about everything some more, having more time than she'd have preferred to admit. Even while working on the psychiatric inpatient ward at St. Paul's hospital in Vancouver, she was constantly reminded of the physical sensations of the pain she'd endured. She sometimes thought on the long-term consequences of a life filled with strain and stress, on the damage she must've, might've been doing to her own body and mind by *living* through all this could've been worse than smoking a pack a day. Even the city beyond her, the city that surrounded her at all times, it was an utterly disinterested place, seeming to have become less provincial and much more confused in all the years that'd passed. But Stephen seemed determined to continue on his own path. The falling out he'd had with his friends, Darlene thought to try and help him mend those fences he'd broken. It broke her heart to see him struggling to find friends, as she'd once struggled to meet new people, and she began to fear as though he'd become lost. But so was she paralyzed, hardly able to help him, consumed as she was in her own problems.

And what Cherise had said to her seemed to resonate over the next two years, while Stephen kept on working his way through the tenth, then eleventh grade. Still, whenever Darlene thought to take decisive action, to do something, anything at all, she'd become paralyzed by the sudden and intense bursts of fear and self-loathing, thoughts and feelings she'd experienced before but only in mild doses. By the time she'd next hear from her son Stephen again, little would've changed in his life even as everything wouldn't have changed at all.

2

A couple of years after moving in with Marcel, Darlene became pregnant. It was an unplanned pregnancy. Marcel tried to pressure her into getting an abortion, but Darlene refused even to consider it. After a few months of subdued arguing over it, he relented, agreeing in any case that he probably wanted children anyways. Some couples work these things out beforehand, but Darlene and Marcel hadn't, save his assurances that he'd marry her and give her a family. At that time, they were still only a relatively young couple living somewhere in the city of Vancouver, one of the many young couples trying to make their way through one of the most expensive cities in the world. In many ways, the city they lived in was as rudderless and confused as they were. Although Vancouver purported to be urbane and cosmopolitan, in reality it was just deeply confused. Marcel kept on cross-dressing through this time, and kept on escalating his sexual and psychological manipulation and abuse of Darlene, until one night this became an assault. They were in the midst of acting out one of his fantasies, one in which he'd taken to striking her repeatedly with various instruments, like wooden paddles, fly swatters, and a frying pan. On this night, he'd goaded her into using the small strap-on he'd bought for her on him, penetrating him anally, demanding that she push into him harder and harder, faster and faster, seeming to critique her every move even as he purported to submit to her like he liked. "You're not doing it hard enough," he said, after her first few movements against her. "It's uncomfortable for me," she said. "It's supposed to be uncomfortable," he said, "that's the whole point." She stopped moving, and withdrew from him fully while they spoke. "Don't stop now," he said. "I'm trying," she said, before managing to re-enter him with the small plastic strap-on. He cried out in melodramatic fashion, causing her to flinch. "That's it," he said, "treat me like a bitch." At exactly the moment of his choosing, he pulled away, then turned around and grabbed her before forcibly and roughly wrestling her down to the bed. She cried out, but her cries seemed only to goad him on. Unexpectedly, she tried to get away, shivering and shuddering all the while. In the confusion, they both fell off the bed, landing awkwardly on the floor next to the bed, his massive bulk landing on top of her slender frame. He began to strike her harder and harder, under the pain became too much for her.

He backed off, kneeling above her as he panted heavily. It was dark, too dark for her to see much of anything as she slowly turned over and looked back up at him. All she could see was the whites of his eyes, slurred a blood red. All she could hear was the grim, repetitive sound of his heaving breath, her own having quieted. Forcibly, he picked her up and put her back on the bed, forcing himself on her again, finishing inside her before collapsing on top of her. A few moments passed before he rolled off her, then sat up. A few more moments passed before Darlene sat up as well. "Will that be all, mistress?" he asked. After catching her breath for a few more moments, Darlene managed to say, "yes," feeling as though she was croaking the words through the solid lump in her throat. With that, he let out a wicked laugh, a low, guttural laugh, then stood and turned to make for the other side of the room. Some time passed, it seemed to Darlene as though it was hours but in fact it was hardly half a minute. They slept that night together, as they slept in their shared bed every night, with Darlene still nursing the pain from his heavy body falling over her. She thought to go to the hospital, but decided against it. It was the first but not the last time she'd have ended up deciding not to seek medical attention for the injuries he'd inflict on her in his sexual frenzy. But that night, that night was only one of many, as the months passed into years, Darlene decided it was best to look past these moments and focus on the good. A few hours after subjecting her to this latest sex act, he approached her and said, "thank you for helping me." She sort of looked away and said, "it's fine." He put his armed around her and hugged her, while saying, "you're the only one who can help me be myself. Without you I'd be lost." Still young, Darlene took this as a sign of Marcel's enduring goodness, and chose to look past the pain and the bruising.

After Darlene became pregnant, they married. It was a small ceremony, attended by Darlene's family and friends from nearby parts of Vancouver and British Columbia, but few of Marcel's. It was the first time she'd met many of the latter, including Marcel's only brother, a similarly large yet lanky man who seemed to delight in towering over her in a way that seemed to her eerily similar to Marcel. His brother's name was Guy, and he'd flown in from their childhood hometown in Quebec. Even these times were hardly any different from the months and years that'd preceded them, at least for Darlene their wedding a small moment of happiness. It wasn't like the wedding she might've wanted, but she enjoyed it anyway. After the ceremony, the reception was held at a small hall nearby, and Darlene spent most of the occasion sitting at her table, too exhausted to do much dancing. But Marcel soon stopped pestering her to take part in acting out the sexual fantasies he'd concocted after Darlene had become pregnant. He once told her that he found her pregnant body disgusting, something which deeply confused her. She gave birth three months after they married, the first time she held her son Stephen one of the happiest moments in her life, a memory she'd cherish for the rest of her life. Marcel was there too; although he'd tried to pressure her into having an abortion, the first time he held baby Stephen seemed to Darlene a happy moment for him too, one of the moments when she saw him with a smile of genuine warmth and happiness. If she'd known what was to come later, if she'd known what she'd never find out, she might've later looked back on this moment as a chilling and surreal foreboding of the absolute worst.

They moved into a bigger place, an apartment with two bedrooms so as to reserve one room for the baby. On both their combined incomes, it was possible for them to afford a two-bedroom place in Vancouver, although it took some creative accounting of their combined finances. It also involved divulging every cent she had to him, or rather, every cent she didn't have. Their cat Barney came along with them into the new place. Through this period, she observed Marcel continuing to indulge in his fantasies. Sometimes her observations came through happening upon him in their bedroom or in their living room, always finding baby Stephen alone in the second bedroom instead of being tended to by Marcel. Sometimes her observations took the form of her discovering Marcel's internet search history; even sometimes she sat at their desktop computer and turned on the monitor only to find fetish pornography left open, which she sometimes thought might've been left strategically open by Marcel. Even during these early times when Marcel had only begun introducing her to the dark side of his life, she still wouldn't have imagined what she'd find. The first time she saw him watching pornography with baby Stephen in the room, she objected. "I wish you wouldn't look at that," she said. "It's fine," he said. "It's not appropriate to expose the baby to it," she said. "He doesn't know what it is," he said. "That's not the point," she said, her voice quivering even as she summoned the courage. "Fine," said Marcel, before shutting off the computer's monitor and turning away.

For so long as she had her baby Stephen, she thought, she'd been given a new reason to keep going, a new reason to put aside her doubts and work through every difficulty that presented itself. Although she was entitled to take a year's maternity leave in the province of British Columbia, the amount she was paid was far less than what she'd made as a nurse working for the local health authority. Her first night back, she was almost relieved to be out of the apartment again, to be back in her element, even the slow and mostly boring night shifts that were common at Vancouver General Hospital. But when one of her older co-workers, a middle-aged woman named Danielle, asked her if everything was alright at home, all Darlene could do was look back and quickly but firmly say, "everything's fine," before turning away, back to her work. She'd learned that many new mothers are eager to get out of the house after feeling like they'd been locked away for many months following childbirth. This is one reason she wanted to return to work as soon as she could manage, the only obstacle being the need to find an affordable daycare. When at home her time was consumed in taking care of baby Stephen, she had precious little opportunity to indulge in reading. Even still, between diaper changes, feedings, and tending to one outcry or another, she found the time to sneak in a few pages here and there. At some point, it occurred to her that she could read *with* Stephen; she began to read novels out loud to him, half-hoping to inspire a lifetime love of books in him as well.

What her father knew she couldn't have said, even then. After having grown up largely without a mother, Darlene hadn't been prepared for what she'd find. It was one of Darlene's days off that week, and he came home when she was quietly reading on the living room couch. After dinner, after the evening had passed more or less uneventfully, she put their son to bed and then turned back into their apartment. It wasn't the first night they were to have had sex since she'd given birth, but it was the first time Marcel had made some rather cutting remarks. The way he said them suggested to Darlene that he'd thought them up in advance, that he'd been ruminating on her appearance, on the way her body had changed even after having given birth. After taking her into their bedroom, he sat her down on the edge of the bed and had her watch as he took off his clothes, then piece by piece put on his women's clothes. All

Darlene wanted was an attentive lover, one who would make her feel loved and who she could make feel loved in return. They had sex that night, of course they had sex that night, but it seemed to Darlene as though the posturing and the preening in the bedroom in front of the mirror and in front of her was more important to Marcel than was the sex act he was to put her through later. "I think I look beautiful," he said, while dressing himself in women's clothes in front of her. "Sure," she said. "sometimes I think I look more beautiful than most women," he said. To this Darlene said nothing at all.

As soon as Stephen was sleeping through the night, Darlene found herself again subject to Marcel's attentions. She learned this was to be after she'd put baby Stephen to bed one night, then turned out the light in his room and gently closed the door as she left. As she quietly made her way back towards the living room, she was set upon by Marcel, her husband having silently emerged from the darkness of the master bedroom wearing a latex miniskirt, fishnets, and bright-red lipstick. "Do you like it?" he asked, grinning wryly. "It's late and I'm tired," she said, quietly. "So you don't like it, mistress?" he asked. He'd taken to playing the game where he'd feign submissiveness, goading her, then employing psychological trickery and compulsion to force her into doing things she didn't want to do. "Just be quiet," she said, herself speaking quietly, "don't disturb the baby." Marcel looked wickedly at her and said, "yes, mistress." He liked to draw her into playing the dominant role in his fantasies, then switch roles for the final climax.

Soon, they were at it again, she beginning to cry softly while he took on the demeanour, the character of the monstrous ogre reappearing as quickly as it'd disappeared. The sex they had that night was typically violent, but not yet harshly so, when he finished the act. Even as they acted out Marcel's fantasies, in the background the sounds of the city faded in through an open window, through a window left only slightly open. She wasn't made to do anything physically painful that night, but felt as though the discomfort in acting out one of Marcel's fantasies was painful in a different way. But she played along. She played along.

1

The shelter where Darlene spent the night following that climactic encounter with Marcel, it proved to be a longer home for her than she'd have expected. If her original plan, conceived of and executed hastily, had worked, she'd have been preparing to leave the house for Vancouver again. Instead, she stayed with her two young sons at the shelter for a few more days, before finally taking up the courage to get in her car and drive far, far away. In the days before informing Marcel she was leaving him, she'd reconnected with her old friend Cherise in Vancouver, her old friend who she'd never really lost touch with but who she hadn't spoken to in years. The car, Darlene was to have taken the car with her, it was the older and more worn-down of the two they'd owned. It was possible to have taken the other, the big, almost brand-new pickup truck Marcel usually drove everywhere, but she'd chosen the car she'd brought with her all the way from Vancouver. But the night was dark, too dark, so dark that even Darlene could look off into open space and imagine the tumult of red and blue and black turned against itself like the churning of the ocean behind a slowly-steaming ship. Even now, only so soon after having achieved that decisive confrontation with her to-be ex-husband, she was lost, she felt as though she was lost. Even now, as she spent those few days living out of the only women's shelter in the area, all she could think of, all she could worry about was the ever-present threat that he'd come after her again. Having reconnected with her old friend Cherise was only the beginning of something far more difficult.

All throughout those days, she wouldn't have known what to do about the constant fear that gripped her. When she rose in the morning and looked out into the street, she felt herself become paralyzed, a strange sort of paralysis that seemed to envelope her. The sons she'd brought with her to Quebec, young Stephen and younger Stuart, both slept quietly as she kept awake, tortured and tormented as she was by the thing that she imagined was turning against her. She didn't know it yet, couldn't have known it yet, but the thing she imagined wasn't there, was entirely the product of her own imagination, an imagination shaped by a psyche wracked by so many successive traumas. She kept on watching the darkness, staring into it with the stare of a veteran recalling an intense barrage of enemy fire. No, even that wasn't accurate, wasn't quite the way it was. Even then, with Darlene not at all imagining something that wasn't there, she managed to keep an even keel, failing to sleep only for all the adrenaline surging through her veins, for her heart that continued to pound even hours after her confrontation with Marcel had ended. At some point in the evening, Darlene checked on her two young sons, again finding them sleeping quietly. They both slept on the bed that night, leaving her to sleep on the room's little sofa, both pieces of furniture having been donated among the community some years ago already worn. Darlene didn't dare ask for anything more, although the next day one of the volunteers would tell her a cot had been found and would be brought into the room for her to sleep on.

Eventually, she determined to carry out her original plan. She worried that it wasn't legal to take her sons and move to the other side of the country, back to the west coast, but knew she couldn't live anywhere near Marcel. As he'd never been all that interested in helping her raise the boys, Marcel had always been at least somewhat distant, although this'd grown worse over time. The days passed slowly, while she was in regular contact with the police, this awkward and uncertain in-between time seeing her caught in a kind of limbo, leaving her paralyzed in ways she'd never felt paralyzed before. It was a waking nightmare, one where she was forced by something she couldn't see to remain in place even as her every instinct screamed at her to run away and to keep running until there was nowhere left to run. But, then, she knew, there would've been someone, if

116

not Marcel then someone to attack her, to take her children from her. She was in this delirious yet almost-catatonic state where she wanted to leap into action but felt ineffectual and lost. That night, that night at the shelter took a long time to pass, each excruciating moment seeming to Darlene like an hour. She looked over at the clock on the wall, saw a time, and then after she was sure an hour or two must've passed she looked over again to see only a minute or two had gone by.

Finally, morning came. It wasn't to have been so simple as just showing up and asking her to come home. He couldn't come in at all, couldn't even set foot on the property, strict as the shelter's rules were about admitting only women and children. But there was a part of her that expected him to come anyways, to try and brute his way in and attack her, somehow, someway. It was all so deeply confusing to her, having planned her escape so differently, so cleanly in her own mind, to now be forced to consider confronting him again, this time as he'd seemingly become a completely different person overnight. As Marcel wasn't allowed on the grounds of the shelter—the shelter was still women only, even excluding men who said they were women—they had to meet somewhere else. Already feeling vulnerable, Darlene wouldn't agree, not at first, not until she could be assured that she'd be allowed to leave. Even thinking about it caused her to fall into a deep depression, deeper than anything she'd ever experienced, even at the height of Marcel's depravity and terror. There came one day when she wouldn't get out of bed in the shelter at all; the volunteer brought her food which she ate grudgingly. But then there was the next day, when she was up and about, seeming to be bounding here and there, powered as she was by a sudden burst of energy and strength. That first night, though, she stayed awake all through the night, even in the morning her nerves frayed and her whole body aching but sleep continuing to elude her. At her side, Stephen and Stuart were awake already. Stuart asked, "are we going home today?" But Darlene only shook her head and said, "I don't know." Stephen said nothing. She hugged him.

There were to be more meetings, more apparent non-confrontations over the coming days. It recalled one of those moments from that particular night, the night when she'd announced her decision to leave him and to take the boys with her. She felt as though he wouldn't let her go, he wouldn't let her go, and she continuously worried about him acting on the many, many threats he'd made in the years that'd led up to her finally breaking away. All those times her mother, Marilyn, had broken down right in front of her had left a lasting impact on Darlene as a young child. At school, the other children always seemed to know there was something different about her and the way she lived, even if they could never have known exactly how. They teased and bullied her relentlessly, and her teachers never offered much in the way of help. There were anti-bullying campaigns in school, but they only resulted in increased bullying. But she never learned not to stop fighting back, never. There came one particular occasion when a group of other girls followed her as she walked home from school. She only made it halfway before turning to confront them, like her father had taught her to. Words were exchanged. A fight ensued. Darlene got in her licks before they swarmed her. When her father came home from work to find her badly bruised and bleeding from her face, he was furious. He called the school, then went to the police. But nothing changed. The girls kept on bullying her, and she kept on sticking up for herself. By the time her mother finally came home from her convalescence in the interior, too much had changed at home and outside the home for them to pick up where their lives had left off.

She envisioned Marcel coming. She envisioned herself meekly, timidly, even quietly saying, "thank you," to whatever he might've said of her, something that would've surely produced a wicked grin on his face, that same wicked grin she'd seen many times over, whenever made to perform the most horrendous sexual acts with him. But even that couldn't have been so simple. It'd still be some time before Darlene could leave for Vancouver with their sons, in that time Darlene receiving much grief. There weren't so many busy moments during that vague and impossible in-between time when she was waiting for help that might've never arrived. Most of her time at the shelter, those days before she was to finally leave for Vancouver, was spent watching over her sons and otherwise desperately passing time that never seemed to pass. The walls in her room at the shelter seemed to have never been cleaned, still dirty in places Darlene might've thought no person could've ever reached. There were cobwebs in the corners of the ceiling. The window, the one window in her room looked scuffed and scratched, but only on one side. At school, the children always seemed to know Darlene was unlike them, in the way children can know these things. Her mother was never seen at school, at miscellaneous events that parents sometimes attend, only her father, which made her the target of rumours. Even in elementary school, kids could be cruel. It might've been the case that the other kids would've teased her had they known the truth, but she was still too young to know these things. Eventually, she worked up the courage to tell someone, to tell another classmate she'd become friends with what was really happening. She put it in the way a child can put such things, telling her friend that her mother was sick and had to stay away. But her friend, another girl, said it wasn't a big deal. This emboldened Darlene to tell more people, something she would later regret.

Even the policewoman, the French-speaking policewoman couldn't have seemed any less sympathetic, or so Darlene had thought. She'd wind up going over that confrontation many times during her subsequent life, during the long and painful rebuilding she'd undertake, as if to extract from it any hidden meaning that'd eluded her. The way the policewoman spoke of her, spoke to her in a language she couldn't understand, it'd seemed so casual, so disinterested. She'd have expected this to continue after making it into a shelter, if her original plan, such as it was, had called for her to flee into a shelter. Back when Darlene was still in elementary school, she'd always been vaguely aware

Darlene

that her teachers and counselors knew what was going on at home. It was a mistake to have told that one friend she thought she'd had in her class. This was a key moment in her learning not to trust anyone outside a core group of people. Soon, the whole class knew, the bullying and the teasing escalating as classmates made fun of her for having a crazy mom. Still young, she fought back the only way she knew how. A fight ensued. Young Darlene lost, but got in her licks again. After it was over, her father came to the school to pick her up, exasperated but on her side. But sometime soon her mother would be there for her, making it even more difficult for her to try and live a normal life. Soon other events in their lives would overtake Darlene's problems at school, the fights at school continuing while the fight at home seemed never to end.

But even this was wrong, she later came to think, wrong for her to blame herself. She was deeply confused and afraid. Sometimes the summer's heat threatened to break, threatened to give way to unseasonable cold and rain, the kind of cold and rain she'd lived most of her life through on the west coast. Demonstrating her need to achieve even some small measure of closure, Darlene couldn't possibly have envisioned these events when planning her escape from her husband's clutches. As difficult as it may have been for her to have conceived, this was something she'd needed to do for a long time. The night, that night, had been unusually warm and humid, even for the Quebec townships this particular summer hot and humid. Throughout the church she stayed

121

in, a small Protestant church in a region of the province filled even in the twenty-first century with Catholics, she saw few other people. Throughout her time at the shelter, she'd learn very little about herself, but so much about the things that were to come. In the morning, in one morning, she finally managed a few hours of uninterrupted sleep, of sleep in which she dreamed. In her dreams, that morning, she was running, running not from something but towards something that was always in the distance, always out of reach. And then she woke up.

Chapter Six

2

A few months after their newborn son Stephen began sleeping through the night, Marcel's sexual torture and manipulation of Darlene became commonplace again. She'd come home after lengthy shifts at the hospital to find him dressed in his women's clothes. She'd tried to set boundaries by getting him to agree to keep his women's clothes in a separate drawer, only to begin around this time finding his oversized bras and panties mixed in with her modest, much smaller bras and panties, his cartoonishly large skirts and tops alongside hers. Every time she went to get dressed in the morning or put away her clothes after a wash—he never did the laundry, not even his own—she was confronted with evidence of his rapidly deepening confusion. Every now and then, he'd return home from a night out with the friends, only to turn right into the bedroom and practice dressing in his women's clothes, parading himself in front of the bedroom mirror even as the baby cried in the other room. When she timidly asked why he hadn't tended to the baby's cries, he chuckled and said that he hadn't noticed. But then there'd be the nights when he'd seem like a doting father, feeding, changing, and cleaning the baby, even singing lullabies or reading books in seeing young Stephen off to sleep in the evening. It was all so deeply confusing for Darlene. It was all so deeply confusing for Darlene. She chose to continue believing in the part of him that was in love with her, that'd been in love with her, recalling as she could the moments when he'd been a sweet and attentive lover and companion, as well as the thrill of being with someone who could introduce her to something new.

But even she was so deeply confused, remembering as she still could, still did the sweet and sensitive yet outgoing and confident young man Marcel had been when they'd first met, when they'd been only dating, long before the monster he was becoming had come out. As there were moments when that young man still showed himself, she always found a reason not to do anything she thought might've upset him. She kept on coming home in the evenings, sometimes very, very late, most nights finding him already home from his nine-to-five job, most nights finding him in the living room dressed in his ordinary clothes, seated on the couch, book open in his hands as he welcomed her home from a long shift at the hospital. Even during this early time, it was exhausting for Darlene to have to so constantly readjust her expectations. Even then, during that relatively early time, she knew nothing of what to expect. Their little apartment was hardly big enough for their family, for their new family, but all they could afford in Vancouver. Such a small place felt to Darlene like a little box within which all her troubles could've been sealed, but she knew even this was a lie, a lie she couldn't have told to herself. Sometimes neither of them could be around to care for young Stephen, necessitating a babysitter or a regular daycare, something Marcel seemed to take only a passing interest in. "It's up to you," he said, when she tried to talk about their options. "You're going to have to pick him up sometimes," said Darlene. "So I'll pick him up," said Marcel. She wound up choosing a small daycare not far from their home. Later, a few weeks later, Marcel seemed to become passionate about attending to Stephen, seeming to spend every spare moment holding their son, cradling him, feeding him, even volunteering to change his diapers. "I love my son," Marcel would say, "he's the most important thing to me in the world." And to this Darlene could only say, "me too," before approaching and laying a hand gently on the side of young Stephen's head, caressing him as Marcel held him. It was a mystery to Darlene how his attitude could change so rapidly. It came to frighten her that she couldn't predict it.

And then there was the fact that their young son, Stephen, still too young to even remember anything that was happening to him or around him. When Marcel forced Darlene to perform increasingly demeaning and humiliating sexual acts in their apartment's larger bedroom, she sometimes was able to grit her teeth and put herself through. Then there were those moments when Marcel demanded she take the active role, demanded that she become the wicked disciplinarian he referred to as 'mistress' in order to act out his deranged fantasies. One night, he demanded she use the term to refer to herself in the third person, then complain when she wouldn't use the proper tone. He seemed like a petulant child. "Don't you want me to be happy, mistress?" he asked, pouting slightly. When she didn't reply right away, he went on to ask, "you know you're the only one who can make me happy, right mistress?" To this Darlene managed to weakly say, "I know." Marcel asked, "when I'm happy you're happy, right mistress?" And Darlene only said, "of course." Then she resumed striking him with a paddle he'd bought, as per his instructions pausing to grab his genitals with one hand and manipulate them quickly. Later, the following morning as she was getting ready to leave for work, he approached her in the kitchen and said, "you had better be ready to put more effort into it than you did last night." She asked, "why's that?" She noticed he was holding Stephen, and although she was already in her scrubs she took Stephen from him for a feeding. "I won't be happy if you don't," he said. After feeding Stephen and the cat Barney, she left for work, not sure what to make of what Marcel had said.

Darlene's thirtieth birthday came. Marcel insisted on being involved in planning something for her, and complained when she wasn't to have everything the way he wanted. This particular part of Marcel, the controlling part, she hadn't ever seen it before. She had a small party, attended by a few friends from work, along with Cherise and Marcel. But not all was so listless or despondent. The young man she'd fallen in love with only some years earlier had a habit of reasserting himself at some of the most unexpected moments. Even though he was still a young man, a young man only a couple of years older than Darlene, Marcel began to seem much older. The question of their future together, of the family they intended to build, it all seemed to have come to a head with the sudden

Darlene

conception and birth of their first child. Their young son, Stephen, demanded much of Darlene's time and attention, all or nearly all of her energy. Although Stephen was sleeping through the night, Darlene wasn't. Most nights Marcel made no demands on her, made her perform no sexual acts she was uncomfortable with, even sometimes their increasingly-infrequent sex rather ordinary, closer to the slow and intimate lovemaking she would've preferred to the violent and deranged fantasies he liked to act out. It was around this time that he told her. "I think I might be a woman," he said, sitting on the couch next to her as she cradled baby Stephen. She said nothing. "I mean," he went on to say, "I don't believe I'm a woman all the time. I just might be one." Still she said nothing. "I'm going to try it out," he said, before explaining what was to come. By the time Darlene put baby Stephen to bed, she was unsure what to think. It'd been only several years since they'd met. Already Marcel was becoming someone different, right in front of her, seemingly in real time.

It was always to have been difficult for Darlene to discover not only that her husband was bisexual but that he was transgender as well. Even as he only indulged in his cross-dressing at home, it became a difficult burden to bear, knowing as she did that her only safe space had been compromised by his worsening fetishizing. A confrontation ensued, one night, after a lengthy shift at the hospital saw Darlene come home to Marcel wearing one of his dresses. But her exhaustion was the kind that frayed nerves, never leaving her utterly spent but draining her energy slowly, over time. She came home to find him wearing one of his dresses, posturing and preening in front of the large mirror in their bedroom even as their son was in the other room. "Oh, you're home," he said, continuing to look at himself in the mirror as he spoke, holding up different items of clothing, different bras and blouses as he spoke. "It's been a long day," she said. After she'd fed Stephen, she approached Marcel. She held Stephen in her arms as she went into the bedroom, Marcel continuing to posture and preen in front of the mirror. For some reason, Darlene felt bold. "I wish you wouldn't do that with my clothes," she said. "I can't do this with my own," he said, "they don't make them in my size." Darlene said, "still…" Marcel asked, "don't you want me to be happy?" Darlene said, "well, I…" But then Marcel turned to face her and snapped at her, saying, "then stop telling me how to do it!" She was taken aback. She stepped back, and when she did Marcel reached out and slammed the door, shutting her out of her own bedroom. Baby Stephen started crying, and it took Darlene the evening to calm him.

The few sources of information Darlene sought out all seemed to indicate that she should've supported her now-husband's sexuality and gender fluidity—those were the terms these sources used to describe his habits, not terms that she used, or would've used had she ever spoken to anyone about it back then—and that any reservations she might've had were hers to overcome. Sometimes he said he thought he was a woman, while other times he said he only liked dressing as one, and even then only in private. After their recent confrontation, only the first time she'd questioned his deepening madness, she felt as though the better part of him, the part she'd fallen in love with only some years ago, was beyond help, beyond recovery. Even she didn't fully understand it, and never could've. As the long shifts at the hospital seemed to draw longer and longer with each week that'd passed, something, at some point, snapped in Darlene, something that'd made her better able to adapt to the man her husband was becoming. But then there were those moments, those moments in the darkness of the night when he'd unexpectedly set himself on her. Darlene began to feel as though she couldn't know what to expect at home. Even despite these moments, Darlene thought it would be best for her to accommodate Marcel's growing obsession with himself, for a variety of reasons. Marcel was still in that early stage of his deepening fascination and experimentation with ideas of his own femininity, in that early stage where he'd yet to come to think of himself of as truly feminine. Still she kept on reading with the very young Stephen, the novels she was reading to him meant for an adult audience but still there for her anyways. Sometimes it was difficult to get Stephen to sit still, but she tried anyways. There were still too many books in their apartment for her ever to read, especially at the slow pace she was able to manage while taking care of young Stephen.

She'd had a small porcelain heart for years by then, kept in a plastic holder that sat upright on her dresser in her apartment's living room. When she'd moved in with Marcel, she brought it with her of course, and continued to place it on the bedroom dresser next to the mirror both she and Marcel used every day. Sometimes, when she was feeling discouraged or uneasy about the future, she looked at that small porcelain heart and remembered where it'd come from, the words she'd heard from the man who'd given it to her. Such a small memento, something that couldn't have cost more than five or ten dollars, but which Darlene had kept for years as a cherished symbol of valued memories. Sitting on the dresser in the bedroom in which Darlene was subject to increasingly violent and confusing behaviour by a deeply confused Marcel, it was like an oasis of calm to sit on the edge of the bed and look on that small porcelain heart. After their recent confrontation, only the first time she'd questioned his deepening madness, she still felt as though she could rely on the small part of him that was still loving and kind, gentle and strong, even as he continued his descent into gender confusion and mental illness. There was still that part of him, she reasoned, that loved her. And this part of him seemed worth the struggle whenever she sat on the edge of the bed and looked on that small porcelain heart.

But Marcel seemed more confused than ever. He hadn't yet become the overtly evil person he was fast becoming. There was still that hint of the kind and sensitive, yet exhilarating young man that Darlene had fallen in love with, hidden behind the man he was fast becoming. Sometimes he came home from work with small gifts for her, gifts like a box of chocolates or a little teddy bear, gifts that might've reflected a lack of imagination but which she genuinely appreciated as well. Later, many years later, she'd come to wonder whether these small gestures reflected a genuine confusion on his part or a cruel manipulation of her. She'd never know for sure. Although she was fast losing any love and respect she'd once had for Marcel, the love and respect that'd caused her to take to him some years earlier, there was still a little bit of life left for her to have lived for them both, for their new family. Stephen had given her a reason to live again, a reason to persist through the rapidly worsening sexual torture and emotional abuse she was being made to endure. This time, he demanded she tie him to their bed and then paddle him with a special leather paddle he'd ordered online and spent far too much money for. She complained that she wasn't feeling very well—this had become her usual complaint when asked to do something in the bedroom she didn't want to do—but he was insistent. Already changed into some of his women's clothes, he too to lying face down on the bed. Reluctantly, she complied with his requests, tying him up, then hitting him with the paddle while he purported to beg her to stop. But then, in the middle of the act, he stopped and complained that she wasn't striking him hard enough. Finally, he asked her to untie him, after which he grabbed the paddle from her and threw it hard across the room. Then, he took her.

But even this reason was fast dwindling in the face of repeated assaults on her by the man *and* woman her husband seemed intent on becoming. Marcel came to her one night and told Darlene that he intended to live as a woman, and that she should learn to accept him as a woman. By the time he was finished, Darlene had a new set of wounds from the abuse she'd endured. This time she wasn't cut, but was bruised severely; the bruises wouldn't fully show until the next day, by which time she'd cover them up with clothes and a bit of makeup. She didn't know, couldn't have said why she kept putting up with this treatment, aside from perhaps the desire to keep the family together and spare the children. That didn't matter. She felt alone, she felt alone but for the sound of her own crying. But even during these early times, these times when her abusive relationship with Marcel was still escalating in intensity and frequency of the abuse, Darlene felt as though there was something in him, some part of him worth fighting for, that it was her responsibility at least in part to keep fighting, not only for her but for him as well. She still loved him; but as she looked at herself in the mirror that next day and saw the bruises on her body, she had to convince herself she still loved him for the first time.

1

The policewoman who'd been one of those attending to the scene, Darlene had thought her cold and unfeeling. These police were trained like all other police in handling domestic disturbances, but this training was rote and mechanical, entirely lacking in empathy or connection to the people they were attending to. Even as Darlene was clasping her sons hands and looking out for any sign of Marcel coming after her, still the policewoman kept on speaking with another office in rapid-fire, coded French. When the only English-speaking officer stopped to say something, anything at all to Darlene, she could hardly hold her focus, her eyes darting back and forth as she clutched her sons' hands, pulling them in tighter at her sides, looking for any sign at all of Marcel coming out after them. It'd all gone wrong, it'd all gone so horribly wrong. She was still, at that exact moment in time, in survival mode, filled as she was with a mix of adrenaline and fear that'd made it possible for her to have slowed down and observed every moment that passed as if it'd been stretched out over hours and hours and hours. Both Stephen and Stuart were crying, like children cry. "Why aren't you letting me leave?" Darlene asked, speaking with the policewoman, that one English-speaking policewoman who seemed like the others utterly uninterested even in being there. "We have to make sure the children are okay," said the officer. "You have to let us go," said Darlene, tears streaming down her cheeks even as she spoke.

The flashing of red and blue lights against the darkness stained the night. It was a mystery to Darlene what the police were doing, why they seemed so determined to hold events in place for as long as the night could've taken to pass, for as long as it could've taken to get her to change her mind. The English-speaking officer explained, in halting, broken English, their point of view, such as it was. "Did he hit you?" asked the officer. Even in her excitable state Darlene couldn't answer directly, a thousand thoughts rushing through her mind all at once, images flashing of him striking her with his hands, with various instruments, not that night but nights before, many, many nights before. "N—no," she said, "n—not—not tonight, but…" The female officer seemed unmoved, pressing the issue by asking, "when?" But Darlene still wouldn't, couldn't answer directly. She wouldn't tell them, couldn't tell them about the years of abuse, of Marcel's cross dressing, of the forcible rape that she'd experienced just a few weeks earlier. Even if she'd wanted to talk about these things with complete strangers, she couldn't have just come out and said that her husband had been torturing her, had been dressing in women's clothes and forcing her to act out his most depraved fantasies, there would've still been that block about it, that thing in the back of her throat that might've forced her not to speak whenever she'd wanted. Even she didn't understand it fully. She didn't understand it much at all.

Even Darlene, as alone and frightened as she was, couldn't help but wonder whether something else was going on. Shivering and shuddering even in the midst of a hot summer's night, Darlene clutched her sons' hands, one in each of hers, having been allowed by the police to sit with them. She might've wondered what the police had said to young Stephen and Stuart while separated from them, but even this thought was beyond her, so consumed as she was in the fear that she could hardly move. Even to be stuck in a state of fear, with every muscle in her body seized in an electric paralysis. "Just, just let me go," she said, "I don't need, I d—don't need to be here." But the policewoman seemed still unmoved. "He doesn't say the children can go," said the officer, "so right now we need to make sure the children won't be abducted." Although she hadn't yet taken any decisive steps in fleeing Quebec, besides announcing to Marcel that she was leaving him. It was still dark out, still too dark out to see much of anything for the lack of streetlights on either side of the road, leaving Darlene still only just able to make out their neighbours that kept on gawking at them. "Why don't they let us go?" asked Stuart. "I don't know," said Darlene, clutching both her sons hands tight. Again, Stephen said nothing.

She couldn't understand why this was happening, why she wasn't being allowed simply to take her sons and leave. There was no need, she thought, for the police to become involved, to have inserted themselves into the situation with all the grace and tact of a brick to the face. The police had proven themselves in past encounters to be the enemy, not these particular officers but the police on the whole. Even the sight of those deep blue uniforms was enough to recall in her mind's eye memories of having been ignored. Their voices, their voices were so deep. Even the policewoman's voice seemed unnaturally deep. "You must know the children need their father," said the policewoman. In her agitated state Darlene couldn't have comprehend anything but the imminent threat. She thought of everything in terms of short-term survival, a habit learned over years of extensive experience. "Has he been assaulting you?" asked the officer. "Well, it's just," she said, thinking of that most recent time when he'd attacked her, when he'd forced her down onto the bed and taken her. "He's a very bad man," she said, tears beginning to form around her eyes again, blurring her vision. She didn't know what to say to the officer, what could've made the officers bring the confrontation to its necessary conclusion; she only feared they'd force her back inside, that they'd take her sons from her and return them to their home, after which she'd feel compelled to join them. At some point, she began to feel as though she was going to die that night. It seemed to her that the walls were closing in and the darkness was slowly advancing on her.

The flashing of red and blue lights against the darkness strained the night until the darkness itself seemed to threaten to burst at the seams. Although Darlene's focus was scattered everywhere at once, she was thinking, thinking, always thinking of the next step she could take away from that place. "Let me go," said Darlene, "let me go with my kids. Please just let me go." But the policewoman was unmoved, saying, "they say you have committed an assault." Darlene wasn't still carrying the can of Lysol she'd used to spray Marcel in the eyes. All this was something, something too much for her. She panicked. She was panicking. She wouldn't understand why this was happening, not for a long time, not until she'd managed to get some distance and perspective on events. Even at the time, she began to feel the aching of fatigue behind her eyes. She was tired, too tired. But the fatigue had been counteracted by the adrenaline coursing through her veins, blotting out all but the most basic and visceral of thoughts. The side of the road in the small city they lived in was no place for any kind of breakdown, she knew that.

The flashing of red and blue lights against the darkness drained the night of its colour, to Darlene exciting the senses and clouding the mind. "Don't let him come near me," she said. In the darkness of the night there was something unseen but definitely there, something that lingered in the night even as the hours dragged on and the morning drew closer. It was a night where so many memories could've all come to a single point, when Darlene could've felt as though she might break down and agree to anything Marcel had demanded of her. But she knew, she knew if she did that then she wouldn't make it through much longer, nor would her young sons. She believed Marcel might've come under the influence of some insidious new aspect of his long-worsening state, some new aspect that could've led him to kill her and her sons before taking his own life. But she struggled to explain this to the police, struggled even to gather the wherewithal to put these fears into words, so overwhelmed as she was. It got to the point where Darlene couldn't even speak, couldn't speak to the officer even when asked a direct question, so consumed and overwhelmed as she was by the fear that'd seized every part of her body and mind.

But after withdrawing to the shelter where she'd spend the next few nights, Darlene couldn't calm down, that night sitting awake, clutching at the couch she sat on while looking off into the darkness. In the darkness of the inside of that little church, she saw the flashing red and blue churning up the night, along with the sounds of sirens wailing in the distance. There were a few books for them to read at the shelter, along with an old TV for them to watch. Hooked up to the TV was a VCR, the TV sitting on top of a cabinet that had inside a box of VHS tapes containing movies the boys had mostly never heard of let alone seen. She kept on thinking about the night and the events that'd led up to it, events sometimes more distant than even she might've considered. Even after Darlene's mother, Marilyn, had come home from her extended time away, Darlene kept on getting into trouble at school, kept on getting into fights with some of the girls who were relentlessly bullying her. Her father, Wayne, commended her for standing up for herself, and continued to deride teachers and other school officials for failing to protect her. But whenever the young Darlene came home from school bruised and bloodied from a recent fight, her mother seemed altogether uninterested in what'd happened to her. But when next her mother tried to kill herself, actually tried to kill herself, it was Darlene who discovered her after coming home from school. Marilyn had overdosed on some of the medications she'd been prescribed, and had drank some vodka as well, and was lying unconscious on the couch when Darlene walked in. Darlene didn't call 9-1-1, but her father, who called 9-1-1 before rushing home from work. Another commitment to the psychiatric ward for Marilyn ensued. It was a lot for a young girl to go through. And through it all, Darlene kept on going to school, kept on getting bullied, kept on standing up for herself. And then she stopped standing up for herself.

Darlene

She lived in that shelter for those days until deciding it was time to take her two young sons and leave for Vancouver at the earliest opportunity. Even this was a lie, a fraud, as the earliest opportunity had come and gone already, and would continue to come and go with every moment that passed while she and the boys remained firmly stuck in place. Marcel would eventually consent to her leaving the province with their sons, for reasons she couldn't have known at the time and wouldn't ever come to know, not even in the years that were to have passed. The Quebec town where they lived together for the past several years were ardently Quebecois, hostile and alien to a western Anglo like Darlene. She'd never learned much French, although this wasn't her own doing. He'd gone through her mail, even mail specifically addressed to her, and thrown out anything he hadn't wanted her to see. Ample free time at the shelter prompted Darlene's recollections to continue. Having seen her mother almost die many years earlier ought to have been a turning point in Darlene's life, one way or another. This time her mother, Marilyn, spent almost a month on the psychiatric ward at the Royal Jubilee Hospital in Victoria. Darlene's father took her to see her mother several times during that span, although each visit was equally awkward and uncertain. Most of the time her mother said very little to her, sometimes nothing at all. It made Darlene, still very young, feel guilty, as though there was something about her that'd precipitated the sickness that'd seized her mother even before she'd been born. Finally, there was one visit where Darlene must've said something to elicit something of a reply. Marilyn said to her, "there isn't anything you can do to help me." Her father, Wayne, wouldn't leave the two of them alone. But when they were driving home, her father said to her, "none of this is your fault. It's no one's fault, not even your mother's." Darlene, still unsure what to say, said nothing. The next time the other children at school bullied her, she didn't fight back. She didn't fight back. She just let it happen.

3

Although Darlene might've thought herself basically good, the current turn of events had forced a re-examination of this belief. After her oldest son Stephen had had a falling out with his group of friends, there was little she thought she could've done to patch things up. At least the younger Stuart seemed comparably well-adjusted, earning good grades in school and keeping out of trouble with his friends. In East Vancouver, where they came to live after moving back from Quebec, this was well enough to help him stand out in good ways. For the years they'd been away, it seemed to Darlene as though much of the city had been torn down and built anew, simple, functional apartment blocks demolished to make way for gleaming, glass-and-steel towers that were always for sale even though they were said by the managers to be one hundred percent sold. Even in the working-class—formerly entirely working-class, at least— parts of the city, these towers were advertised with elaborate, colourful displays. Sometimes construction seemed to stop for months at a time, crews leaving machinery in place while behind the scenes all kinds of financial or legal wrangling took weeks or months to resolve. But it'd always resolve, one way or another. The nearly-continuous development bothered Darlene because she felt as though her sons' futures were being stolen from them, that they'd have bad jobs and sky-high rents to contend with when they came of age and had to strike out on their own. But even sometimes Darlene found her attention drawn away from these things, drawn towards the war at home, a war that'd never really ended but had only taken a new form.

Darlene wanted to go into the school both her sons attended and ask if Stephen's teachers had known anything about the struggles he was experiencing. It was difficult for her to get the time off from work, her work at the hospital in downtown Vancouver always on the night shift. She knew very little about his grades, only seeing the occasional marked assignment poking out of textbooks or binders he left scattered around the home. It didn't help that most of the time she wasn't home before school got out for the day, which made it possible for Stephen to intercept any mail that came from the school's administration. Even when there weren't any extra shifts to be had at the hospital, Darlene still had to volunteer for extended overtime on her regularly-scheduled shifts. Sometimes, sometimes the moments where she was overwhelmed came at her suddenly, without warning, only to leave her unmoved, apparently stuck in some catatonic state. And then she'd reappear, sometimes a few minutes and sometimes a few hours later, apparently having been in full control of herself throughout the intervening period but having no recollection of where she'd been or what she'd done. If Darlene had thought herself basically good at one point in her life, she must've come to the realization that nothing could've been further from the truth, that she, like everyone else, was fundamentally something other than what she was. The halls at the hospital, they were made of linoleum on the floor and squares of drywall on the ceiling, squares of drywall interspersed with the occasional flickering light. "Don't worry about it," said one of her co-workers, a porter named Duane who could always be seen with a smile on his face and a spring in his step.

They sometimes made her feel guilty for having so little spare time. She was home on a rare Friday off when Stephen arrived after school with his girlfriend in tow. Darlene didn't even know the young woman's name, despite having seen her around the house more than a few times over the past few months. "You said your mom wasn't going to be here," said the young woman, seeming to have said it almost playfully. "Don't worry about it," said Stephen, shooting a quick glare at Darlene before continuing to say, "she's not going to do anything." At that moment, Darlene felt disarmed and vaguely threatened. The two bounded up the stairs, their steps tracking across the second floor above her. She let it be, turning instead to the television, pausing only to get herself a glass of wine from the box she had open in the fridge. It was by some coincidence that Darlene received a call on her cell phone right then, a call from her best friend Cherise. Darlene answered readily, and they talked about everything but Stephen, Darlene deciding she needed the distraction. "You sound off," said Cherise, before asking, "is this a bad time?" Darlene sighed softly before saying, "as a matter of fact it's the best time you could've picked." But Stephen seemed lost in his own world, a world made of things Darlene was intimately familiar with but powerless to do anything to change. "I know you'll do it anyways," said Cherise, "but you shouldn't worry about it so much." They went back and forth for a little while, eventually moving on to other topics, their conversation blending seamlessly into a single continuous part. "It's not that I don't want to be there," said Cherise, "it's just that it's a long way to go." Even Cherise's problems, her ongoing loneliness and her frustrations life, she often wouldn't disclose them directly to Darlene. And Darlene, Darlene was okay with this.

Soon, she would later learn, Stephen met a girl. He was in the twelfth grade by this point, and nearing high school graduation. He found a part-time job at a pizza place. The girl he met and soon after began dating had been struggling with her friends just as Stephen had been, something they'd bonded over one afternoon under the bleachers around the football field behind school. Darlene didn't know this, of course, but came to suspect something when she found a pack of cigarettes and a lighter in Stephen's room. She confronted him over this, intending for her confrontation to amount to something, anything at all in the way of an intervention of sorts. But Stephen had his girlfriend there at the time, and she couldn't summon the courage to confront them both at the same time. "What's she looking at?" asked the girlfriend, in a voice just loud enough to be audible to Darlene but quiet enough that suggested she thought Darlene couldn't hear. "Nothing," said Stephen, "just ignore her." He turned to face the door, shooting Darlene a mean look, a look that she saw the beginnings of a wickedness in, only the very hint of a growing maliciousness she'd once been terrified of in Marcel. That familiarity was enough to cause her to lapse back into her own habits, that night, a night she had off, seeing her take to quietly drinking in the living room while listening to music that'd been known to her as Marcel's favourite.

But the drama involved in teenaged relationships like Stephen's never seemed to end. The fighting and the crying and the screaming never seemed to end. Sometimes she'd come home from another lengthy shift at the hospital or from running errands on a day off to find the two of them going at it in his bedroom, sometimes arguing about something, sometimes having sex in his room or kissing on the living room couch. When she came home one evening to find Stuart doing his homework on the kitchen table, she asked him whether his older brother was home. "He's upstairs," said Stuart, seeming rather exasperated, at least as exasperated as a twelve-year-old boy could be. Darlene set her things down on the table, then went upstairs, knocking lightly on the door to

144

Darlene

Stephen's bedroom. "Stephen, are you in there?" she asked. She couldn't think of anything else to say. "Hurry up, she's home," said Stephen, his voice slightly muffled even from behind the door. When he came to the door and opened it, he walked right past Darlene, leading a girl past her as well. The girl, Darlene didn't recognize her as the most recent girl he'd spent some time with. They bounded down the stairs, and seemed to be making for the front door. "Dinner's at six," Darlene said, calling out after him. When she came back down, Stephen was gone. Stuart asked, "don't you know he won't be back tonight?" After thinking about it for a moment, Darlene said, "finish your homework." Then, she went into the kitchen, and before Stuart said anything else she found a bottle of booze in the top cupboard and took a swig.

So close as he was to graduating high school, but Stephen had yet to give any hint to Darlene of what he intended to do afterward. She wanted him to keep on studying, but his grades were too poor for him to get into any university. She thought this might've meant him enrolling in a local community college, hoping he'd be able and willing to put in the effort to get grades there good enough to transfer to UBC or SFU, although inwardly she doubted even this would ever happen. She couldn't press him; every time she thought to try, she'd look at him and see an angrier person hiding behind his eyes, an angrier person than even she thought might've been lurking there. The moments when he showed the kind and sensitive young man he used to be were growing scarcer and scarcer. He liked animals. He always liked animals. When she brought up the topic in conversation of the cat they used to own, he spoke fondly of the affection the cat used to show him, the way he used to scratch the cat behind the ears just so. There was no one moment when she began to become afraid of Stephen. At some point she just started seeing that look in his eyes, that painful and angry look, that look that threatened something much, much more. He was never violent at home, not yet, and he never threatened her in any way. But that look in his eyes, it was too much for her to ignore.

Still, she thought work was the answer. A third time she'd tried to interrupt Stephen in his playing games with friends. It'd been only so long since they'd come to live back in Vancouver again, and it was as if nothing had changed at all. There weren't a lot of decent jobs out there for young people like Stephen, as wages in Vancouver were too low and the cost of living was too high. Sometimes she didn't blame Stephen and many others in his generation for not having much of a plan for their own futures, as there seemed little to be worth planning for. All through the night, on nights around this time, there was still that all-familiar anxiety provoked only by the loneliness and by the darkness of the night. Darlene slept with the covers pulled up to her neck, even on the hottest of summer nights. She sweated through the nights, and often had to wash the sheets multiple times a week. Even she was tired, too tired, always so tired from working so much and having seemingly so little time to spend at home, even as home as the source of nearly all her fixations. She felt frustrated even as she felt empowered. Not for the first time in her life she was caught between extremes, straddling the boundary between two parts of her life, with hardly the energy to get through the day much less thrive. But she always managed. She always managed to get through the day. Whenever she felt as though she'd reached the end, there was always something that inspired her to do what she needed to do, to make dinner, clean their apartment, shop for one thing or another, or just be there to see another latest crisis come to an end.

This time seemed for Darlene to pass even slower than it'd come to pass. In those few months between Stephen's having struck up a relationship with this new girl and his having graduated high school, something still off in his immediate future, there was endless drama. Stephen could be heard to shout and yell on the phone, his girlfriend coming over to continue the yelling and shouting. This was known to Darlene only from the moments she was at home, on those days off from her lengthy shifts at the hospital, those days off when she hadn't or couldn't have volunteered for an extra shift. She might've said something about it, anything at all to try and calm her son or at least get him to cut the noise, but every time he raised his voice and got into it with his girlfriend she had these flashbacks to her own relationship with the boy's father, Marcel. They hadn't heard from Marcel for some time, and Darlene had begun to wonder if she might've never heard from him again.

Chapter Seven

1

After spending a first night at that shelter, back after having left Marcel for the final time, Darlene was uncertain and exhausted. Being on edge, being constantly alert for any possible threat to her safety and to the safety of her two sons, it drained her so completely. At some point that night, in the space of a moment between one heartbeat and the next, Darlene took to quieting her racing thoughts and stilling her thumping heart by looking off into the darkness and trying to imagine what might've been there. The boys kept on sleeping, softly. Even in the dead of night Darlene wondered whether Marcel was to come after her, whether he could've materialized out of the darkness and come after her and her sons like a ghost or a demon. Living holed-up in the shelter for a few days would do little to help their state. Both Stephen and Stuart, on the other hand, seemed to acutely know where they were, even as they must've known nothing at all. It made Darlene feel like an utter failure to have been so unable to have protected them, and she immediately began to blame herself, began to castigate herself for having been unwilling to protect them for as long as they'd lived. Sitting in that little room in the dead of night, she was able to recall the past. After Darlene's mother, Marilyn, attempted suicide, after Darlene had come home in the afternoon to find her mother unconscious on the living room couch, nothing changed, not right away. Under the strain of Marilyn's chronic mental health problems, her parents soon separated, eventually to divorce. By this time, Darlene was in the next grade over. The girls kept on bullying her, but she grew more passive, less likely to stand up to any one instance of bullying. The bullying became less physical and more verbal. Her father, overburdened with a litany of other problems, took the fact that she wasn't getting into fights anymore as progress, and stopped protesting her treatment to the school. The culmination of this came when she was standing at her locker, at school, and a girl walked past, shouting something obscene at her, causing her to simply shut her locker and walk away. By this time twelve, Darlene was on the cusp of adolescence, her mother having disappeared from her life for reasons she still struggled to understand more than twenty-five years later.

More than a few thoughts were to occur to Darlene in the stillness and quiet of the night, that night. Her sons slept still through the night, she knew exhausted by the ordeal they'd been through. By the time she'd been able to calm down, Darlene had begun to feel the creeping onset of an insidious guilt, the very same guilt that'd once made her blame herself for what she'd been through, what she'd been subjected to at the hands of her monster of a boyfriend, then fiancé, then husband. It was all an elaborate sham, a fraud, the way the night had made her into something other than what she was. She'd planned to have been long gone by then, to be in Vancouver after having flown out. Even this wasn't true; she'd planned to drive to Quebec City, then perhaps on to Montreal, where she'd have flown direct. After having moved to Quebec some years earlier and succeeded in making no friends during the intervening years, Darlene had come to be totally isolated, alone, without anyone to help her. It was that way during her final years before adolescence, when she felt as though she had no friends and no one to rely on except maybe her father, Wayne. Although she was about to enter high school, all she could thing about was the battle at home. Teachers offered no help, no sign of understanding, seemingly no desire to make her feel any less alone. Wayne didn't ask. Her grades kept up, however. Still so young was she that even the next few years would've seemed like an infinite stretch of time, had she even been able or willing to look ahead. She saw her mother less frequently; at one point Marilyn took to self-medicating, having given up on prescribed psychiatric medications, and disappeared for months at a stretch. All this was too much, too much for a young girl like Darlene even to process, and she withdrew even further. But she remembered everything, remembered everything in the way a twelve year old can, remembered it for future understanding, her adolescence beginning at exactly the wrong time.

Back during that climactic confrontation, when Darlene had been in the midst of announcing her decision to leave her husband, it'd been something just to have made it out of there alive. "You have no idea what you're doing," Marcel had said, "you're killing me. You're going to kill me if you do this." But these were the same threats he'd made before, their having been made so many times effectively neutering his intentions. "You can do what you want," Darlene had said, "but I'm leaving, and I'm taking my sons with me." He'd towered over her and said, "you'll kill them, too. You're going to kill my children." There was something in Darlene at that moment that'd emboldened her, causing her to rise to meet him as she said, "they're my children too." There was more weeping and wailing, more shouting and screaming, until the final decision had been made and the tipping point had been reached. That was what'd happened between Darlene announcing her intention to leave and Marcel trying to stop her by physical intimidation. For all his posturing, for all his pretension to femininity, he could only be a hulking ogre of a man. She might've imagined him threatening to kill her, but after he'd raped her and beaten her so viciously only a few weeks before she had every reason to fear for her life.

But that was then. As the night ground past, the first night she'd wind up spending at that little shelter, Darlene began to feel no less discomfort. She was fed out of the shelter's cafeteria, which was closed after hours. She managed to sip on a glass of water over the late night hours, but ate nothing as she wasn't hungry. Stephen and Stuart both slept through the night, exhausted as their limited endurance was by the night's events. She took to praying at some point in the night, not long before she'd eventually manage to fall asleep. The pastor from the nearby church came to greet her in the morning. She spoke very little English, requiring the attendance of the caretaker who'd spent the night along with Darlene. She felt

Darlene

thankful for the caretaker, a humble, elderly woman who spoke perfect English without the slightest hint of an accent, but spoke French as well. When Darlene complimented her and asked where she'd learned such fluent English, she simply shrugged and said she'd spoken English and French all her life. For the first time since she'd resolved to leave Marcel, she felt a genuine, albeit passing, appreciation for someone else, as though she couldn't help but wonder. A pastor who volunteered at the shelter was a black woman who said she was born and raised in the Democratic Republic of the Congo, and came to Canada as a refugee fleeing decades of civil war with her family.

The Congolese pastor's name was Amelie Nzuzi, and she seemed much older to Darlene than she was. Amalie explained this was because of her lengthy experiences in fleeing persecution, having come to Canada as a refugee during the Congo Wars of the 1990s. "But I always want to give my time to help other women," she said, speaking with a thick accent Darlene could only just understand. "I see in some of the women in Canada a fear," she said, "and it is the same fear I saw when I was younger." Darlene said, "thank you." It was all she could think to say. Amelie hadn't said it, but she'd been raped as a girl growing up in the Congo, during the wars where many women and girls had been raped. The two spoke while Darlene was with her sons in one of the shelter's common areas, in the middle of the day when there was little for her to do but sit and wait for things to happen. It was midway through the summer, a time of the year Darlene had been fortunate enough to happen

153

upon for the most important decision she'd made in years. During the day, that day, it was as hot and sticky out as it'd been during the earlier parts of the recent summer heatwave. The shelter had no air conditioning. During the sweltering summer's heat, the building was reliably ten degrees hotter inside than out, leaving Darlene and the other women living there sweating profusely all through the day and sometimes through the night. Stephen and Stuart both kept by her side. "When will we get to go home?" asked Stuart. "I don't know," said Darlene. Again Stephen said nothing. Again Darlene said nothing.

"You know there is always a place for you," said pastor Amelie. "Thank you," said Darlene. It was still all she could think to say. Amelie went on to describe her difficulty in adjusting to life in Canada after having come from a war-torn country. Although Amelie never directly compared her experiences to Darlene's, she sometimes said things that made Darlene feel as though she could see right through her. "You have a lot of pain in you," said Amelie, "and it's okay because you're always going to be safe here. If you need to have someone to listen to you, then I will be here for you. If you need someone to listen to then I will be here for you as well." Still Darlene could think of little else to say but to thank Amelie for the comfort. Looking back, Darlene couldn't help herself from looking back even as she'd been forced by circumstance to keep looking forward. Without her car—Marcel's car, actually, as both of their cars had been registered in Quebec in his name and not hers—she couldn't go anywhere during the day, not that she would've wanted to.

"There will be a service tomorrow," said Amelie. It was Saturday afternoon. "Where?" Darlene asked. "Here at the shelter," said Amelie, "it will be held in the living area." The living area was a small room, with seating only for a few people. "I will come over in the early afternoon," said Amelie, "I come every Sunday to give a service to anyone who wants. Sometimes there is only one or two women who like to listen. Sometimes everyone in the building comes. I give my sermon regardless." Darlene thought about it for a moment, and then said, "I'll be there." Even through those days after her anti-climactic confrontation with Marcel, Darlene couldn't help but keep herself all but grounded in the there and then. For how long it'd take her to get out of that little church Darlene might've imagined there was something else waiting for her when she returned to Vancouver with the boys. Even still, she might've imagined Marcel going back on his promise to let them go, the promise she'd won only after several days of inner turmoil.

Even still, leaving Quebec and heading back to Vancouver once and for all would only heighten her anxiety and provoke more anguish. If her father had still been alive when all this happened, she wouldn't have had to think about what to do or when to do it. She wouldn't have had to figure it all out on her own. All she'd have had to do was make one call to him and he'd have given her all the help she'd needed. Even this was true throughout all the years Marcel's escalating psychological and sexual abuse had been driving her slowly to her breaking point. By the time she'd reached that point, she had few options left to escape. But she tried, she tried.

3

Darlene's son Stephen graduated high school without incident. He kept on seeing the girl he'd been dating for the last few months, and kept on working at the pizza place for minimum wage. But the dramatic changes she'd seen in him hadn't yet abated but accelerated. The changes she'd seen in Stephen over the earlier months, Darlene didn't like them. But as she hemmed and hawed over what to do, over how to broach the subject after her previous efforts had all failed, she felt as though she was wasting valuable time, paralyzed like she'd always been, utterly helpless. The place they lived in, it was starting to grow a little old and a little stale after having been lived in by Darlene and the two boys for several years, the carpet fraying in placing in places, the pain thinned and scratched, the smell of cigarette smoke lingering even in the suites where no one smoked. Sometimes in the apartment Darlene shared with her sons she could smell the foul smell of marijuana smoke, coming in through the windows from the street, the summer forcing her to choose between shutting herself up in the season's searing heat or allowing the noxious stench from people smoking to enter throughout their suite. "You can't smoke in here," said Darlene, when she confronted Stephen with a pair of his friends in his room one evening. "Yeah right," Stephen said, before drawing a drag on his joint and exhaling right at her. His friends laughed. "That smells horrible,"

Although Darlene didn't like all the drama, she hoped that both Stephen and his girlfriend would keep on helping each other learn. After all, she thought, it's normal and natural, even healthy to be so given to melodrama at such a young age. That summer was hotter and more humid than most summers on Canada's west coast, leaving Darlene even less able than usual to fight the fights that'd seemed to need fighting every month, every week, sometimes even every day. Once, Stephen came in with a bottle of something that looked suspiciously like hard liquor. When Darlene managed her way into his bedroom, she took the bottle of liquor and went to pour it out. But she paused at the sink to take a whiff, the stinging smell of vodka, the smell that smelled more like nail paint remover. She felt the flare of temptation, and after instinctively checking to see if anyone could've been looking she took a swig. "Hey!" It was Stephen. He'd come home. "You can't drink this," she said. "But you can?" he asked. It was then that she realized she'd taken more than one swig, that she'd paused for longer than she could remember to drink from Stephen's bottle. She said, "I'm old enough, and—" But Stephen reached for the bottle, Darlene struggling to hold it back, in her struggle fumbling with it before finally dropping it. The bottle fell onto the edge of the counter, then to the floor, shattering. "Why did you do that?" he asked. But he seemed to her more upset than angry. "Just go upstairs," she said. "Fucking shit!" he said, before turning and bounding up the stairs. She heard the thumping of stairs across the upstairs floor, then the slamming of a door.

Eventually, a few months after they both graduated from high school by the slimmest of margins, Stephen and his girlfriend broke up. This Darlene only found out when she suggested to him that the he and his girlfriend should find an apartment or basement suite together, even going so far as to suggest they look in the somewhat cheaper city of Surrey to the southwest. "We're not together anymore," he said, his tone of voice suggesting disinterest even in the subject. "I don't think I like girls anymore," he said. This was shocking enough to Darlene, but what Stephen said next shocked her even more. He said, "I think vaginas are disgusting." Even she didn't know what to say to that. "I'm not gay," said Stephen, looking at her with a half-sideways look that suggested he knew what she was thinking. "That's okay," she said, unsure what else to say. "I just don't want to be with anyone right now," he said. "That's your choice," she said. Soon, he moved out, finding a room to rent in a house somewhere else in Vancouver. She'd later learn exactly what these accommodations were like, but that's to come. Although she continued to worry about him, now that he was at arm's length it became easier for Darlene to process what was happening to him.

Even still, young Stephen's fascination with violence had continued to concern Darlene. When he was still in his teens, he'd read obsessively about war and the military, and for a time Darlene had encouraged this to the extent that she had. She tried to give him books and have him watch movies about historical incidents and periods related to some of these; if he was reading about violence in the Vietnam War, for instance, she tried to get him to watch movies like *Platoon* or *Full Metal Jacket*. He seemed to delight at watching the graphic violence in these movies, which led her to believe her efforts had backfired. But then there were the moments when he demonstrated he still could've been the sweet and sensitive young boy he once was. Every now and then, when she had a day off in the middle of the regular work week, she saw him stop at a neighbour's place and pet their cat that was allowed to roam freely outside. The cat was known around the neighbourhood as unfriendly and ill-approachable. When she asked about it, he replied that he liked cats, and that he liked cats because they didn't care about any of the things people cared about, like how much money you had or what kind of clothes you wore. They only cared, he said, about how good you treated them. When he said this, Darlene wasn't sure what to say, moved a little as she was by the unexpected display of his kindness.

As it was time for Stephen to be studying for his provincial exams, Darlene didn't want to do anything to upset him. She would later feel guilty about always finding a reason, always finding an *excuse* not to do or say anything, but at the time she was still hoping only he'd get through this challenge and make it through the other side in one piece. The next time Stephen and Darlene were home at the same time, something that was happening less and less as he'd taken to working part time at the pizza place until closing late at night, she sat at the kitchen table and looked up from a book she'd been reading to watch him march into the kitchen and search through the cabinets for something. She heard the repetitive sound of a lighter flicking, then Stephen exhaling deeply. She smelled the foul odour of cigarettes, an odour that suddenly recalled memories of Stephen's father, the recollections so strong that it was as though she could feel Marcel's stubble against her cheeks or her inner thighs. It inspired in her an instant revulsion, an instant revulsion she had to work hard to keep under control. "I don't like it when you smoke in here," she said. "I know that," he said. But she thought it was a good thing he wasn't smoking marijuana; the smell of cigarettes was far less pungent.

The St. Paul's hospital in downtown Vancouver was to be replaced in the coming years. The replacement hospital wasn't to be built on the same site, nor anywhere near it, but further to the east, well outside the city's downtown core, on a property currently occupied by a great empty lot directly north of the city's central train station. The site of the old hospital, where Darlene continued to work during this time, had already been sold to a developer, the hospital itself to be torn down and replaced by still more gleaming, glass-and-steel luxury towers that were always to be for sale yet always to be fully sold. Although Darlene had moved back to Vancouver with her sons and started working at the St. Paul's hospital after these decisions had been made, she quietly resented them like everyone else. Even these thoughts sometimes lingered after she'd come home, after she'd come home and found young Stephen smoking in the kitchen or playing loud music in his bedroom.

A lot of grumbling could be heard around the hospital, in the little private conversations that nurses, orderlies, doctors, even some of the cafeteria workers or janitors sometimes had in the few spare moments that presented themselves on shift. The new hospital was said by management to be larger, better equipped, and better staffed than the old, as well as better able to withstand a serious earthquake, but these reassurances fell flat. The billion dollars made by the health authority in the sale, it was supposedly to be put to use in funding all manner of services that people like Darlene and her co-workers wouldn't make a difference in their lives. It all seemed to them like an unmistakeable yet impenetrable morass of blackness. Even these thoughts sometimes lingered after she'd come home, after she'd come home and found young Stephen drinking in the living room or watching movies too loud on his computer.

Regardless, Stephen was on his own. She would continue to see him, every now and then, for the next few years, until he'd break the news that'd break her heart. By then, much was to have happened, little of which Darlene was to have seen but the effects of which were to have had a profoundly disturbing impact on her own life. No matter what her oldest son did, it affected Darlene double, the pain and the confusion in his life manifesting as if by some subconscious link in hers.

2

Eventually, Marcel lost his job. The exact circumstances under which he lost his job were unknown to Darlene. It must've had nothing to do with his still-escalating sexual perversion, she thought, because of his propensity to restrict those activities to the bedroom and the bedroom only. In recent months, he'd spent an increasing amount of time at home, alone save the company of their young son Stephen. Even as she went to work at the hospital twelve hours a day, four or more days a week, Darlene began to feel as though she shouldn't have been leaving Marcel alone with their young son, that Marcel might've exposed their young son to some aspect of his cross dressing. But despite his having become unemployed, Marcel seemed to be a doting father, although sometimes lacking in earnestness, in any real clue what he was doing. It became necessary for Darlene to pick up additional shifts wherever possible, just to keep a roof over their heads. Even still, through this time she observed not only this good side to him, coming home to find him sometimes playing with Stephen on the couch, in the living room, sometimes reading to him, sometimes even cleaning some mess their son had made in the kitchen. It was these little moments that made Darlene not forget but almost overlook the darker side to him, the darker side that she'd begun to feel she was becoming lost in.

He continued his cross-dressing, spending much of his time alone at home on it, when the boys were at school. He'd frequently buy new

outfits, using credit cards—both his and hers—
while trying them out at home. Unemployment
soon provided Marcel with ample time to conceive
of his next fantasies, soon his fantasies seeming to
compel him to subject Darlene to something
newer, something more perverted. He began to
concoct new scenarios involving role play. He
came up with an alter ego, a feminine identity to
use in the sexual acts he kept compelling Darlene
to act out. The name of this alter ego was Betty
Brilliance, something Darlene couldn't help but
laugh a little at the first time she heard him say it.
"You don't like it?" he asked. Even this put a
frown on his face, wounding his pride. "I'm sorry,"
she said, "I want you to be happy." She knew what
he was thinking. "This is a part of me," he said,
"and you know that I need you to help make me
happy. If you disapprove of this then you'll be
taking away my happiness." Keeping in mind his
sometimes-attentive care for their young son, she
sought to placate him. She said, "we can both be
happy." But he stuck with it, that night, that very
night forcing her to act out his next fantasy,
dressing her in a latex miniskirt that was at least
two sizes too small before beating her over, again
and again. In this fantasy, she was made to play the
role of the street walking prostitute, while he
purported to be the wealthy businessman who'd
picked her up. Later that night, he struck her
violently, leaving marks on her bottom, causing her
to cry out in pain.

Soon, Darlene became pregnant again. At first,
she was relieved to have become pregnant,
knowing that Marcel's revulsion for her pregnant

body would've led to his lust for sexual violence and abuse relenting, at least for a little while. She stopped drinking while she was pregnant, as she'd stopped when pregnant with Stephen. Her alcoholism wasn't so bad back then, such that she was still able to stop drinking whenever she wanted. With Marcel having mostly ceased his voracious and perverted sexual desires on her, it became possible for Darlene to get through the days again without need for booze. But even this reprieve couldn't last. Eventually having to take off work, at a later stage in her pregnancy, she was largely confined to home for several weeks, several weeks in which she couldn't do much not because she was physically unable but because Marcel insisted on her remaining at home. Their family, now of four instead of three, seemed to Darlene as though it was fast becoming a prison. After coming home with their second son, Stuart, and after having stopped breastfeeding him, Darlene took to drinking again, more moderately than before but regularly enough. Although there were still those moments when Marcel seemed like a doting, caring father, those moments were fast becoming rare. He seemed selectively uninterested in their children. "Your son is crying," said Darlene, when she came home one evening to find him on his computer, while young Stuart cried in his crib. "He's been crying all day," said Marcel, not even bothering to look up from his computer. "Have you been feeding him?" asked Darlene. "Of course I have," said Marcel. He turned to face her, and asked, "do you think I would let him starve?" But his tone of voice was short, although he didn't yell. "I'm sorry," she said, having picked up Stephen and begun to coddle him, "it's been a very long day." Marcel mumbled something and turned back to his computer, while Darlene changed and fed young Stuart. Stephen was there and saw everything, but said nothing. At only two, two and a half, Stephen was too young to know what was happening around him.

At some point after Marcel lost his job, he seemed to fall into a deep depression. He was still in bed when Darlene left for work every morning, and some days he was in bed when she came home. He still kept up with feeding their boys; this she could tell from Darlene felt as though she was doing nothing, absolutely nothing to arrest their family's descent into madness. Now the only working member of their household, she had assumed the entire mantle of the provider for the family. Even still, the birth of her second son had provided Darlene another very powerful reason to keep going, to keep on trudging through the days and nights, to keep putting one foot forward and pulling herself through the still-mounting pain, her having taken to drinking again notwithstanding. One evening, one Saturday evening saw Marcel preening in front of the mirror, dressed in some of his women's clothes, while Darlene sat in the living room with baby Stuart on her lap, Barney the cat at her feet, and a glass of wine in her hand. "I bet I worked harder than you here at home," Marcel had said, of the things he'd been up to all week. "I'm not sure what you mean," Darlene said, trying to avoid getting into an argument. "I have to work at home right now," he said, "feeding and cleaning the children. I'm so much better at it than most women." But Darlene said nothing in response, only letting an exasperated sigh escape her lips. "You don't like it?" asked Marcel. "It's fine," she said, "I'm just tired." He seemed to take notice. For a while, a little while, his antics tapered off, and she saw him less and less in his women's garb at home. But this was only one of many false improvements.

Several months passed between the birth of their second son and the return of her body to normal, more or less. She lost most of the weight she'd gained, and except for the stretch marks her abdomen shrunk back into itself. Betty Brilliance returned, Marcel even going so far as to demand that she refer to him by that name when they were in the home, alone with the boys, alone so that no one could see them. She thought to ask him why this new identity was so important to him if he was bent on keeping it a secret from the outside world, but knew better than to provoke his rage by doing so. At some point, the beatings and the whippings and the sexual torture resumed, always under the guise of acting out his latest sexual fantasy, always involving one of them playing a domineering role while the other played the role of the submissive. For Darlene, who only wanted sensual, nurturing, mutually-loving sex, these fantasies were gruesome and grotesque imitations of sex. One night, he dressed as Betty Brilliance, with a red wig, lipstick, and dress, a dress he'd haphazardly cut out in strategic places to allow access to his genitals. While dressed like this, he pushed Darlene down into the bedding, face first, and pounded her hard

166

from behind. He clutched at her hair and worked one hand to her throat, grabbing at her tight until she could hardly breathe. She tried to cry out, but could hardly gasp the words for his grip. He was choking her. And then he came, holding himself still, buried inside her to the hilt, tightening his grip on her throat until she couldn't breathe at all. But then he released her, and they fell forward onto the bed.

Then, he came up with an idea: the whole family should move clear across the country to the small city in Quebec he'd been born and raised in. At first resistant to the idea, Darlene felt as though she was rapidly losing the ability to assert herself, as though he was killing her. Moving to Quebec, she thought, would only hasten her own destruction. They'd wind up leaving a little over a month later, renting a house owned by Marcel's parents in a small city in the Saguenay region, a part of Quebec north and northeast of the capital and one of the most ardently pro-separation parts of the province. (Even referring to Quebec as a province rather than a nation might've offended some of those who lived in the area). In the most recent referendum on separation, which took place in 1995, the region had voted overwhelmingly for the province of Quebec to separate from Canada and become an independent country. Although Darlene held her tongue on the topic, had anyone asked she might've told them she favoured a whole Canada, and opposed Quebec separation. Darlene feared extreme culture shock and isolation, so she hesitated to agree right away, her agreement coming only later, after he'd subjected her to an escalating regime of sadism and sexual misery. Marcel's younger brother Guy still lived in Quebec. Although Darlene had only met him the one time, at her wedding, she'd seen in him much the same confusion and disorientation she'd come to see in Marcel, perhaps absent the self-delusions of femininity. The way Guy had looked at her, the way she'd seen him looking at others, it seemed he had some of the same mean-spirited harshness lurking deep inside him, the same darkness just behind his eyes. But Darlene said nothing on that day, not wanting to ruin her wedding by causing a fuss, keeping quiet, keeping quiet, always keeping quiet, always not wanting to upset anyone who might've been watching.

While she told Marcel she was thinking about the move, she kept on reading, kept on trying to delay a decision by burying herself in the pages of one book or another whenever the opportunity presented itself. This was her way of avoiding the issue, although as she read her novels with both sons Marcel began quietly laying plans to move. When she came home and saw Marcel going over cross-country truck rentals, she ignored what she saw and took to reading one of her books, even going so far as to wake baby Stuart from a nap so she could read with him. Even then, it would've been hard for Darlene to imagine what it might've been like to live in such a place. She'd never actually asked why Marcel had come to live in the west anyways; she knew he was attending BCIT, but not what'd motivated him to choose to attend BCIT in the first place. Although she didn't know it, Marcel had come to British Columbia seeking to

168

become a different person, after having inwardly wrestled with his own sexual desires, desires that were coming to consume his entire identity. At least, that's what she might've suspected, had she not been so given to quietly putting herself through everything that seemed to happen. By the time he realized he'd failed, it was too late for Darlene to escape quickly or easily, ensnared as she was in worsening pain and suffering.

Chapter Eight

3

Shortly after Stephen had told Darlene point blank that he wasn't interested in women anymore, he moved out. At first, this came as something of a relief to Darlene, as it meant less conflict at home. (Her younger son Stuart was still in the eleventh grade, and was a model student with a bright future ahead of him). This even meant having her friend Cherise over for their late-night coffees more often, as often as their busy work schedules would allow. Although Darlene wouldn't have ever admitted it to anyone, much less to one of her own sons, Stephen having moved out seemed to have calmed things. But still there were those nights when Darlene found herself unable to sleep, sometimes staring into the darkness of her bedroom and suddenly imagining herself somewhere else entirely. One night she'd left the closet in her bedroom open, she suddenly found herself back in that night, back in that little church, staring off into the darkness as if it was the same darkness staring her back. By the time she managed to bring herself back, she'd sat up, sat up on the edge of the bed, clutching at her bedspread, skin stretched white against her knuckles, breaths coming hard and fast, heart pounding in her throat. Even these moments, these little moments when she felt as though she was being thrown back ten years to some of the most traumatic experiences of her life, she felt as though she was someone other than herself. That night, that night she made sure to get up and shut the closet, but only when she felt as though the moment that'd set itself on her gave some time to think, some time to breathe. At some point, she began to try and reach out from under the bedspread, as if she could've reached across the way to shut the closet from where she was. But her reach wasn't far enough.

Eventually, Stephen told her that he'd enrolled at a local college—which one was unimportant—in an animation and design program. She knew nothing about the subject, nor its potential career applications, but inwardly joyed at Stephen's having apparently gotten himself on the right track. They had very little contact through this time, aside from the occasional message shared through social media. If Stephen wanted his space, she reasoned, then she'd give it to him. After he'd graduated high school and found work, he seemed to have been doing well enough for himself that he didn't need Darlene's regular attention, not at first. Even still, she couldn't help but text him now and then, sometimes waiting hours, even days before sending another text. The pull of having thought what might've been, it was too strong to ignore. There was something there, she knew, she thought she knew, that she had to do. She just couldn't for the life of her figure out what it was. Around the time she finally heard from him, she knew something had changed. "I'm really busy," he said, "I don't have a lot of time." He said this after she'd asked him to come over to her apartment for dinner. They were speaking on the phone. "Then I'll come to you," she said. He paused for a moment, then said, "no, no, it's not a good time." She could detect the struggle behind his voice, an almost-strain that was barely there. "Okay," she said, before letting him go. Later, much later, she'd come to regret this as one of many opportunities to have pressed the issue and helped him before it was too late.

But there was more to it than that, as there always had to have been more to it than that. She remembered the way the rain had fallen, the way the air seemed to hold in moisture like a thick but somehow transparent fog, but only October through April, maybe a little longer if the winter was unseasonably long. The mountains that towered over the city in the north, as well as the forest of glass and steel that made up the city itself, they all seemed to disappear into the distance, obscured behind a haze that wasn't really there. It was strange, it'd been strange to Darlene, living in the city for the first time without anyone since even before she'd met Marcel. She drove, once, after coming back to Vancouver, by the first apartment she'd shared with Marcel, finding it as it'd been: square, grey, still standing, seeming exactly as it'd seemed when last they lived in it. But like with the darkness in the closet at night, she suddenly found herself consumed by something that wasn't there. The next thing she knew, she was driving away, without any recollection of having done anything at all in the intervening time. Sometimes, during these moments, she was consumed in recollections instead of conversations she'd had with her oldest son. "I've got something to do," he'd said, after she'd invited him over for Christmas dinner. "Your brother will be there," said Darlene, "I'm sure he'd love to see you." There was a pause, before Stephen said, "yeah." And then Darlene said, "I would too." There was another pause, before he said, "sorry." And that was the end of that. This she recalled, only to run through every aspect of the call in excruciating detail, from his strained voice to the sound of silence in spare moments when neither of them said anything.

Even still there were those other occasions, such as those moments when she was in the kitchen, cooking something on the stove, only to be interrupted by the ringing of the phone. But the phone seemed to ring at exactly the wrong moment, inspiring in her recollections of a specific time when she'd been blamed by Marcel for something, anything at all. And this time, this time, by the time she regained control of her runaway thoughts, the phone had stopped ringing but the smoke alarm had sounded out, the pot of rice she'd been cooking burning on the stove. Sometimes Darlene took to deliberately provoking these experiences, whether leaving her closet open at night, driving past some remembered spot in the city, or along some street she'd used to drive along every day or nearly every day. The city she'd returned to with her two sons several years earlier had changed so little yet had become something so different. The roads were still just as bad, ridden with potholes and covered-over in those black stripes, so uneven as to wear out a car's suspension in just a few years. But flanking either side of some roads were freshly-built but mostly empty glass and steel towers, signs still up that boldly declared every unit sold even as the balconies were bare and hardly more than a few cars could be seen coming and going from the parkade every day. It was when driving past one such tower, not altogether far from the dumpy, old apartment she still lived in, that she recalled one of the last conversations she'd had with Stephen before he announced his transition. "I really want to see you," she said. "It's not a good time," he said. His voice sounded emptier and more mournful than usual. "When will be a good time?" she asked. "I don't know," he said, "I'll let you know." She wouldn't hear from him again for months after that. That'd be when he'd break the news.

Even with Stephen having moved out, and soon afterwards his younger brother Stuart, Darlene never quite felt as though she was alone. "I'm sure some of this is not my fault," said Darlene. "None of it's your fault," said Cherise. "Yes," said Darlene. "You might have to just let it go," said Cherise. "I don't know if I can do that," said Darlene. "You can't control everything," said Cherise, "some thing aren't your fault." Even Cherise, at this time, was having her own problems, seeing a therapist, taking psychiatric medications to help with a lingering depression that'd set in at some point. Sometimes Cherise complained about her difficulty in finding friends, but always couched her complaints in expressions of gratitude for having a friend like Darlene. Darlene, so consumed in having escaped from Marcel and trying to manage her oldest son's increasingly unmanageable moods, felt compelled to empathize with Cherise's problems, to the extent that she could. Darlene finally said, "it matters to me whether it's all my fault." And Cherise, Cherise said, "it shouldn't, because it's not." This same non-argument they'd been having for some time, Darlene seeking to unburden herself the best she could, Cherise counseling her better than any paid therapist or psychiatrist ever could.

"But I still think it is," said Darlene. "You can't think like that," said Cherise. After she'd taken her sons and moved back to Vancouver, with Marcel's blessings, it became necessary for Darlene to work out a permanent custody arrangement with him, pending their divorce. Although Marcel had allowed her to go, he hadn't contented himself to lead her life. There was still the question of working out that permanent custody arrangement, which was to eventually consist of the boys living in Vancouver with her but sending them off multiple times a year on visits to Quebec. In the time after Stephen would 'come out' to Darlene, she'd look back on those visits, on that time after she and Marcel had separated as probably the key in Stephen having been led astray. But she'd never know, she'd never know the truth of what went on in the family's home. If she'd known, it might've made no difference. She might've been just as paralyzed, just as horrified, just as she was when she finally learned what her son Stephen had thought he'd become.

2

A few weeks passed. Uncharacteristically, Marcel didn't demand an answer from Darlene on his notion of moving to Quebec right away, asking instead that she think about it for as long as she needed. Even this made her vaguely suspicious, a suspicion that only mounted as he continued to assault her on a regular basis, continued to coerce her into doing things she didn't want to do not on a nightly basis but close to it. It wasn't clear even to Darlene when exactly these assaults had escalated from the initial perversions, from his initial experimentation with women's clothes to compelling her to act out various increasingly elaborate sexual fantasies in bed, only that it'd seemed happen over night. To her, it was as though she'd gone to bed one night and then woken up in a completely different world, one that looked the same at a glance but upon closer examination seemed something alien, utterly baffling, disturbing in its hostility and in the pain it caused her. There came a night, one night, when he asked her to wear a dress far too tight, uncomfortably tight, as part of a particular fantasy of his. She was not yet recovered from having given birth to their second son, Stuart; it took her several weeks to begin to lose the weight she'd gained and for her abdomen to shrink. She complained how uncomfortable the dress was for her, but he insisted she wear it to act out his latest fantasy, one where she played the role of the older woman and he the younger lesbian she was to help awaken his sexuality. "You have to take the lead," he said, instructing her step by step on what to do to satisfy his fantasy. "Okay," she said, "I'll get on top of you." And she awkwardly laid on him, while he lay on his stomach. "You're not doing it right," he said, after a little while. She was trying to avoid resting her full weight on his back, as her stomach was still a little distended from pregnancy and childbirth. "I'm sorry," she said, before gritting her teeth and letting her full weight fall on him. She cried out in pain. The strap on she was wearing buried inside him. He cried out in pain. A little while later, they spoke. "Only you can teach me," he said, "only you can help me find myself." Still in pain, she only said, "it's fine," and looked away. Eventually he fell asleep, while she couldn't sleep until hours later.

As the weeks turned into months, Marcel's depression seemed to worsen. He had seemed to have perked up when he first presented the idea of moving across the country to Darlene, but when she continued to delay a decision, he resorted to increasing pressure to try and make her agree. There were nights when she'd come home from work and find some of her things—hers, never his—in a suitcase in the bedroom, or in boxes labeled in felt pen. Even the very idea of moving to Quebec made her feel uncomfortable, given that at this time her father was still alive but getting older. Marcel seemed to continue to spend his days mostly in bed or on the computer looking up ways for his sexual fantasies to involve some element of coercion. There came a night, one night, when he tried something else he found online, coercing Darlene into fulfilling his fantasy of a teenaged cheerleader groomed by an older teacher. In this fantasy, he was the cheerleader, while she was to be the teacher. He wore the skimpiest outfit he could find online, still looking like an ogre stuffed into an ill-fitting garbage bag. He laid on his back, while she was on top of him. It was awkward and painful to manipulate the apparatus she wore while in such a position, but he didn't care. "Fuck me, mistress," he said, while urging her to move against him. "I'm doing that," she said. He grumbled a little, but urged her on. She moved against him, penetrating him repeatedly, at an erratic pace. At some point, he began to manipulate his own genitals. "Yes, that's it," he said, hissing as she moved against him last time. Then, suddenly, he pushed her off him, rolled her over onto her back, and pushed inside her. The pain caused her to cry out, but it was over quickly.

As the months ground past, she began to lose sight of the sweet and sensitive young man Marcel had once seemed to be. She sometimes found herself looking through old pictures of them, from when they were first dating, sometimes even from after they'd first moved in with each other. Those pictures, of the happy, young couple at the bar, at a restaurant, partying with other young couples in Vancouver, they seemed to be of completely different people. She hardly recognized herself. She hardly recognized him. There was more to it than that, as there always had to have been more to it than that. There came a night, one night, when Marcel set himself on Darlene, even before she'd had the chance to put the boys to bed. This had come to be so common that she even began to think little of it, as though it'd become a fact of life. He called her into the bedroom, but she wouldn't leave the boys' room, not right away. Instead, she switched off the light and stood in the darkness, waiting in the doorway while her husband continued to call out her name. Finally, after shutting the door to the boys' room and making for the bedroom in which Marcel waited for her, she heard him again call out, this time in the guise of the submissive woman he'd made himself out to be in his fantasies. "Have I done something to displease you, my mistress?" he asked. Although it was dark, she could see his teeth bared and the whites of his eyes as thin slits. "Yes," she said, knowing the character he wanted to play. "Are you going to punish me, mistress?" he asked, grinning a mischievous grin. Exhausted, she complied.

A few days later, she agreed to move. She was just too exhausted and worn out to hold out any longer. She was able to insist they took the cat, Barney, something she expected Marcel to put up more resistance to than he would. It took a few months to arrange and complete the move, eventually culminating in them driving across the country with the boys in the back. It took over ten days, something either Marcel or Darlene might've been able to accomplish in as little as four days when they were younger and without children. For the first few months after arriving in Quebec, they lived at Marcel's parents' place, taking up residence in the basement suite that'd been rented out to miscellaneous tenants for much of the last twenty years. It was a small place, essentially two rooms, too small for a family of four. His parents let them store most of the possessions they'd brought in the house's garage, though, and that left them enough room to live. Even through this early time, Marcel left her more or less alone, his voracious sexual appetite having abated. But she knew this was only

Darlene

a temporary reprieve, to end as soon as they were on their own again. Although she hated his family, hated his brother Guy in particular, at least their company afforded her a momentary protection from her husband's voracious appetites. That first night living in his parents' basement passed quietly. She slept well for the first time in months.

Eventually, Marcel found work as some sort of IT instructor at the local CEGEP, a kind of pre-university school only found in Quebec. She might've thought to ask him what the salary would be, so as to see if it was enough to support the whole family, but by then had learned not to ask any probing questions. All she wanted to do was move out of his parents' basement, away from their prying eyes. She was in this curious mentality where she wanted to leave the company of others even as she knew full well it'd mean the assault and the rape would resume, inasmuch as Marcel had doubtless come up with many new sexual acts to force her through. And so it was. As she helped move their belongings again from the basement suite beneath his parents' house to the modest townhouse he'd arranged to rent for them, she was caught in a kind of waking sleep, a daze where she was fully aware of everything she was doing yet had been removed from her body and was only watching from a distance. Her lack of fluency in French meant she was unable to put her education and experience in nursing to work in finding a job locally, despite the desperate shortage of qualified and experienced nurses with the local health authority. This left her staying at home, tending to Stephen and Stuart when they were around, sealed

181

in a little box of house, the whole world outside a completely alien culture that seemed hostile towards everything she'd ever known and loved. So she drank.

Sometimes Guy came around, both while she and Marcel were living with his parents and after they'd moved into their own house. At first, she felt as though Guy had been making something of an effort to be good to Darlene and her two young sons, better than she'd have expected at least. He came over for dinner once or twice, and brought gifts for the boys both times. He spoke passable English, better than most in this part of Quebec. He drank with Marcel after dinner both times, beers in the living room. He smoked in the living room, and ignored her requests that he smoke outside. But then he turned against her, too. He came over and cruelly mocked her, telling her that the meal she'd cooked was horrible, even in front of Marcel mocking her. "What kind of woman doesn't know how to cook?" he asked. "It's the same as I've always cooked it," said Darlene. Although Marcel had cooked for her before, she'd been doing all the cooking since they'd moved over from Quebec and moved into their own place. She wasn't much of a natural cook; but in her youth her father had done all the cooking, and had made no big deal about it. "She's trying," said Marcel, although he didn't seem convinced himself. "She should try harder," said Guy. To this Darlene only nodded. After dinner was over, she was thankful to wash the dishes by herself while Guy and Marcel smoked and drank in the living room, as it left her alone with her thoughts. After she'd finished the dishes, she said she was going to check on the boys, to which neither Marcel nor Guy reacted. As she walked away, she heard them laugh, about what she didn't know.

But even after moving with her husband and two young sons to a small city in the heart of nationalist Quebec, very little changed for Darlene. Without anyone to help her, without anyone to reach out to, she believed she had no choice but to accept the state of affairs she found herself in, for the time being at least. It was hard for Darlene to reconcile the conservatism of the Saguenay part of Quebec with her husband's sexual habits and appetites, but then she had very little reason to even try. That night, after Guy had mocked and belittled Darlene's domestic habits, Marcel wasn't have another go at her, instead coming to bed and falling asleep without saying much of anything. It'd become impossible for Darlene to predict when he'd set himself on her, when he'd appear out of the darkness wearing women's clothes, makeup, and a wig before demanding she act out his latest sexual fantasy cooked up from something he'd read or watched on the internet. The only thing she knew was that it wasn't to have been long before he had at it again. Even after moving to Quebec, though, she still sought to distract from the things going on around her by retreating into the pages of one book or another, her taste in reading changing according to her worsening marriage. While the boys were both about to enter school and no employment in her near future, she felt as though she had no reason to do anything at home but keep on reading and drinking all day. So that's what she did.

As far as she knew, no one else in Marcel's hometown knew anything of his sexual habits, as it'd been in Vancouver. But at least Vancouver, the supposedly urbane, cosmopolitan city, had seemed like the sort of place in which someone might've developed habits like his. In the Saguenay region of Quebec, the local economy had been in a state of transition for many years, manufacturing and resources still the backbone but receding in importance. Although parts of Vancouver had been in the grips of an endless decay, there was much worse poverty and decay throughout some parts of Quebec. In the midst of this decline into poverty there was a crisis of conscience, a crisis that meant nothing at all to Darlene when next Marcel appeared in a dress, makeup, and a wig to act out his latest sexual fantasy.

1

Those few days after having moved, effectively, into a battered women's shelter outside a small city in one of the most ardently nationalist parts of Quebec were slow, yet harried. The small shelter had communal showers in the back, along with a small cafeteria, providing Darlene and her two young sons the facilities they needed for a few days. Even during this early period, during those early few days after that anti-climactic confrontation with Marcel, Darlene kept on looking for him around every corner, peeking out through the shelter's storefront-like façade onto the street. He might've come driving along at any moment; in fact, she couldn't have known but he drove past several times in those few days. With memories fresh in her mind of his most recent attack on her, of the most recent time he'd held her down and viciously raped her in their bedroom, while their sons slept just a few metres away, Darlene was still in survival mode. Her heart was beating steadily, but the sight of a car coloured the same off-grey as his rolling down the street in the distance was enough to harden her veins and send her heart pounding in her throat, as well as making her reach for her young sons' hands and clutch them tight in hers. But it wasn't his car that she saw, never managing to be looking in the right direction, out of the right window on those few moments when it really was her husband's car. It'd seemed to Darlene as though she'd never be free, as though she'd never leave. At some point in her days-long stay at that shelter, she began to fear as though she'd never leave. The police had asked her not to leave while the matter of their children was sorted out, and she'd agreed.

The confrontation which'd provoked Darlene's having fled to that shelter, she kept on going over it in her mind, replaying every moment again and again, looking over every miniscule detail in search of some hidden meaning. But there was no hidden meaning, not that she would've accepted any. That first day spent staying in that shelter, very little happened. As it was the middle of summer, the boys didn't have school to attend, so it wasn't necessary for Darlene to keep them out of school to stay at that shelter. But the room she stayed in was too small to be comfortable. Even this provoked a runaway train of thoughts. Back when Darlene, a young, pre-teen Darlene had defended herself from relentless bullying by fighting against her bullies, she couldn't have ever escaped the teasing. The other children, both the boys and the girls made fun of her for her troubled home life, knowing as they all did in the way such young children could and always did. The next time she saw her mother, Marilyn, was on a visit to Marilyn's new home in a halfway house of sorts. It wasn't far, less than two blocks from the Royal Jubilee hospital in which Marilyn had been confined on the psychiatric ward twice. The supervision was court-ordered, as part of her parents' divorce proceedings. (It wasn't her father, Wayne, who would supervise, but a social worker from the hospital). The whole hour spent there was awkward and uncertain, neither Darlene nor her mother speaking much. Nearly the whole time, Marilyn had a look on her face and an unconcerned restlessness about her that reminded Darlene of the way she'd behaved when at home, months and years earlier, alone. Still only twelve but almost thirteen, Darlene didn't want to be there. She could've refused to go, but hadn't.

At the shelter she busied herself by looking over Stephen and Stuart, making sure they were properly bathed. (There was a shower in the shelter, but no bath, and neither Stephen nor Stuart had begun taking showers instead of baths before coming here). But even through this early time the tension was slowly escalating, so slowly that to Darlene it was hardly noticeable from one moment to the next, only perceptible if she should've stopped to realize it. She never heard voices, never heard voices that weren't there, only sometimes imagined as though she was in the middle of a conversation, without context, placed somewhere other than where she was. The reason Darlene, at twelve, didn't refuse to go see her mother was that she genuinely wanted to see her mother, her mother she hadn't seen in months. But by the time that particular visit was over, Darlene came away more confused and restless than ever. On the awkwardly quiet drive home, her father, Wayne, seemed like he wanted to say something, but never managed it. After they'd arrived home it was close to dinner time, and he said to her he'd call her when dinner was ready, then turned away, leaving her to her own devices. It was a feeling she'd become used to in her youth, only a feeling that was about to be upended by her coming time in high school. Having seen her mother in the psychiatric ward, in a halfway house, even in the grips of a suicidal episode in their own home, it was to have left an indelible impression on the young Darlene, something she couldn't possibly have been aware of when she was so young. Inwardly, she was headstrong and utterly confident of herself, even as she withdrew into a shell of depression and loneliness, a shell that wasn't to have been opened until after she'd graduated college and found herself somewhere else altogether.

The food available at the shelter wasn't very good, but Darlene accepted it gratefully. She still hadn't stopped thinking, hadn't stopped letting her thoughts run wild with flights of fear and fancy. In the night, even while she was staying at that shelter, she determined to leave open the door to the room she and the boys slept in, recalling as she could the beatings and the rape she'd endured, particularly latterly. It made her shiver and shudder all over, even without tears streaming down her face the sensations of crying replicated even when there was no proximate cause.

Although Darlene hadn't worked in years, having been unable to find work since they'd moved to Quebec together, she'd saved a small sum of money through the strategic withdrawal of cash, here and there, no more than twenty dollars at a time. She looked into the mirror and saw someone she'd never seen before, someone completely unfamiliar to her. The woman looking back at her, the woman on the other side of the mirror was utterly broken, with hair that was a tangled mess, her face drained of its colour, even the bags under her eyes seemingly faded a ghostly white. She looked as though she'd died. She felt as though she'd died. She was too tired even to stand up for long, within a few minutes sitting back down on the little chair in her room. After a few more minutes had passed, she fell asleep. Her sleep had become completely erratic and unpredictable; sometimes she managed to sleep for no more than ten or twenty minutes before leaping awake, other times hours passing in the blink of an eye. It was frustrating for her to be so utterly spent, so completely defeated, so totally reliant on the charity of others. In that shelter, waiting for a social worker to help her, she felt as though there was nothing more she could do, that she was to be permanently and irrevocably shackled to the man who wanted to kill her. He wanted to kill her, she'd come to well and truly believe. By the time morning came, she'd run through every scenario possible, every eventuality she could conceive of, and they all led towards the same conclusion.

The night, that night, when she'd announced her decision to leave Marcel and take their two young sons with her, at some point it occurred to Darlene that she couldn't recall the colour of the sky. Of course it was black, but it was a particular blackness that haunted. And the police, the red and blue lights that flashed instantaneously into the night, they lent the blackness a surreal character that Darlene couldn't have described even if her mind hadn't been occupied by the overwhelming urge to flee an imminent danger. But those lights, those red and blue lights that flashed into the night, they seemed surreal. In those days she spent at that shelter, Darlene couldn't help but sometimes see those red and blue lights flashing into the darkness even when they weren't there. Throughout the time she was sitting with her two young sons, waiting for permission from the police to leave, Darlene couldn't help but contemplate the urge to leave anyways, to bolt for safety, any safety, anywhere but there. That night had been over quicker than she'd have thought, even as it'd seemed to her, then, as though the night was passing over the course of a lifetime. But as the police came back to speak with her, she instinctively knew that something had changed, that something had been changed around her.

"He says you are trying to abduct your children," said the police officer, the only one who spoke any English at all. "No!" said Darlene, reflexively clutching her sons' hands in hers as she shook her head and shouted out. Tears had been streaming down her cheeks, dripping from her face, Darlene unable to let go of one or both of her sons' hands to wipe the tears with her sleeve. It was at this moment, at this very moment that the police officer who seemed to speak only halting, broken English that she was at her absolute lowest. "You are not trying to abduct your children?" asked the police officer. "No!" said Darlene, before going on to shout, "no, no, no!" The night slurred into the all-familiar darkness, leaving Darlene to wonder if there was anyone out there who could or would help her at all.

Chapter Nine

2

At some point after they'd moved to Quebec, Marcel began to insist that Betty Brilliance was his real name. He insisted this only in private, only around Darlene. He insisted this while wearing one of his most-recently purchased outfits, an outfit that looked like a Japanese schoolgirl's uniform he might've seen somewhere on the internet. Even after having moved to Quebec, he continued to spend much time online, she couldn't know but suspected him of finding communities on certain websites, message boards and social media outlets and the like, where he could immerse himself in gatherings of people who would reinforce his increasingly deranged and severe delusions and violent tendencies. He insisted that his real name was Betty Brilliance after having forced Darlene to act out one of his latest sexual fantasies, one in which she was a shackled slave who would escape and try to overcome him, only for him to overpower her and force her back into her shackles for his final climax. These fantasies, Darlene was aware they were all scripted by Marcel, Marcel having scripted them after having been inspired by one internet posting or another. "Don't you think I'd have been more popular if I was a girl?" he asked. But she didn't know what to make of these questions, and only shyly said, "that could be true." She'd taken to giving vague and evasive non-answers when asked impossible questions. This particular conversation was had in the evening, one evening, after he'd put her through the paces of his shackled-slave fantasy the night before. "I think I would've been," he said, turning back to the pornography he'd been browsing on his phone. "Mmm hmm," Darlene said. She saw her cat, Barney, on the other side of the room, and felt embarrassed that he might've seen her and Marcel have sex. She put that thought aside and fell asleep.

In Quebec Darlene was more alone than ever. When she spent too long talking on the phone with her friend Cherise, still in Vancouver, Marcel took the phone from her and threw it hard against the wall, the phone breaking into three or four different pieces. He then turned to face her and stood over her, threatening her with a menacing scowl and a clenched fist. This time, he wore ordinary clothes, a pair of jeans and a t-shirt, having lapsed out of his alter-ego, Betty Brilliance, for the moment. Sometimes he chose to play the role of the cartoonish, sexually aggressive woman, instead playing himself, only himself. It seemed as though the kind and sensitive young man she'd fallen in love with had disappeared entirely, what little traces had been left discarded entirely when they'd moved across the country. Given that she was unemployed, Marcel had declared her responsible for the children, and forbade her from hiring a nanny to help out around the house. The life of a stay at home mother didn't come naturally to Darlene; when she forgot to run the dishwasher while he was at work, he yelled at her after he came home. "I give you this responsibility and you don't do it," he said, taking one dirty plate out of the dishwasher and holding it in front of her, before throwing it on the floor, smashing it into a hundred pieces. "I'm sorry," she said, "I'll remember next time." Soon, as she took to drinking more heavily to cope with the pain and loneliness, she began to forget more and more daily chores, which resulted in further verbal abuse. This caused her to drink more heavily, increasing her forgetfulness, inviting more abuse. It was a vicious cycle she felt powerless to break out of.

The next time Marcel—he who would insist on himself as the woman named Betty Brilliance—took to his alter ego, it seemed a little different to Darlene even as it seemed exactly the same as it'd been. She was sitting on the living room couch, watching as the boys played with their toys. He'd come home from a day at the CEGEP to encounter Darlene in the living room of their little house. She was watching over the boys, who were playing with their toys. Marcel seemed to reluctantly tolerate the boys being in the main room for at least as long as he had to, somewhat diplomatically waiting through a light supper before sending them off to their rooms. It was once the doors to their rooms were closed that the vicious monster he'd become came out. He emerged from their marital bedroom dressed in his pantyhose, in his high heels, in his thigh-length miniskirt and in his restrictive blouse. The blouse only seemed to emphasize his masculine chest, along with the wireframe bra. But even the blond wig seemed most ridiculous of all to Darlene. He asked, "am I pleasing to you, mistress?" In response Darlene sighed and said, "I don't want to do this tonight." To this Marcel pouted and said, "what have I done to displease you, mistress?" He took a step closer to her, his lanky frame towering over her. She said, "Marcel, please…" But this only seemed to enrage him. "Don't call me that," he said, raising his voice, a threatening scowl forming on his face in an instant. She said, "please…" He declared himself to be Betty Brilliance, that he'd always been Betty Brilliance but'd only just realized it. He said it was people like her who'd be the way of the future.

Another instance came when Marcel's brother, Guy, was visiting for dinner. When Marcel and Guy began drinking beers, Darlene knew she was in trouble, but did nothing to stop it, nothing to try and escape as she knew there was nothing she could've done but grit her teeth and bear it. At some point, Marcel and Guy ran low on their beers, prompting Marcel to shout out for her to bring more. Darlene brought out beers from the fridge, setting the beers on the living room table and taking the empties. But just as she was about to turn back and make for the kitchen, Guy could be heard in broken English to say, "you had better train that woman properly!" The two of them broke out into uproarious laughter, but not before Marcel had looked her right in the eye with a menacing glare. The laughter only began after Darlene had broken the stare, turning away, as she turned away a wick of fear licking up from a pit at the bottom of her stomach, the kind of fear that made her dizzy and nauseous. She got herself a drink and went to one of the boys' rooms and started reading a book, managing after the alcohol had set in to lose herself in the pages but only just long enough to forget her fears for a half second; it was the half-second that made her able to withstand what was to come. That night, after she'd put the boys to bed, she walked out of their room and closed the door, then turned to face Marcel. There to ambush her, he looked her right in the eye, their shared gaze forcing her to look away before she'd feel like vomiting. He was dressed in some of his women's clothes, that night seeming to take particular joy in forcing her to act out his then-current sexual fantasy.

Even as he was doing these things, Darlene couldn't help but cling to some small hope that something uncertain and unknowable lay in her immediate future. It wasn't as though she believed Marcel would suddenly snap out of it and begin acting like a sane person again, only that she thought each moment could've been the worst, could've been Marcel's nadir, with each successive moment better than the last. But still she loved Marcel, in an awkward, roundabout sort of way, as if there was some small part of her capacity to love that hadn't yet been snuffed out in her like the last flame in a still-smouldering campfire at the end of a long night. That night, his particular fantasy involved violently smacking and striking of Darlene's body, hard enough to cut her, hard enough to leave bruises that only began to show the next day. He held her down and continued to strike her and smack her even as he continued to violently penetrate her. It was painful and awkward and it seemed to Darlene as though she was being made to experience that pain. Later, much later, she'd think about it, she'd replay the moments over in her mind again and again, realizing that whenever she cried out in pain he seemed to seethe with pleasure. He held her down and drew her back, her whole body manipulated like a doll.

It was as though Darlene was under some kind of strange waking hypnosis, hardly able to fathom the situation she'd found herself in. Yet, she still clung to the small amount of love she felt for Marcel, something which even she couldn't understand. It wasn't so easy for someone like Darlene, who wanted nothing more than to be loved and to love others. In the aisles at the grocery store, she sometimes looked up to see perhaps-sympathetic looks being cast her way by workers or other shoppers, only for those looks to be averted whenever her eyes met theirs. She felt so lonely, loneliness a feeling for her that was like being caught outside in the cold. But her sons, Stephen and Stuart, were the light in her life. No matter what happened, no matter what she was put through by the husband she'd once seen as someone else, her sons were there to give her a reason to push through it. That night, his particular fantasy was the fantasy of her resistance. That night, for the first time, he asked her, he told her to try and act as though she was fighting back.

1

But even after having escaped Marcel's clutches that night, the police came back in the morning, this time bringing that same English-speaking officer, the only English-speaking officer the entire department must've had. "We are checking on the children," said the officer, "for to make sure they are still here." By this time she'd calmed down enough to know what the officer meant, but her having calmed hadn't meant being any less upset. "I won't ever leave them," she said, "I won't go anywhere." She only realized after the fact that she'd been crying, still as she was stretched past the breaking point. "Please stay for your husband to come," said the officer, "and to speak with the children." To this Darlene could only nod, inwardly cringing as she thought of Marcel coming to the shelter. She didn't know exactly what they meant by this; she was confused as the shelter's no-men policy had been explained to her. She had to prepare for it, though, and as soon as the police left she felt relieved, as relieved as she could. It seemed to her as though this short time living in that shelter was adding up to nothing, was amounting to nothing but the relentless suffering and stigma of having been made to take refuge in among the other women who were at their lowest. The social workers that came by erratically had much to do but little to do it with, the need for an English speaking social worker preventing them from offering much help to Darlene until one could be made available from the nearby regional centre, something that was taking days. "I don't want to stay here," Darlene would tell the officers, "I can't stay here forever." But the officers, even the English speaking policewoman seemed to take this the wrong way, smiling and speaking with each other in a rapid-fire French as they jotted something down on their notepads. They thought she was indicating her intent to go home; but she didn't know, couldn't have known this.

But the fluently English-speaking caretaker helpfully minded her, as did the French-speaking pastor. Neither were there to defend her from attack, given as they were to non-violence. She'd later learn the pastor had asked the police to let her be, insisting on the security of the shelter and the women inside, something the police were more-or-less reluctant to deny. Even the police knew, although Darlene didn't, that this shelter had once been an ordinary liquor store, whose owners had sold to the non-profit that now ran the shelter in order to move to a larger place nearby. But the police, those police who'd forced Darlene to remain at the shelter, they seemed as uninterested in what'd gone into forcing her here, in the things that'd happened to her over the past months and years to drive her to this desperation. For the next few years after Darlene's mother, Marilyn, had attempted suicide, things stabilized for Darlene, at least outwardly. She began high school neither outgoing and assertive nor introverted and passive, stuck in an awkward and uncertain place between the two. The move from elementary school to high school meant an entirely new set of classmates to become lost among, a set much larger and more diverse. There was still the odd incident, but these mostly amounted to the same taunting and bullying, without ever escalating into the physical. She saw her mother, Marilyn, less and less. She managed to make a few friends. Her grades improved. But still there came an occasion when she wanted the attention of a boy she liked. She asked her father, Wayne, what to do. He told her to go right at it, telling her any boy would love a girl who took the initiative. So she approached him in the hallway at school when he was standing at his locker with a group of other boys, and summoned the courage to ask him on a date. He looked at her and blinked, stammered something, and said he'd think about it. But as she walked away she heard first him, then the others laugh. She felt her stomach turn to ice. She didn't know what to do, but she felt humiliated.

Although the province of Quebec had mostly secularized, like the rest of Canada through the turn of the millennium, it was still steeped in a tradition of Catholicism that'd survived in at least some small way. The pastor, despite her lack of English fluency, managed to convey to Darlene in his limited contact with her and her sons that she was welcome to stay as long as she wanted. It occurred to Darlene at some point during her stay at the shelter that Marcel could've put on some of his women's clothes and claimed to be a woman in need of help. This threat would occupy her thoughts for the remainder of her time in the shelter, only a few more days. But in her youth Darlene's having learned to keep her father and everyone else away from her life at school brought her no peace or happiness. The bullying continued, but she didn't tell her father, Wayne. So young as she was, she didn't want to disappoint him by admitting to her that she was still a social pariah, that she'd taken his advice and squandered it. Of course she wouldn't have ever said this; she was at that age when her thinking was so distorted by the utter confusion and trepidation from so many conflicting feelings that seemed to be pulling her in a thousand directions at once. She lied to Wayne and told him that the boy she'd asked out had turned out to already have a girlfriend and had politely declined her offer. She said this to him when they were sitting over dinner and she was poking at her meal, eating little, saying little. At the time, she felt bad for lying to her own father, but she'd later come to realize he saw right through her. She was just too young to see it.

But Darlene was stronger than this, stronger than even she could've realized. There was something coming, something she couldn't see but that was definitely there. Her imagination was powerful, too powerful, having not been dulled the slightest by the relentless assault on her body and her mind. Even still, Darlene was thoughtful and pensive, prone to lapses in concentration even as she seemed determined and able to devote the full force of her energies to the problem in front of her. After all was said and done, Darlene would wind up securing her freedom after what would seem like an eternity of living at that shelter. But so long as she had her two young sons to look out for, she knew, there was something to struggle for. That summer, although unusually long and hot, had proven to be the perfectly wrong summer to try and escape. While living in that little shelter for those several days, she devoted herself to the care of her two young sons, Stephen and Stuart. She kept them properly bathed, using the facilities there, and clothed from the donated clothing provided by shelter volunteers. Even as she was doing this, the fear of Marcel appearing out of nowhere in one of his women's outfits paralyzed her, a kind of waking, fully aware paralysis in which she was still able to physically move and conduct herself as any other day but was hollowed out by a pit of fear that was welling up from the bottom of her stomach, making it harder to walk, harder to talk. She didn't know what to make of it. She couldn't bring herself to express her fears to shelter staff and volunteers, had any of them been able to speak English anyways.

All it did was make her think again about that night, replaying every moment as if to learn something new, as if to uncover some hidden meaning in the events that'd transpired only a couple of nights earlier. Even before the flashing of the red and blue lights that'd lit up the night, before even she'd fled outside with her sons to the car in some vain attempt to flee, reminded her on the powerful isolation she was subject to. As Marcel had towered over her, menacing her with that awful scowl she'd come to fear, she'd felt a surge of strength. So soon after that night, she was still capable of not only remembering it but living it, as though that evening was every evening, every moment of every day. "I'm going to kill myself if you leave me," Marcel had said. This wasn't exactly what Marcel had said, wasn't the exact words he'd used, but it was what Darlene recalled him as having said as she put the full focus of her energies to her imminent survival. For as long as it'd taken the police to arrive that night, Darlene had been on her own, effectively charged with managing a crisis she couldn't have managed on her own. "You're killing me," he'd said, "you're going to kill me if you leave me." Again, these were only the best recollections she could manage, as she sat in that little shelter so late at night, already her memory having begun to play tricks on her.

"You're killing them too," he'd said, referring to their sons, "they'll die if you leave me. Do you want to kill them too?" So fragile and so broken as she was, even this threat hadn't registered as what it'd been. Although Marcel had come and visited—or tried to visit, at least—her in that little shelter, she was still a few days away from being able to leave for Vancouver, in keeping with her original plan, such as it'd been. For those few more days, she'd have plenty more time to reflect on the things that she'd seen, the things she'd been through, all this coming out to be something more than nothing at all. "Is there anything I can get for you?" she heard someone ask. It was the one of the shelter's volunteers, approaching her from behind. Suddenly she realized it was the middle of the night, the middle of a Saturday night, the boys sound asleep while she was looking over them. "No," she said, "I'll be fine." The volunteer asked, "are you sure?" Darlene hadn't recognized this particular volunteer, and felt too uncomfortable even to speak with her for more than this brief exchange. But by the time the volunteer had left, Darlene was trapped.

3

It was then that Darlene placed one of her many calls to Stephen, expecting this particular call, like nearly every other, to go unanswered and without reply. But after two, three, four rings, Stephen picked up. And it was during this conversation that Stephen finally announced to Darlene that he'd decided he was a woman, that Stephen was to be referred to as Stephanie. As much as Darlene would've wanted to emphasize her own fragility, even this was a moment when her son Stephen might've needed her most. And she wasn't able to be there for him, separated as they were not by so much physical distance as by a casual energy. Darlene hadn't much of a clue what he'd been up to in the many months since their last real conversation, only that he seemed to have wanted to be left alone. As she was struggling with her own problems, she decided to let him be. Even still, listening to her oldest son angrily describe himself as truly a woman, hearing him accuse her of all sorts of horrible crimes against her, even hearing him stop just barely short of outright accusing her of abusing him, it was all too much for Darlene to manage, too much for her to stand. She took to sitting on the edge of the couch, crying softly at first, then louder, until she was bawling, gasping for breath through her sobs. It was hard for her to do anything but sit there and cry, for a little while at least, the memories overwhelming, the pain suddenly made real, again.

After having finished speaking with Stephen, Darlene felt lost. Her first instinct was to reach for the bottle, but something inside her made her instead reach back for the phone. She called her long-time friend, Cherise, and they got together for one of their regular evening coffees. "What have I done wrong?" she asked. "You haven't done anything wrong," said Cherise. Her long-time friend was much older than when they'd first met, and herself had been through a lot of adversity. Although Cherise had never married, never had any children of her own, the years had seen her encounter her fair share of problems. "Sometimes I envy you," said Darlene. "Why's that?" asked Cherise. Darlene took a sip of coffee before replying. Her face was still red and raw from having cried so hard after that phone call with her oldest son. It was only a few hours later, later that night. "I shouldn't have said that," said Darlene. "No, it's fine," said Cherise. It was too late at night, and Darlene had already made up her mind not to ask.

As she'd done when dealing with Marcel's mounting obsession with his transgender identity, she took to searching the internet for any signs of help. Unlike what she'd done when living with Marcel, she wasn't optimistic about what she would find. Indeed, there were a lot of websites that urged unconditional and uncritical acceptance, including many public health websites from the local health authorities. "Sometimes it seems like the whole world wants it to be this way," said Darlene. "You're doing the right thing," said Cherise. Stuart wasn't living at home anymore, having recently graduated from high school himself and enrolled in the University of Victoria, roughly ninety minutes by ferry and an hour or two by car from her. "Have you always done the right thing?" asked Darlene. "Not always," said Cherise. They went on to talk at length about Cherise's own problems, about her persistent and pervasive loneliness, problems Cherise had always been open about but which she'd rarely explored. She admitted, both then and earlier, that she'd felt stuck, hardly able to reach out and get help. "I really miss having these talks with you," said Darlene. "We don't get together often enough," said Cherise. "I remember when you used to help me look after the boys after I first came back to Vancouver," said Darlene, "I can never thank you enough for that." But Cherise shook her head and said, "you never had to thank me." Darlene didn't know, couldn't know that Cherise felt a little bad, a little guilty about being unable to help Darlene through her current crisis.

But there were other websites too, not many but at least a few that offered something in the way of solace for Darlene. She wouldn't, couldn't simply *accept* that she'd done something wrong, even as she was made by her own thoughts and feelings to confront this very possibility. Although most, nearly all of the sources of information she'd had available would've urged her to see her oldest son as her daughter, she couldn't, wouldn't. There were a lot of reasons for this, some of which even Darlene couldn't understand. "I don't think I'd be doing him any favours by agreeing to accept him as a woman," she said. "Well you know him best," said Cherise. But they went on to talk about Cherise's loneliness. As they spoke, Darlene began to feel a relaxation, a comfort she'd not felt since even before she'd met Marcel. She could offer no solutions, but none were expected. Cherise didn't know, couldn't know that her being there, her comfort was enough of a help for Darlene, to help

Darlene through the latter's current crisis. There was always a crisis, there was always a crisis, Cherise had learned. Although she'd never say it to Darlene, sometimes observing her best friend's latest crisis gave Cherise pause to consider her loneliness better than relentless conflict at home. These things, these things were left unsaid between them, conveyed only through the slight twitches of hands around cups of coffee or looking away and then back at the mention of one name or another. But at least they were there for each other. that was something Darlene would never take for granted and would never forget.

By this time, it was well past the point when she'd have heard anything from Marcel. Since they'd separated, since she left him and began the long process of divorce, Darlene had been subject to numerous acts of stalking by Marcel. Most of the time, she had little real evidence that it was him, but had quickly surmised it was him or his brother, Guy. Sometimes there'd be the phone calls that came at strange hours, like three in the morning. These phone calls often consisted of breathing, just heavy breathing, although sometimes they consisted of music played at a low volume, the kind of music Darlene was known by Marcel to hate. The first time this happened, she listened to the message for a little while, confused as she was; when she realized it was either Marcel or Guy, she deleted the message. Every time after that, whenever she listened to a message and heard music playing, she deleted it immediately, just a couple of seconds in. She never asked if Stephen or Stuart knew anything about it, and she never tried to raise the issue with Marcel. It was too mortifying at first even to consider asking anyone else about it. She just put up with it. After some years, it tapered off; she didn't know this was because even Guy had moved on. Things like these, she let them be, thinking it was more trouble than it was worth to pursue them. Besides, she thought at the time, there was no way to prove it was him.

Then there were the emails addressed to her, even after she'd changed email addresses repeatedly still the emails coming at a steady pace. A few times a month, she'd receive pornographic images from anonymous addresses. At first, she thought about complaining to anyone who would listen, to the lawyer she'd had help her through the divorce and custody battles or even to the police, but something held her back from doing so. Eventually she confided in Cherise, who listened to her and gave her sympathy. Even still, there was a part of her that was sure there was no way of knowing these emails came from Marcel or Guy, no way of proving anything at all, no way of knowing it was worth the effort. The lawyer she'd used, he came from a charity service operated by a women's foundation, and he said at some point that allegations that couldn't be substantiated even weakly weren't worth anything at all in court. These things, she kept on letting them be during those early few years, choosing to ignore them rather than be seen to come to hysterics, as she knew she would've. Darlene had been struggling with her own problems, not infrequently making it through the day only by the slimmest of margins.

Even still, there were the pictures, the pictures she'd sometimes receive by phone. It was hard for her to imagine how she could've done anything about it. She changed her cell number during those few years that this behaviour came up, but every time there was only a few weeks, maybe a month or two of peace before the images and texts would come again. At the time, Darlene continued to disregard them, at least as much as she could. It was obvious to her, it was just obvious these must've been coming from Marcel. He'd shown her pornographic images and videos before she'd left him, shown her these things to demonstrate one fantasy or another he wanted her to help him act out in the bedroom. The lawyer she'd used, the one who came from the charity service operated by the women's foundation, she supposed he'd have told her the same thing about the emails: there was no way to prove or even substantiate that these texts were coming from Marcel, and so it wasn't worth pursuing in court. Every time she received such a text message from Marcel, the sender's number hidden by some kind of technology she thought Marcel might've had access to given that he worked in IT, she was reminded of what the lawyer had said, that no one would believe her, that no one was well and truly on her side but her.

These things only happened every once in a while, and only in the first few years after Darlene had left Marcel and took the boys with her. Then, sometime around Stephen's twelfth birthday, it stopped. At the time, she had no explanation, could come up with no explanation for the sudden cessation of the harassment. If she'd only known, she might've done nothing different, nothing at all. She'd never learn the real reason her ex-husband and his brother were to stop harassing her because her oldest son would never tell.

Chapter Ten

1

After having spent only a couple of nights at the shelter, Darlene had already begun to feel as though she was dying, dying inside. Even the police weren't allowed to enter the shelter, unless the officers were women. The police had a policy of cooperating with the shelter, referring women and their children as well as generally abiding by the policies and procedures set by the shelter. When the police came to check on her, to make sure she hadn't absconded with the children, and to try and interview her for the ongoing case file, she was still too vulnerable and too agitated to cooperate much. She spoke with the officers briefly, very briefly, their visit supervised by a member of the shelter's staff and another of the shelter's volunteers, only the latter of whom spoke English. Some part of her wondered what they must've thought they were there to do, as she didn't have any weapons and hadn't displayed any aggressive or violent tendencies towards anyone at the shelter or to the police. The other part of her, the better part believed, fully believed they were there to make sure she stayed at home, that she felt the pressure to return home. Despite the shelter's foyer being filled with people, still she felt the chill of loneliness, like a shivering sensation that ran the length of her spine, as if she should've bundled herself and her young sons in the warmest, tightest clothing she could find before running with them somewhere, anywhere at all. It was the same vague but powerful sensation that she'd felt when going to make for her escape, the same vague but powerful sensation that'd given her a momentary but unexpected surge of courage. But it wasn't for want of courage that she'd been unable to break free until then. "We understand you are having difficulty," said the officer, that same blonde policewoman who'd been there that night when she'd tried to break free. "I'm not going back," said Darlene. "I understand," said the policewoman, but for the case to see the children, we would like to have some mor information." This caused Darlene to instinctively clutch at her sons' hands, as she'd come to instinctively clutch whenever the ever-present threat suddenly intensified. "I won't go back," said Darlene, fear overcoming her, leaving her unable to say anything else. "For bringing charges we need more information," said the policewoman. The policewoman went on to say they'd arrested Marcel only recently, in the days since that confrontation. But he'd been released without bail, on strict orders not to go near her until things had settled down. The upshot was that Darlene couldn't flee the province until the case had been resolved, one way or the other.

But there was some small part of her, some little unheard voice inside her that urged her to go back home. It was as if she'd gone to the top of a tall building and looked out over the side, that little unheard voice urging her to jump off, promising that she could fly. This was one of the most distressing parts of this time to Darlene, that she could've found some reason to justify putting herself back in that personal hell. "He tried to kill me," said Darlene. "We can use this," said the policewoman, writing down every word Darlene said. Her stomach churned, even as she felt it turn to stone. "He'll try to kill me again," said Darlene. "Did he try to kill your children?" the policewoman asked But even this thought made her stomach churn. The shelter staff and volunteer both listened intently; even though the staff member couldn't understand English she still seemed to be listening to every word Darlene spoke. Even the slightest turn of phrase or the barest of transgressions, she thought, could've wound up leading her right back into the hell she'd escaped from, she was trying to escape from. Even the police could've arrested her at any time, she thought, for any number of crimes, like the attempted abduction of her own children. In the afternoon, that afternoon, the shelter seemed so small to Darlene, as though it'd shrunk to the size of a locker, she imagined Marcel so close she could smell the alcohol on his breath as though it was really there. So powerful was her imagination and so constant her stress that she smelled that familiar smell that'd so often emanated from his mouth and his body when he'd set himself on her.

Soon, the police left. Even Darlene couldn't have explained why she'd refused to tell any of the officers any more about the truth about what'd happened, the truth about why she was in the shelter. They must've assumed the worst, she'd later reason, although she could never account for their motivations in choosing to urge her to reconcile with him. The shelter wasn't a place where anyone could live, not for more than a few days, maybe a week or two at a time. Outside, cigarette butts and broken hypodermic needles littered the street. For Darlene, the pain and awkward young teenager, her having asked out one of the most attractive and popular boys in her grade seemed to have only provoked a renewed bullying. Soon it felt to her as though the whole school was laughing at her, mocking her, bullying her again. Most of the time this took place behind her back; sometimes she would walk into a room and the room would fall silent, many of the students turning to look at her as she took her desk. Then there were the times when she'd go to her locker and find it scrawled over with hurtful slurs, once or twice even pried open and vandalized inside with paint or whiteout. It was this singular experience that convinced her not to try and step outside her own shell, but neither to lash out violently and physically as she'd done when she was even younger. Even though she wasn't even sixteen by the time she'd made this determination, the years of relentless bullying and teasing had taken their toll. She was left, still, with one last hope, a young man who would give her a chance.

After the police had left, Darlene was mostly left to her own devices again. The English-speaking volunteer spoke with her for a little while, offering her comfort. "You'll always be safe here," said the volunteer. "Please," Darlene said. "Your children are safe here too," said the volunteer. "I don't know what you mean," she said. Fear had crept back into her voice. There was still that part of her that believed they were going to take her and force her to do things she didn't want to do, things she knew weren't best for her or her children, things that were in essence no different from the things Marcel had made her do many, many times over the years. The one young man who was to give her a chance when she was in high school, she'd met him, but wasn't sure if he even knew her name. The high school they went to wasn't particularly large, with around a thousand students. Fewer than two hundred were in the tenth grade with Darlene. It was the late-nineties. Eventually she was to work up the courage to approach him, and strike up a relationship with him, the kind of high school relationship that amounted to hanging out in the halls together between classes and eating lunch together in the school cafeteria, along with the occasional spending of time together at the mall on weekends and such. He asked about her family, one afternoon when they were trying out cigarettes under the bleachers by the football field, and she freely told him about her father. But when he asked about her mother, she stammered for a moment, then said nothing at all. She wouldn't see him for a few weeks.

But Darlene was too caught up in the moment, as anyone would've been in her place, too caught up in the moment to know anything about the caretaker. That Sunday, Darlene attended pastor Amelie's service in the main living area. Although the service was mainly conducted in French, pastor Amelie roughly translated her remarks into English as well, strictly for Darlene's benefit. "...they did not believe the women, because their words seemed to them like nonsense," said Amelie, reading a quote from the

Bible. "It is hard for many women to feel believed," said Amelie, speaking in the same heavily-accented English she spoke to Darlene in private, "but we can always feel as though we are listened to by the Lord. We are in very good company now because many other women have felt not listened to in their experiences." This wasn't a precise translation of her French sermon, of course, but a rough approximation. It didn't exactly make Darlene feel inspired or comforted, but she was able to sit in the company of a small group for a length of time. After the sermon, Darlene spoke with pastor Amelie for a little while, Darlene feeling no more optimistic or assured but a little safer, physically at least. For so long as she remained at that shelter, Darlene would speak with pastor Amelie a few more times, reluctant to overtly talk about what she'd been through, about the things she'd been subject to, relying on pastor Amelie's kindness to avoid directly broaching the subject. This small connection would help her get through the days, along with the friendship Darlene was about to forge with a young woman she was about to meet. Despite this, the terror and the horror, the relentless terror and horror of her own memories and the scars and bruises to her body and mind would continue to haunt her, for so long as she was kept up in that shelter and in the many, many years to follow.

Following Darlene's talk with pastor Amelie, Stuart asked, "can we go home tomorrow?" And Darlene said, "I don't know." She sat on the bed in her room while the boys played with some old toys donated years ago to the shelter, toys with paint worn off and stuffed animals missing patches of fur. Stephen said nothing, so Darlene said nothing to him. She couldn't think of anything to say. But her time living in that shelter was closer to its end than its beginning. Although she was eventually to leave Quebec for Vancouver and take their sons with her, a lot of things had to happen before she could escape back to the west coast. Darlene knew very little of what was going on beyond that shelter's walls, so caught up in the moment as she was that she couldn't have known anything of what was to transpire. Without booze to sustain her, Darlene had begun to suffer from acute withdrawal; she felt the shakes all the time, and her thinking was dulled. She took to drinking some of the alcohol-based hand sanitizer that could be found around the shelter, and managed to get drunk. She thought no one noticed. Almost no one noticed. It was only after she became violently ill from drinking too much hand sanitizer that it was noticed; she became so ill that she vomited blood and had to be taken to the hospital, transported by ambulance with her sons along for the ride. She'd spend only a day in the hospital before returning to the shelter, returning to find all the hand sanitizer gone from her room, from the common areas, from wherever she and the other residents could get to it. Although no one said anything about it to her, she felt ashamed, she felt as though everyone was watching her and seeing right through her. She didn't drink anything at the shelter from then on.

3

Some time after Darlene returned to Vancouver with their sons, she and Marcel began to work out a definitive custody arrangement. It was a foregone conclusion that Stephen and Stuart would live with her, but how much time they were to spend visiting Marcel in Quebec was still an open question. Knowing as she did that Marcel was a monster, a horrible, horrible monster, Darlene knew the best thing for the three of them was to simply wash their hands of him as best they could. But the world wouldn't let it work that way. The first time she drove Stephen and Stuart to the airport to see them off on their flight to Quebec City via Toronto, she managed to keep herself composed until the time came for them to board the plane. They both seemed reluctant to go, Stuart crying but Stephen quiet and pensive, as quiet and pensive as so young a boy can be. Ever since they'd moved back to Vancouver, Stephen had been quieter than usual, the rambunctious and energetic boy he'd been seeming to have disappeared, replaced by a boy far more quiet and brooding. For the four weeks they were away, Darlene was in a constant state of internal crisis, seemingly every little bump in the road, every unexpected noise enough to precipitate a major episode. At times, she'd find herself transported somewhere else, as if by some force of magic back to those most frightening moments when it seemed as though she was about to die. She couldn't understand what was happening to her. "You're hurting me," she said, one night, sitting alone in bed. She didn't hear

218

voices, but sometimes found herself overtaken by memories, and spoke out to nothing in particular. "Don't leave me," said Darlene, controlled by memories, by horrible memories that left her barely able to function at times. But when she would once or twice speak quietly to herself at work—not in response to voices but as expressions of her own nervous tics—someone once heard her. "Fuck, I'm worthless," she said, only to realize she wasn't alone. In the hall at work there was another employee who was close enough to have heard her. "It's been a long day," she said, forcing a smile and a laugh.

It was during these episodes that Darlene learned she was experiencing something known to the world and to the medical community in which she worked as post-traumatic stress disorder, something she might've, at a younger age, thought limited to shell-shocked veterans. By the time they'd returned, she hadn't calmed herself much, having spent the entire four weeks they'd been away fretting over them. Stuart practically leapt into her arms as she greeted them back at the airport in Vancouver. Stephen was less enthusiastic, smiling, reaching out for a hug, but seeming altogether someplace else. She gave them both small gifts on returning; she managed a small stuffed animal for Stuart, and a book on the history of the Vancouver Canucks for Stephen. Stuart gladly accepted his gift, thanking her. Stephen seemed uninterested, but accepted his anyway. "There are too many things to do," she said. She was speaking with another co-worker, one who'd asked her whether she had any plans for the

J.T. Marsh

weekend. "That's too bad," she said sometimes, when asked to go out with the other co-workers, "I'd love to make it but I just can't." Most of them quickly learned not to ask her to come with them anymore, though every now and then a new person would try. It was as though she'd reverted to the withdrawn person she'd once been, only now as a much older person with scars to hide. The summer, that summer, had been unusually hot, Darlene's workplace air conditioned but her home reliably ten degrees hotter than the outside air.

She wouldn't learn for some time exactly what'd gone on in the boys' visit to their father in Quebec. That wasn't important right then. What'd mattered was preparing for the beginning of the new school year, Stuart entering the third grade, Stephen the fifth. While Stuart had already begun to distinguish himself as a good student, Stephen was falling behind in his studies. Even Darlene could tell there was much more going on that met the eye. "I'm happy to have you back," she said to the boys, after meeting them at the airport right outside the gate. It was still possible for non-passengers to visit gates to see off and welcome home passengers under certain circumstances, like parents with children who were travelling as unaccompanied minors. Stuart said, "I wanna go home," after hugging Darlene. "Then let's go home," said Darlene. She turned to Stephen and said, "I'm so happy you're back," while offering a hug. Stephen said nothing, and seemed to only reluctantly hug her back. She could instinctively tell something, something was wrong. But she couldn't tell what, and he wouldn't say. Some part of her thought it might've been something serious, but the better part of her thought he was a little moody, a little uncertain of himself being that he was on the cusp of adolescence, and that the best thing she could do to comfort him was just be there for him. So she determined to be there for him.

This coming school year was to be a year of much change, not so much for Stuart who continued to be a top student but for Stephen who began to change. In the first week of classes Stephen got into a fight with an older boy, earning him a three-day suspension. This forced Darlene to scramble to find him daycare for those three days. She thought he might've been old enough to handle these things by himself, but couldn't resist the urge to try and fight his battles for him. Even while this was happening, there was something lurking in the background, not anything real but something altogether imagined, something that was driving her oldest son to fall behind. When she stuck up for him in a meeting with his teacher, she thought she was doing the right thing. But when she came home a few days later from another lengthy shift at the hospital, she found a young Stephen despondent. In his room, he seemed to be crying. There was rock music playing, but at a volume low enough for Darlene to hear his apparent crying through the door. After listening for a few seconds, she knocked on the door. "Stephen, are you alright?" she asked. But his only response was to turn up the music quickly, and Darlene could hear nothing else. She knocked again and asked, "what happened today?" This time she spoke louder. But still he said nothing. She wanted to enter his room and try again, but she thought the best course of action was to let him be and try later, try later. But she never did.

Things continued to deteriorate. It was strange for her to accommodate even the notion of having made the wrong choice, even as she always suspected herself of having made exactly the wrong choice in everything she'd done. Still, every night she came home from working one of her lengthy shifts at the St. Paul's hospital in downtown Vancouver to find both of her young sons at home, one night Stephen alone in their room, Stuart alone in the living room watching TV. When she asked Stuart what was going on, he told her that Stephen had kicked him out of their room. Still in her scrubs, still wearing the backpack filled with her work things, and still holding the bag of groceries she'd picked up on the way home, she had come home late. She made her way up to the second bedroom and knocked on the door, quietly at first, then louder, soon pounding on it to try and make herself heard through the noise of the music blasting from the other side. It was music in French, both Stephen and Stuart having picked up enough French from their father and from their lives in Quebec for them to understand things like French music. Sometimes when Darlene heard the French language, whether in the music the boys sometimes listened to or the language they sometimes spoke, she almost had to stop herself from thinking she was back in Quebec again. The study of French was mandatory through grade eight. It didn't matter what they were saying, or

Darlene

why. "Could you please do your homework upstairs?" she asked, speaking to Stuart after hearing him recite French aloud. He was sitting at the kitchen table. Stuart said, "no, Stephen's up there." Darlene said, "he's not doing his homework, I bet." And Stuart only shrugged, then went back to his French homework. Darlene went to the kitchen and poured herself a drink rather than confront Stephen.

But even despite these problems, Darlene felt as though she had no choice but to keep on working through the problem, whatever the problem might've been. The school year continued much as it'd started for her sons, Stuart earning good grades and accolades from his teacher, Stephen always getting into trouble. There was more to it than that, as there always had to have been more to it than that, now not so much for Darlene as for her sons. She wished for her father to have been there still, to still have been alive to help her through this. As the school year continued, Stephen seemed to settle into a groove, never doing very well but more or less avoiding trouble. Darlene found him falling behind but still in school. "You have to do better," she said, once trying to go over his schoolwork with him. "I'm doing fine," he said. "No," she said, "you're not." She was trying to be firm, but it just wasn't in her to be so firm. "I'm doing the best I can," Stephen said, before asking, "so why don't you get off my case?" She was taken aback by this, and let him be. They'd been talking after he'd come down to the kitchen to get a coke from the fridge, she stopping him to talk about it. She'd received a letter from his school noting that he'd fallen behind, although this letter was sent out automatically as determined by some software on a computer in a counselor's office. She'd been nervous when he came into the kitchen, nervous at the prospect of another confrontation. These letters, they were soon to be followed up with a meeting or two, the last concern anyone would show for her oldest son at his school before he was well and truly out there. "I just worry about you," she said. "Don't," he said, before turning and leaving the kitchen, leaving her alone again with her thoughts.

Still, something else was happening, something she knew must've been there but something she felt powerless to do anything about. Stephen wouldn't tell her anything, wouldn't tell her about any problems he was having at school. For a time, Darlene was sure Stephen must've been bullied, that this was the only possible explanation for his sudden and dramatic turn. But even she couldn't have just barged into her son's school and demanded to know what his teachers were doing to stop it. The truth was that even Darlene couldn't have suspected how hard it was, how little anyone cared about even her oldest son. If not for the fact that he was constantly getting into trouble, he'd have received no attention at all.

There was violence, there was always violence, Stephen simply responding like a scared and cornered animal, doing what he needed to do to survive. And for all the work she'd had to do, for all the time she'd have had to spend outside the home, it was inside the home that the biggest and most threatening problems would soon rise. But she'd never know the full truth about what'd happened to him, about what he'd been through. If she had, though, she might not've done anything different, for no other reason than she couldn't have, paralyzed as she was by her own maladaptive coping. It rained that night, as it rained many nights until that school year ended and it was time for Stephen and Stuart to head off to Quebec again.

2

Life in Quebec continued to be the source of much frustration and anguish for Darlene, who began to regret her decision to move out there with her husband and two children. It was impossible for her to find work in the most ardently Francophone part of the province, one in which she was the alien, the foreigner even. Although she'd read that many people spoke both French and English even in this part of the province, she came to find virtually no one spoke English around her. At times, it seemed as though there must've been some elaborate conspiracy against her, from the way the other people acted around her. At the grocery store checkout she'd stumble her way through her own very broken French, before lapsing into English, out of the corner of her eye catching the customers in line behind her staring at her as if she was a leper. Every time it was a deeply humiliating experience for Darlene, trying as she could to learn French in the few years they'd been living in the province despite her own personal lack of employment and socializing outside the home. Although she could stutter and nod her way through these basic conversations necessary to survive, she'd still come to be totally and hopelessly reliant on Marcel, something she was beginning to suspect had been his intention in moving the whole family to his childhood home in the first place. But after managing to establish something vaguely resembling a routine—rising in the morning, tending to the boys, chores, errands, and going to bed at night—Darlene was left wondering when he'd come for her again. She distracted herself, as she'd come to, by drinking and reading, even though her sons no long young enough to be willing to sit and read for her. But even as she read, still the books she'd read had the power to take her far away from wherever she was, the booze helping a little bit as well. She'd managed to bring over from Vancouver most of the books she'd owned; they became her most prized possessions.

Still, so long as she had her sons, Stephen and Stuart, she thought she might've been able to make life work. All she had to do, she thought, was to keep pushing ahead, keep working forward. At the school they'd enrolled in, Darlene would go to meetings with the boys' teachers, sometimes on her own, other times with Marcel. When she went on her own, she found the teachers knew only passing English on their own, as with the clerks at the grocery store Darlene having to stumble her way through her own broken French, all the while the teacher seeming frustrated and bored with her at the same time. Sitting in one of those hard plastic chairs, the ones with metal legs and coloured red, orange, blue, or purple, she tried to listen, tried to pick out one or two key words she'd picked up, but

Darlene

hardly managing through the teacher's very thick, regional accent. She guessed it wasn't any easier for the Francophone teacher, who spoke only a little English and seemed at times to stutter and stammer through his limited vocabulary before lapsing back into French. Eventually it became easier for teachers to simply had her documents written mostly in French, with an English invitation to have it translated. At one point, a teacher managed to get through a question, asking if the boys' father could come to one of these parent-teacher meetings, if only to help translate. It was a rather pointed question, one that made Darlene feel acutely aware of herself even as she realized it was probably meant only as an honest question. Earlier, Marcel had declined to come to these meetings, leaving her to feel as though she was flailing about all on her own. She felt her only friend was her cat, Barney, who loved to be near her in the way cats do.

After Darlene had suggested to Marcel that she attend the local community centre to take up French lessons that were offered for a very small fee, he became angry with her even for making the suggestion. "That would be a waste of money," he said, "and it's my money." He was dressed in his ordinary, men's clothes as they spoke, their conversation taking place in the dining room of their little house. "It would make it a lot easier to run errands," she said. She sat at the kitchen table, while he stood, his lanky frame seeming to tower over her. "You can run the errands already," said Marcel, "it makes no sense to spend so much money for you to do something you can already

227

do." "It's not that much money," she said. Suddenly she found herself unable to look him in the eye. "It's my money," he said, "and I say whether it's a lot or not." He was drinking, having come into the kitchen to get a beer from the fridge. He took a swig from his beer, then shot a sharp look at her. "It would help me make friends," she said. But this only seemed to set him off. After finishing his beer, he threw the bottle on the floor, shattering it into a hundred pieces before growling out a reply. "You don't need to make any friends," he said, "you have everything here." She meekly accepted this, determining to defuse tensions and avoid provoking him any further. She apologized to him, and he said nothing in reply. He got another beer from the fridge before turning and making back for the living room. As she swept up the broken glass, Darlene noticed the boys both peeking into the kitchen from around the corner, the boys watching her intently. She said nothing to them. It was all she could think to do.

But her difficulties continued, as if they could've ever stopped. There were the moments when she'd had to take the car to be fixed at an auto shop. The receptionist she went in to see spoke no English, nor did the mechanics she wouldn't speak to at all, forcing her to rely on translation apps on her phone. The French these apps translated into was all but unintelligible to a fluent speaker, she came to learn. And when she came home with the car, hours later she was interrogated by Marcel on the money she'd spent at the shop. "You waste my money when you spend so much," he said. He was going over the receipt line by line. He found instances where she'd purchased items that weren't store brand, that weren't on sale, that he thought weren't needed at all. "I bought everything we need," she said. "You don't know what we need," he said. He'd spent all day, that day, on the computer, seeming to have been intently watching pornography or researching some sexual act she knew he wanted her to perform. What'd set him off was when she asked him not to watch pornography during the day, when their sons were potentially watching. "I'm tired of your complaints," he said, "and I know more than you do about what the children need." But he'd said this in an ominous way, an ominous way Darlene wouldn't fully appreciate until years later, when going over this moment among many others in the back of her mind. "I'm sorry," she said. "As you should be," he said, suddenly seeming to become someone else. It was hard even for Darlene to follow, Marcel's mood swings so violent that they hurt her more than anything else.

She had the power to reveal the full extent of Marcel's degenerate habits and urges, but didn't realize it. Even if she had, there were others who would stop her. Marcel's brother, Guy, kept coming around, in the evening, on weekends, always seeming to bring with him the same boisterous energy. She wanted to ask whether Guy had a girlfriend of his own, but never thought it a good idea. When he came over for beer with Marcel one night, he kept on making so much noise in the living room that Darlene and the children were disturbed. She asked him to keep it down, but he and Marcel both angrily told her off.

Later, when she was in the washroom, she was set on by Guy, who stepped close to her and threatened her. "You should know your place," he said. It was always some small wonder to Darlene that Guy spoke English when so few people in this part of the country did. "I'm sorry," she said. "You should be," he said, before adding, "I don't know why he puts up with you when you don't even show anyone the proper respect." She was suddenly nervous, her heart pounding and her breath short. She felt as though he might reach out and strike her, right then and there. Then, then, Marcel appeared behind Guy. He said something in French to Guy, who responded by looking quickly over his shoulder and saying something back. But then Marcel took a step closer and said something again, still in French, this time Guy saying nothing but looking at Darlene again one more time before stepping away. Guy walked past Marcel, who looked at her in a cross sort of way. Guy left right away, and wouldn't be back for some time. Darlene would never know what was said between them.

But soon after Darlene would face new pain and suffering. A few days would pass, and soon Marcel would find one reason or another to get angry with her. He'd accused her of telling someone about his sexual predilections; who he thought she'd told didn't matter, nor what she'd done to provoke the accusation. He screamed and shouted at her, accusing her of trying to out him, of wanting to have him dead. "No one has that right but me," he said, still shouting at her, still seeming to tower over her as he always had. "Please," she said, "the children…" But this only

Darlene

seemed to enrage him further. He took in one hand the figurine, then turned and threw it hard against the wall. The figurine shattered into a hundred little pieces, the pieces making a tinkering sound as they fell on the hardwood floor. "Don't you ever say that again," he said, "you don't know anything about what's good for the children or anyone else." Even in these moments of terror and loneliness, Darlene sometimes remembered the sweet and sensitive young man Marcel had once been, back when they'd met as young adults living and working in Vancouver. "I'm trying to understand you," she said, almost whimpering as she spoke. "You can't understand me," he said, snarling. "Why can't I?" she asked, managing to look up at him while tears streamed down her face. "You're one of those feminists," he said, "you're one of those feminist bitches who wouldn't ever accept women like me." "I'm trying," she said. "Your try isn't good enough," said Marcel, "you're not good enough."

That evening, he took her into their bedroom, locked the door, then told her to wait on the bed while he changed. Piece by piece, he shed his normal, masculine clothes and put on his women's clothes, quickly becoming the woman he called Betty Brilliance, the woman he'd have insisted he'd been all along. On this night he wore his oversized skin-tight PVC catsuit, coloured a deep black that seemed to blend in with the surrounding darkness as soon as he turned off the lights. The squeaking of the plastic he wore against his thighs, against his sides seemed almost like that of a cartoon mouse. This time, this night he wasn't interested in playing the role of the submissive. He pushed her face-down onto the bed and lay overtop of her, inserting himself into her while gripping her by the hair with one hand and by the neck with the other. Over and over he thrust against her, his whole weight seeming to fall on her. When she cried out, he only seemed to force himself harder down onto her. While wearing his women's clothes he seemed this night to be angrier and more violent than ever, pushing her down and choking her, choking her for a moment before letting her breathe again. "You love this," he said, before saying, "you little whore." She couldn't say anything. "Come on," he said, pausing for a moment to forcibly pull her head back up off the bed so he could talk directly into her ear, "tell me you love this, you bitch." She could smell the alcohol on his breath. All she could manage to say was, "please." She felt as though she'd been utterly defeated. She felt as though she had nothing left. But he kept going.

She cried quietly as he finished, as he held himself in place and shuddered. "I love you," she said, unsure what else to say. The next time they were to act out one of his fantasies, he'd insist she take the role of the masochist, the dominatrix, punishing him while he purported to be submissive. These changes, they meant she could never tell whether he wanted to inflict pain on her or have her inflict pain on him. But even when she was made to assault him with whips, chains, and paddles, she was still hurt by the cruelty of it, by the absence of the intimacy she'd wanted. Even now the sex they were having, the sex she was being made to have was so far from the intimate,

Darlene

nurturing sex she'd have wanted, she'd always
wanted. That night, after Marcel had fallen asleep,
she rose from bed and quietly tip-toed out of the
bedroom and into the bathroom. She gently shut
the door and then sat on the toilet for a little while,
crying as silently as she could. She didn't want to
wake the children. She didn't want to wake the
children. When she reached down and felt for
herself, she felt a little numb, a dull pain. She held
her hand back up, and she saw blood on her finger,
only faintly visible in the darkness of the bathroom
at night. She didn't feel much of anything on the
realization at what she was seeing. She was
detached from herself. Even she couldn't explain it.

Although that night was a turning point for
Darlene, she didn't know it, didn't realize it, so
consumed as she was in an unrelenting terror. It
seemed to Darlene as though Marcel's impulses
and fantasies had entered a new phase, one where
he relished in actively causing her pain. It was
deeply confusing to Darlene how Marcel could
purport to submissiveness even while towering
over her like a monstrous giant. But things
wouldn't always be this way, not for Darlene.
Finally, things were to take a turn for the worst, as
if such a thing were imaginable even to Darlene
herself. Everything that she did, every step forward
she took into the terrifying darkness that was the
future she saw, she did it for her sons, for Stephen
and Stuart. Eventually, even this flimsy justification
wouldn't be enough. Eventually, she'd realize doing
everything for them was sometimes a way of doing
everything for him, something that'd make her sick

when it finally occurred to her. But she wasn't there yet.

Chapter Eleven

3

After having more or less routinely come to look past her son Stephen's misbehaviour when he was young, Darlene had thought she'd turned a corner. But there was nothing routine about the way Stephen had insisted on being called Stephanie, nothing ordinary about the troubled young man he was insisting he was really a woman. At some point after that phone call, she'd put herself through the task of going through some of Stephen's old things, some of the toys he'd left over from his childhood in a box in a closet, things Darlene had kept in the hopes that she'd one day be able to pass them on to a grandson. There were stuffed animals, action figures, and even books, some children's books read after they'd stopped being age-appropriate, some adult books read long before they'd become. She couldn't remember bits and pieces of Stephen's childhood, the combined stressors of domestic violence and recurring alcoholism creating holes in her memory. After Stephen had demanded to be called Stephanie, Darlene began to consider there might've been something, anything at all that could've happened here and there, when she hadn't remembered. As she struggled to work her way through this latest crisis, she thought back to her successful escape from Marcel's clutches, a successful escape made possible only by the timely intervention of help by others. She thought, she thought, as she worked her way through another shift at the hospital, there might've been help somewhere, somewhere out there, if only she could've found it. But it wasn't there.

The few sources of information Darlene consulted with all seemed to say the same thing. She was reluctant to search the internet too much, for fear of encountering pornography that she knew would set off her post-traumatic stress disorder, which she still hadn't sought treatment for. If she spent too much time searching for information on Stephen's debilitating mental illnesses and his transgender beliefs, she could only imagine that she'd have come apart at the seams. She didn't know whether Stephen had intended on pursuing any hormone therapy or surgery to try and make himself look more like a woman, and she preferred not to even think about those possibilities. As she went through some of the old things he'd left behind when he'd moved out, even these possibilities seemed too horrific, too grim to imagine. It made Darlene feel helpless and hopeless to find all the public health authorities recommended only 'affirming' her oldest son's delusions of femininity. She knew in her heart that there must've been something, anything at all that'd happened to him that caused him to come to these delusional beliefs; in point of fact, she knew many things had happened to him throughout his youth, that he'd been through many traumatic events in growing up that'd affected him in ways even he couldn't have known. As she worked through another shift at the St. Paul's hospital in downtown Vancouver, she only wished there was someone, anyone she could've reached out to for help. After

her shift was over, she went home to an empty
apartment and fell into bed still wearing her scrubs.
But she didn't sleep.

All this was long after he'd taken that turn,
after he'd demanded she refer to him by the
feminine name he'd chosen for himself, and long
after he'd begun his transition. The way Stephen
had demanded she call him Stephanie, it made him
sound exactly like his father had sounded all those
years earlier. As Darlene replayed that conversation
over in her mind, something she'd done many
times in the months after, she began to recall that
conversation as having been had with Marcel
himself, with Stephen's voice replaced by Marcel's,
as though someone or something had reached into
her memory and reconfigured her recollection of
that call. This made her fear trying to call Stephen
again; she began to try, more than once, but found
herself hanging up after two or three rings, not
even able to leave a message. Eventually, she
couldn't even scroll down her phone's contacts list
all the way to Stephen's entry, fearing as she did
that each second spent talking with him should he
pick up would only immerse her deeper in the pain
and anxiety of her own past. All the progress she'd
made in escaping her former life, in helping her
sons escape had become undone. This came to a
head, one night, when she came home from work
at the hospital to try at another night of unwinding
with a glass of wine, only to come unglued by
nothing more than the sight of an advertisement
for something she hadn't seen since leaving
Quebec all those years ago. As soon as she sat

down on the couch, she reached for the phone, dialed her old friend Cherise, and invited her over.

"I feel so hopeless," said Darlene, "I feel like I've made no progress since I left my ex." In the years after she'd left Marcel and struck out on her own back in Vancouver, things had continued to develop. Stephen's mounting troubles at school contrasted against his younger brother Stuart's earning nothing but praise from his teachers. (Both boys had picked up enough French in the years they'd lived in Quebec to have some basic, conversational fluency, although their lack of use since moving back to the coast meant that fluency was atrophying). At this point Darlene learned something new. Cherise had met someone, someone she'd actually met a long time ago but had only recently reconnected with. Although they spent the better part of that afternoon talking about Stephen, talking about Stephen's declaration to be Stephanie, at some point Cherise mentioned she'd found someone. "I'm happy for you," said Darlene. Exhausted though she was, it was a welcome distraction to hear about Cherise's news. "Well, don't get too excited," said Cherise, "I'm not so sure it's going to go anywhere." After having not seen each other for the years Darlene and the boys lived in Quebec, it'd been a relief to reconnect with Cherise, not simply to re-establish contact with her best friend but to be able to sit in the same room again. But now after having been thrown into a new crisis by her oldest son's sudden emergence into his own imaginary femininity, Darlene felt genuinely happy, at least a little happier to hear that her best friend was making progress, some progress, at least some progress in finding her own happiness.

Later that night, Darlene looked at herself in the mirror, her eyes finding some of the scars she'd been left with. As these scars had been left by the things Marcel had made her do in the bedroom, they were never visible when she was fully clothed, around others. Most of the time she hated even the thought of her own naked body, of exposing herself to anyone, even to any future lover. During these times, she came to believe she'd been damaged too much to ever form that kind of a bond with another person. "I feel like I'm a different person," she'd said to Cherise, "and I'll never be the same again." This wasn't during that conversation they'd had when Cherise told Darlene she'd met someone, but another conversation over coffee. But Cherise had said, "no one will ever be the same person they were." Then Darlene said, "I feel like I'm too damaged ever to really love someone or be loved by someone again." And then Cherise said something, something, reassuring to Darlene or at least meant to be reassuring. It was too late at night, both Cherise and Darlene having gotten off work only a couple of hours earlier, their coffees having become regular enough. "When do I get to meet him?" Darlene asked at some point. "As soon as you want to," said Cherise. But Darlene hesitated, avoiding any commitment to a specific date and time. Instead, she just said, "I'll let you know," and left it at that.

Sometimes Darlene felt guilty for having devoted too much time and energy to sorting out Stephen's troubles, guilty for having neglected

Stuart's achievements in comparison. In those years after she'd struck out on her own in Vancouver, after having left Marcel and taken the boys with her, she kept on managing to survive, but only by managing the best of a series of crises that never seemed to end. The peak of this came when Stephen got into another fight at school, this time taking on two boys from his class in a treed area behind the school. Exact details of the fight weren't known to Darlene; but even Stephen didn't deny his role in starting the fight. When Darlene took off from work to meet with the principal, she was struck by the way the school staff seemed so uninterested in the whole matter. "I don't feel like I can really trust any of them," she'd said to Cherise, "but I can't say that to them. I can't say that to Stephen either." This, again, was said at another one of their regular coffees, late at night on a night both Darlene and Cherise had off. And Cherise had said, "learning to trust again is hard, especially after you've been hurt so badly." Darlene asked, "how do you do it?" Cherise shrugged and said, "I don't know. It just takes time." There was a pause. Cherise said, "just keep doing what's right." Darlene said, "I'll try." Although she was belatedly learning to be more confident, even she couldn't help but allow some doubt to linger in her voice. Still, she was glad to have some support.

But Darlene, Darlene only wondered what she could've or would've done had her father been there to help her, what he might've had to say or do to strengthen her in the way only her father could've. A steadily escalating tension had meant this turn of events were having a debilitating effect on Darlene, who felt as though she was someplace other than herself. That particular school year, some years earlier, would eventually end with Stephen managing to avoid getting into any more fights, something that gave Darlene some hope for the immediate future. If Stephen had managed to avoid fighting, then that must've meant he'd made some progress. Because Stephen was her son, Darlene thought it her responsibility to always take his side, in public at least, which is why she'd always refused to even consider upbraiding him or otherwise punishing him out of view. When she took off work to go and get Stephen from school, or to meet with teachers or counselors, she went in with an attitude to always stick up for him. She missed having read to him and his younger son when they were all a little younger, and there were times she wished she could still read to her sons, if only they'd have wanted to still be read to.

Perpetually exhausted from working as much as she did, Darlene felt as though there was little she could do to help him that she wasn't already doing. This was even as she was determined to do everything she could to help her son. At some point, though, she began to consider whether her refusal to do anything but support him might've been a mistake. Her son having gone through so much as a young child made her look in the mirror and see someone who'd failed utterly to provide a loving and stable home for her sons. She confusedly wavered from believing her oldest son was on the straight and narrow to believing that he was one bad decision away from ruining his last chance at achieving something with his life. Years later, after Stephen had declared himself Stephanie, she felt more confused than ever. Stephen had wanted her to apologize for something, even though he hadn't said as much. She could tell he blamed her for a lot of things, whether they were her fault or not. Producing something even vaguely resembling an apology was difficult for Darlene. Apologizing for something she'd done wrong, even for something she hadn't done wrong was almost impossible. By the time all those years were to have passed and her best friend Cherise was to have reassured her she'd done the right thing, Darlene was growing steadily more confident in herself, even as she felt she was accomplishing nothing at all.

2

Darlene soon learned as she'd already learned many times before, not to speak out. But there were the little moments when even this learned behaviour was challenged, when the small hope inside her pushed through. Although the house they lived in was large enough for a family of four, Darlene knew there was no hiding, no escaping from the changes her husband seemed to have been going through. In the Saguenay region of Quebec, winters were much longer and colder than in Vancouver, stormier too. The darkness that was all around throughout these coldest months of the year made Darlene feel more isolated, like she'd been frozen in place not only by her own torment but by the snow and ice. Even driving through the city in doing the daily errands took greater care in the winter, used as she was to driving in Vancouver's comparably mild, rainy winters. "You don't know how to drive anyways," Marcel would say, "there aren't any cis-women who would know how to drive." And Darlene would say, "I'm sorry." Sometimes she'd add, "I'll try to learn how to drive better," which would only prompt him to glare at her for a moment or two before erupting in laughter. Even these moments were had around the boys, sometimes Stephen and Stuart in their room, sometimes out in the living room or dining room, always within earshot, Darlene feared always absorbing every word that was hurled at her. "Not that you know anything about cooking either," Marcel would sometimes say after eating whatever meal Darlene had cooked for the family. "You know, they say only trans-women really know how to cook," Marcel would say, "because only they really know what a man wants." Again he'd look her right in the eye with a menacing glare, at the table even holding his fork and his knife for a moment or two before erupting in boisterous laughter. Stephen and Stuart, there at the dinner table, seemed awkwardly unsure of themselves, looking at their meals, poking their forks at their food. Stephen said, "I like it." But this only prompted Marcel to say, "you're just a kid," pausing for a moment before adding, "kids don't know shit, right Darlene?" But he said it with an awkward and forced accent that Darlene couldn't place as neither West Coast nor Quebecois.

Although Darlene had been crying all night, she found herself not nearly all cried out. Marcel wasn't to demand sex from her on this occasion, but was to hurl all kinds of horrible, verbal abuse at her, declaring her to be a rude and vicious woman who only wanted to hurt him. "What makes you think I won't kill you before you kill me?" he asked. "I don't know what you're talking about," she said. But even this was only one conversation, against the streak of fear that stretched out over months, even years. To Darlene, it was as though her whole life had become a permanent darkness. Sometimes, sometimes she'd sit in the boys' room, on a chair pulled at the foot of one of their beds, watching them pretend to fall asleep as she resisted heading out into the hall, knowing as she did that Marcel would be there to ambush her and force her into whatever sexual act he'd concocted recently. "I won't let you kill me," he said, "I won't let anyone kill me." She said, "I'm not going to kill you. I don't know what you're talking about." But he didn't mean it literally. He'd been on the internet. He'd read things. Later he'd tell her that refusing to accept his rapidly deepening ideas about himself as a woman was tantamount to murder. "If you don't accept me for who I am," he said, "then that's like destroying who I am." Confused, she didn't know what to say. She nodded along, stifling her fears as best she could. She stifled her fears by turning once again to her books, ensconcing herself in an alcove at home with one book or another while drinking one drink or another. This escape was the one way she felt she could be anywhere other than the prison she'd found herself trapped in.

Later, after some time in the living room sitting on the edge of the couch, Darlene went to get a drink. But Marcel was there, blocking her way back into the kitchen. "Mistress," he said, before asking, "don't you want me to be happy?" He was wearing some of his women's clothes. She sighed, then said, "I think…" But her voice trailed off as she looked briefly into Marcel's eyes, glimpsing at the man he'd become before quickly looking away. "Mistress," he said, his voice turning firmer, "don't disappoint me." Darlene felt at that moment as though she was battered and bruised, as though she was struggling simply to hide her pain. On this night, she was injured by Marcel's sex acts. He was striking her with a paddle, again and again, when he started laughing maniacally. "I love you," she said, hoping to inspire in him the feelings he must've felt for her back when they were still young, back when they'd first met. It was a futile action, as Marcel was too far gone, lost to the impulses he'd surrendered himself to. He began dressing as Betty Brilliance at home all the time, even around their sons. Neither Stephen nor Stuart asked any uncomfortable questions, but neither did they not notice. The first time she saw him dressed as a woman around the boys was a night she came home after running some errands, finding Marcel already home from work.

There were more nights like those, the nights seeming to Marcel to blend together. Her life had become a continuous blur of unrelenting pain, not only the sadness and the sex. There came a night, one night, when he'd insisted on Darlene playing the role of the dominatrix he sometimes insisted she play. But he became angry with her for failing to be so enthusiastic about it as he wanted. "You never do anything right," he said, after she'd stopped for a moment to compose herself. "I'm trying," she said. She'd knelt back on the bed, and he reached for her, taking her by the shoulders and shaking her vigorously. "You're not trying hard enough," he said. He was wearing one of his skirts, one of his blouses, even pantyhose and a wig to complete the look. "I'm sorry," she said. She couldn't even look him in the eye. "It's times like these that make me think you're trying to kill me," he said, before asking, "you want to kill me, don't you?" This she denied vigorously. But her denial was only met with his challenge, to prove she wasn't trying to kill him by helping him act out his then-current fantasy. The rest of the night, that night saw her try again. Mercifully, it was over quickly. After it was over, she rose from bed like always, but rather than going to the bathroom she went to the kitchen and reached into the freezer for a bottle of vodka she'd stashed there. She didn't bother with a glass; she drank right from the bottle, gulping it down, hardly even noticing the sting of the booze in her mouth and throat. Out of the corner of her eye, she saw her cat, Barney, seeming to watch her from a distance. She soon felt the warm haze of drunkenness, and went to pet him. But Barney sniffed her hand, then recoiled from her, Darlene unaware the cat could smell the booze on her.

Even freeing herself from the pain and hopelessness seemed like a fantasy to Darlene, as though she couldn't help but live in this place for as long as she was to live. It wasn't as though the end of her life seemed imminent; but it was around this time that she first began to look beyond. She looked on the internet. As Marcel was at work and the boys at school all day, she had time to find certain things. At some point, she began looking for communities online where she could find some support. She might not've thought about it that way, but when she began posting on an internet message board she found at least some semblance of belonging. Actually, she'd begun posting on this particular message board not long after having moved to Quebec; it offered a connection she couldn't seem to find in a francophone province. This particular message board was devoted to books and literature, with sub-communities devoted to every genre imaginable. Over the few years she'd wind up living with the boys and Marcel in Quebec, she regularly turned to this message board for community, starting out comparing notes and opinions on various books she'd read but soon forming the closest thing to real friendships she'd had in a long time. At first, Marcel either didn't notice or didn't care that she was spending more time online. After all, he spent much time online as well, only indulging in his fantasies rather than pursuing real interests. At first, she didn't reveal much in the way of personal information about herself to any of her newfound internet friends. She wouldn't dare. She couldn't even begin to fathom the possibility of baring her soul to people she hardly knew. But as the weeks turned into months and as the months turned into years, she began to feel more comfortable talking about herself online. She began to drift from the parts of the message board that dealt strictly with books and literature to the parts about other topics, even including relationships and sex. But she couldn't post in those sections, not right away, not while she still nursed the pains and the bruises from Marcel's most recent assault on her body.

But there was a tipping point that was coming, a moment when she'd finally make that critical decision she'd wanted to make for a long time. Darlene's will to live was too strong to be so easily suppressed. Although Marcel had yet to subject her to the most gruesome and vicious assault possible, he was still capable of harming her. This time, she put more of an effort into it. This time, she vigorously struck him with the whip, causing him to cry out in pain. Although she didn't break the skin, her whipping would leave marks that'd last for days. "Oh yes, mistress," he said, after she'd begun whipping him harder and harder. "You speak when I've let you," said Darlene, managing to forcibly inject a stern tone into her voice. "Sorry, mistress," he said, before she struck him again and again. He was on his knees, with his face down on the bed. She grabbed his wig, thinking to pull his head back. But the wig came off in her grip, and she fell back. At that moment, the character of Marcel as the meek, submissive woman disappeared, replaced by the aggressive, disgusting hulk of a man with a voracious appetite. He pulled her back onto the bed, forced her awkwardly down, and entered her, put his hands around her neck and clasping them tight until she couldn't breathe. She struggled for breath. The air in her lungs turned stale, then burned as she gasped out. But he wouldn't let her breathe. He held her down as he rapidly came to his own climax. Then he let her go, and she gulped down air as he fell onto the bed next to her. Darlene had tried this last time to get into it, but couldn't. That night she didn't get up after Marcel fell asleep, but instead lay in bed, on her side, looking into the darkness of the night. She didn't think about anything. She couldn't think about anything. It was hard for Darlene to imagine that this was about to get any worse.

At times, she tried to call her old friend Cherise, the only friend she had left in the world. As Cherise still lived in Vancouver, this necessitated more long distance calls, more long distance calls Darlene was certain Marcel would disapprove of. Even when Marcel was away at work, she felt as though some part of him was there, as if he could've arrived at any moment. On this night, instead of trying to sneak in a call to her one and only friend, Darlene spent the hours before Marcel was to come home looking through boxes of old things brought over from Vancouver. She was looking for something. By the time she found it, though, she'd disturbed too much to put back quickly before Marcel arrived. This was particularly true as sometimes Darlene sat at the desk and sipped on a glass of cheap wine while chatting with her internet friends for hours. The first time she ventured into that part of that message board that dealt with sex and relationships, she was a little drunk, and said some things about herself that she might not've said had she been sober. But when she took to the internet again, she found a private message sent by another poster, offering to listen if she needed someone to talk to. She let that message linger for a few days, neither declining nor accepting the offer but not responding to it at all.

Even this wouldn't be the end of it, though. The next time Darlene summoned the courage to sneak around the house behind Marcel's back, she managed a few more square feet covered, an extra part of a single room explored. As before, every moment she spent looking through her own possessions was spent with her heart pounding and her stomach churning. The smooth tile of the floor slid underneath her feet without making a sound. And it was at that moment that Marcel came home, catching her in the act. That was the first night she almost died.

1

Her few days at the shelter were passing, but slowly. She still couldn't sleep, knowing Marcel was out there, knowing he could return at any time to try and persuade her to come back home. Actually, that wasn't what scared her the most. What scared her the most was the possibility that she could've been persuaded, the possibility that she wasn't strong enough to resist him. Even this was one of the reasons why she'd planned a quick getaway, as every second that her escape was drawn out meant a successful escape was less likely. And she couldn't stay, she couldn't stay in that house for even a minute longer, couldn't live in a house of violence and terror any more. As she sat awake at night in that shelter, she wondered on the possibility of her returning to Marcel's grip, and realized she wouldn't have been strong enough to break free again. At the moment when she'd come into the shelter only a few days earlier, Darlene had felt as though she was at her lowest, unable even to reach out and seek any more help. Even reaching out and taking that first step in leaving Marcel had proven beyond her, in her mind at least, and now she felt as though she was at the mercy of people and forces she couldn't understand. At the shelter, that day, she hardly ate anything, instead watching Stephen and Stuart eat the cafeteria-grade meals served to them, then looking over them as they ate without complaint. "…Are you, are you sure?" asked one woman, one woman somewhat younger than Darlene. This young woman was speaking on the phone, and spoke in French, in a French so thick it was beyond Darlene's limited grasp of the language.

Darlene was still nursing a bruised abdomen and numerous other minor injuries from the most vicious of assault inflicted on her by Marcel just under two weeks earlier; at least, she imagined the pain and the awkwardness in her body was because of that vicious assault. She still hadn't seen a doctor, even refusing—declining—to see one after shelter staff had offered following her admission only a few days earlier. "I haven't got anywhere else to go," said one woman, this woman, like the other, speaking in incredibly thick French that Darlene couldn't understand. But this woman wasn't speaking on the phone, instead with one of the volunteers at the shelter. There were volunteers who were here only to provide emotional support, to listen to the residents in the hopes that this listening would provide some kind of catharsis. But decades earlier, Darlene's mother, Marilyn, hadn't disappeared after having been let out of the psychiatric ward the second time. Her father, Wayne, had wanted her to maintain something of a relationship with her mother, but that was proving difficult. Marilyn moved from the halfway house she'd spent a couple of years in to a small basement apartment in a house further away from the city. Then, she moved to a room in a dilapidated house shared with three others, where she spent little more than ten months. Quickly Darlene lost track. Quickly, Darlene came only to see her mother every once in a while, sometimes as little as a couple of times in a year. The culmination of this came when Marilyn had promised to host a visit for a few hours on Christmas day, though she wouldn't say where she'd be hosting. In fact, neither Darlene nor her father knew exactly where Marilyn had been living for the past several months, the only address they had for a place she'd moved out of more than a year earlier. At sixteen, Darlene was in the eleventh grade. Finally the day came with Marilyn unheard from for weeks; her phone number had been disconnected. That Christmas had been ruined.

At the shelter, there were only a few other women, all of whom were fleeing circumstances like hers. She wouldn't make conversation with them, wouldn't learn anything about any of them beyond what she could see plainly with her eyes, limited as she was by the language barrier. The shelter was said to have been at capacity, even though there were beds empty and many of the residents seemed to disappear for days at a time. "I don't have any money," said another woman, this woman looking a little older than Darlene but no less defeated. This woman also spoke in that same, thick French that Darlene couldn't have begun to understand, even if she'd tried. Even though there weren't so many women at the shelter, it seemed to Darlene as though she was surrounded by something she couldn't see but which was definitely there. When she was only sixteen, Darlene's first boyfriend was something of an enigma, even to her. When she'd stopped seeing him after he'd asked what her mother did for a living, she wasn't sure if she'd ever see him again as anything more than a classmate. They saw each other in the halls, but Darlene wouldn't say anything to him. She was feeling too infringed upon, her personal space too invaded. After having effectively lost contact with her own mother, Darlene wouldn't have wanted to let anyone know what was going on at home. But there was more to it than that. She wouldn't forget about the young man who'd probed too far; in fact, they'd begin seeing each other again soon. After that year's Christmas had been ruined, she continued to keep to herself at school, never less unsure of herself.

Something was happening, something she couldn't see but could feel. There wasn't anything at work there, anything besides her own imagination and the relentless terror waiting beyond. "Many of them are like this," said the counselor, speaking to Darlene in English. "If I leave here he'll kill me," said Darlene, speaking quietly, unable even to look the counselor in the eye. "I understand," said the counselor. Although

Darlene didn't know it, this was something the counselor heard frequently, from women exactly as terrified and desperate as her. Even Darlene was starting to feel the intense cravings that came from suddenly not putting any alcohol into her body for days in a row. She'd been experiencing withdrawal symptoms throughout those days, but the cravings, the raw cravings hadn't hit her with full force until after she'd realized how lonely she'd come to feel. That day, that day, after the counselor had a brief and mostly-unproductive conversation with her, she thought to find booze, any kind of booze, and put it in her body. She wasn't the only woman at the shelter with an addiction. Even the counselor had offered to refer her for addictions services, but Darlene had declined, wanting only to get as far from Marcel as she could, as quickly as she could. But that day, as she wandered the halls and paced nervously inside her own room, suddenly all she could think about was finding that next drink. It was so confusing and disorienting to her, how the cravings hadn't set in during those first couple of days, but that didn't matter to her, not right then. There had to be booze somewhere around there, she reasoned, and all she had to do was find it. She looked in a couple of closets but found nothing. She thought to check the bathroom, hoping someone might've hid something in there somewhere. But after opening the cabinet in the bathroom she stopped, looked in the mirror in the bathroom, and realized herself. Against the cravings, she closed the bathroom's cabinet, turned, and went back to her room. The boys were there, and she sat with them.

Darlene

She wouldn't have wanted to see him, even if he was allowed onto the grounds of the shelter. There were plenty of shelters in Canada, plenty in Vancouver but none that allowed men. Although it'd been only a few days since she'd fled her own home with her two young sons, she feared he'd show up dressed in the women's clothes he'd come to be so fond of. She feared him coming in claiming to be a woman, claiming to be a woman in distress and in need of transitional housing. She was afraid of this even after the counselor had told her the shelter had a strict no-men policy, and that they didn't admit trans-women, men who said they were women. She didn't know the policy in this shelter had been adopted despite pressure from the local health authority to admit these men, that this pressure had even included the withdrawal of critical funding. She couldn't have known this, as she didn't speak or read French, and didn't consume the French-language media this turn of events had been reported in. Even the social worker hadn't told her this, and she hadn't told the social worker of Marcel's gender-bending habits. There were a lot of shelters in Canada that'd come to admit men who said they were women, and as Marcel had said he was thinking of living as a woman full time she had no way of knowing whether she was truly safe but for the policy she didn't know about.

Even this had been unknown to Darlene, the latter living in this small city somewhere in the Saguenay region of Quebec for the years it'd taken to come to this point. Darlene thought it must've been hard for Marcel not to lapse into his alter ego,

Betty Brilliance, that it must've been hard for him not to bristle at the mere suggestion that he wasn't to be allowed into a *women's shelter* because he wasn't a *woman*. But the tension and the fear that'd worked its way into every moment hadn't, couldn't have ceased, even then. The something that was happening, it was happening even as Darlene couldn't summon the courage simply to put one foot in front of the other and pull herself through the challenges she'd become immersed in. She needed help. She wanted help. Even as Marcel was outside the shelter and Darlene consigned to live inside, she couldn't help but devote her thoughts to that night, that night when she'd made that attempt to escape. Even the way the police officers took to looking at her, the little glances and the sideways stares, they made her feel like she was wasting their time, that she shouldn't have bothered to have tried to reason with them. "Are we going home soon?" asked Stuart, this time when they were eating in the shelter's dining room. "No," Darlene said, "we're not going home at all." Stuart asked, "why not?" And Darlene said, she said, "we can't go home." Somehow, someway, Stuart seemed to understand this. But that wasn't the end of it.

There were a lot of things she could've done differently. She thought she might've just taken her sons, piled them into the car, and driven away, driving as far and as fast as she could in one day before stopping for the night, repeating until she made it to Vancouver. But even this would've been impossible, she thought. Still, as she sat on that little cot in the shelter, she wished she'd had the courage to try, no matter the consequences. She inwardly chided herself, using an inner voice trained by so many years of hard living and relentless assault forced on her by others. "I don't want to live here," said Stuart, later that afternoon. "We're not going to live here," said Darlene. "Then why can't we leave?" asked Stuart. "It's not time yet," said Darlene. Still Stephen said nothing, seeming to quietly sit in the room, taking in everything that was happening, everything he was seeing and hearing, letting out nothing at all. But to both of them Darlene said, "I'm sorry for everything." And she meant it, she meant it. By the time they were to have left the shelter, they'd have had this same conversation a few more times, each time Darlene feeling a little guiltier, her guilt drawing her closer to making the wrong choice. She wanted to drink. She wanted a drink more than she'd ever wanted a drink in her life. But she couldn't have it, not in the shelter, not without leaving the shelter and exposing herself to the possibility of another assault from Marcel. She soon left the shelter but not under her own power; so deprived of alcohol had she become that she had a seizure. The staff called an ambulance, which took her to the local hospital. There she woke up about twelve hours later, as frightened as ever.

Chapter Twelve

2

After Marcel had found Darlene looking through boxes of things in one of the house's many closets, he dropped even the pretense and began assaulting her right in front of the kids. He yelled at her, he stomped around the house, and he threw things. He went into the kitchen and tossed plates on the floor, one after the other. He screamed, hurling insults at her, despicable things she'd never heard before, not even from him. Finally, he approached her and put his fist through the wall behind her, his fist crunching the drywall, leaving his fist cratered in the wall for a few moments as he breathed fire at her. It was the alcohol on his breath that inspired her to fear and revulsion the most. He seemed hardly feminine to Darlene, even as he'd come to insist he was as much a woman as she. Later, many years later, she'd look back on this particular moment, seeing it as something of a watershed. He didn't touch her that night. He didn't even threaten to touch her, not verbally at least. Instead, as he accused her for the first time of wanting to hurt him. "You want me to suffer, don't you?" he asked. "I don't know what you mean," she said, speaking quietly, unable even to look him in the eye. "You're doing what the feminist bitches and lesbians have told you to do," he said. As he spoke, he seemed to grind his fist against the fridge's hard surface, his whole body seeming to shake and quiver slightly. His face was red, and the veins on the side of his neck and on his forehead bulged noticeably. "I don't know what you're talking about," she said, hardly able to speak at all. At some point he backed off, allowing her a moment to breathe. She looked over to her side, and saw both the boys seeming to stare at she and Marcel, both Stephen and Stuart peeking out from behind the living room's recliner. "Don't look away," said Marcel, his voice quieting a little before he asked, "if you had your way I'd be dead right now, wouldn't I?" He reached out for Darlene's face and gripped her by the jaw, turning her to look at him. "That's not true," she said, beginning to feel that familiar yet still frightening wick of panic licking up from a pit at the bottom of her stomach. "It better not be," said Marcel, before letting go and turning away. He went into the basement, a place he'd told Darlene and the boys not to go, and left the three of them for the rest of the night. It took some time for Darlene to calm down, after which she went to show the boys to bed, the three pretending nothing had happened. The three always pretended nothing had happened.

It wasn't that night, but a few nights later that Marcel forced Darlene into another of his still-escalating sex acts. Even this time, he didn't wait until Darlene had put the boys to bed, instead waltzing out of the master bedroom dressed in one of the gaudiest and trashiest women's outfits he'd managed. From bottom to top, he wore black high heels, fishnet stockings, a garter belt, and the most obscenely oversized halter top he must've been able to squeeze his massive chest into. "Darling," he said, approaching her as she stood in front of the refrigerator in the kitchen. "Don't you like the way I look?" he asked, still approaching her, causing her to instinctively clench her teeth and look away slightly. Again he had her backed up against the fridge. He put one hand on the fridge, right over her shoulder, and leaned slightly until his face was only inches from hers. She gulped and nodded, which only elicited from him a disappointed sigh. the sex they were having, it was ritualistic and almost hypnotic in that Darlene felt mesmerized a little more each time Marcel put on his women's clothes and took her to bed, Darlene feeling as though she was in full control of her body and mind even as she was paralyzed with fear. He assaulted her that night; but it wasn't the vicious and vigorous assault that'd come later. No, this time he made her do something she didn't want to do. He played the role of the meek, submissive woman, and insisted she play the role of the cruel dominatrix. As he approached his climax by manipulating himself while she struck him, he came prematurely, later blaming her.

Even at the time Darlene was acutely aware of how far she'd come, hardly able to recall as she was the charming young man Marcel had been when they'd first met. She felt so helpless, yet still able to see a way out. After that night when he'd come out dressed in his women's clothes and dragged her back into the bedroom, nothing seemed quite the same. Even Marcel seemed to have almost completely disappeared, replaced by Betty Brilliance, the hulking, grotesque, imitation of a woman he'd declared himself to be, the sweet and sensitive man he'd been having been fully subsumed within the fictional entity he'd created out of the deepest and darkest recesses of his own mind. But Darlene secretly kept on looking for something, anything at all in searching not necessarily throughout the house but wherever she could find an excuse to look. Even she didn't wonder how much more of this she could withstand. It never crossed her mind. After he blamed her for making him come prematurely, thus preventing him from acting out his fantasy of switching roles so he could be the domineering master for his climax. She protested meekly. He slapped her. But later, later, he came to her and apologized. He said, "it's not your fault." She was taken aback by this, and didn't know what to say. "You don't know what to do," he said, "you don't know because I haven't taught you. Without me, you don't know anything. You don't know how to be a real woman." He had a glazed-over look in his eyes that Darlene couldn't understand. She just meekly nodded. "Don't worry," he said, "you'll learn soon enough." But Darlene didn't know what to make even of this, so she only nodded again.

Some time passed. A few weeks, a month or two maybe. To Darlene, all time seemed to have frozen, and her only clues things like the changing of the seasons, the growing of the boys, the holidays routinely prepared for and passed by gritting her teeth and pushing through them. As Marcel had made enough working at the CEGEP to provide for the family, the pressure on her to find a job had abated almost as soon as they'd arrived. But still she found herself lost in a little world of her own misery, the boys at school and Marcel at work. Marcel already spoke French, while

Darlene

Stephen and Stuart were learning French as part of their education, going to school as they were in a French language school. And then he'd come home, sometimes leaving her alone as he preferred to isolate himself. After he came home, she wouldn't have the computer for the rest of the night, having instead to use her cell phone to access the message board she'd come to rely on. But there was a message there, a message from that very same poster who'd once offered to listen to her. They'd been sending messages back and forth; Darlene was reluctant to reply too quickly, for fear of seeming too eager. Too eager to whom, she didn't know, just to someone, anyone who might've been out there.

She wanted to return to Vancouver, but only for a visit to her old friend Cherise. When he'd discovered her rifling through that closet, he became angry. She wanted to take the boys with her, but when she suggested this, Marcel became angry again. He accused her of wanting to abandon him, of plotting to take their sons from him and turn them against him. She insisted it wasn't true, but this only provoked him to accuse her of accusing him of lying. "No one has the right to say that about me," he said. "I'm not," she said, "I don't know what you want from me." Later, much later that night, she quietly found her way onto the computer and opened the last message her internet friend had sent. She read it through again, hoping to summon the courage to reply. But she didn't, she didn't. it was so heartbreaking, for Darlene to think there might've been someone out there she could've had a real connection with. After sitting on the computer for a little while that night, she heard the door to the bedroom swing open, and she quickly closed the browser, hoping that was enough. She swung around in the chair to face Marcel. As he approached, she rose to meet him. She started, saying, "I'm sorry for—" But Marcel took her by the hand and pulled her in close. "You're sorry," he said, "of course you're sorry." She was confused, but she wasn't afraid for herself, not right then. He began yelling again, accusing her of one thing or another, going so far as to declare her lack of enthusiasm for his latest sexual fantasy to be evidence of a future betrayal. At some point a few days later she realized the cat, Barney, had disappeared, although Marcel said he hadn't seen her. She became convinced he'd deliberately let Barney out, intending to rid the house of her only friend. He wouldn't even let her go out and post up notices, not that she could've come up with them in French. The sudden loss of her friendly cat cut a hole in her life that she wouldn't be able to fill, not for a long time.

Earlier, when Marcel had been berating her and accusing her of lying to him, she felt as though he might've reached out and strangled her at any moment. "Why are you this way?" she asked. Her voice was quiet, the voice of a woman defeated and hopeless. "I'm becoming myself," he said, "and you can't do anything to stop me." She wouldn't again take the risk of visiting that site on the computer while Marcel was home. She still visited it on her phone, until Marcel began looking at her strangely when she did so. Although she wasn't sure of the technical aspects of it, she began to fear the possibility that Marcel could access her phone, her phone records, her phone's internet history. She'd gone through their computer's internet history and selectively deleted what she thought he'd find incriminating, silently promising to herself that she'd use her phone from then on. But there was more to it than that, as there always had to have been more to it than that. The steadily-escalating fantasies Marcel was subjecting Darlene to were escalating towards something, Darlene knew it. But the nights at home, the nights at home filled with terror and uncertainty were building, whether Darlene realized it or not. The only relief from the terror continued to be the moments she was able to spend reading her books and drinking her drinks, mostly during the day when the boys were at school and Marcel was at work but sometimes on the weekends as well. Those moments, they were hardly enough to keep her sane as she fell further into darkness and despair, but sometimes she could at least convince herself that she was anywhere but at home.

After checking on the boys, she spent the rest of the night, that night, sitting in the living room. She avoided going to bed, and Marcel seemed to let her be. Eventually, she fell asleep on the living room couch, only to wake up at two o'clock. She found the house dark and empty, everyone else still asleep. She wandered quietly into the bedroom, opening and closing the door as quietly as she could, tip-toeing across the carpeted floor as deftly as she'd learned how. She stepped here and there, avoiding the spots on the floor where the floorboards creaked. Still in her clothes, she got into bed and pulled the covers up around her. Although he didn't wake up, Marcel mumbled something in his sleep. A few moments later, she replied. "I love you," she said, even aware of what she was saying. It was as though she'd fallen under a spell, as though she'd come to selectively and randomly leave her own body, to look down on herself and wonder how it'd all come to this. But she wasn't to feel so helpless or so hopeless for much longer. The time was coming when she'd summon the courage to take matters into her own hands.

1

Still a few hours had passed at the shelter since her last talk with the counselor and still Darlene felt lost. It was only a couple of days later and already Darlene felt as though her stay at the shelter was never to end. The shelter was dark at night, too dark, through the windows a pale orange glow bleeding onto the tiled linoleum floor. Even in the middle of the night, it was never silent, the rustling of the trees in the wind a constant background to Darlene's running thoughts. "I can't go home," another woman in the shelter Darlene had overheard as having said, like the others speaking in French. It meant very little to Darlene at the time, except to make her feel as though there was no one there for her, as though she was isolated in ways none of them could've. The isolation hadn't abated since she'd left Marcel that night, but had intensified, even in the middle of the day surrounded by staff, volunteers, and other residents at the shelter Darlene feeling as though she was all alone in the world. Nearly all the materials at the shelter, the pamphlets for handing out, the posters on the walls, even the magazines and others were all printed in French only. Even after having moved to the Saguenay region of Quebec from Vancouver, it was still oddly disturbing and made her feel lonely to be immersed in a sea of French, of a language she couldn't understand. All the little signs and notes and labels anyone would've normally found and have been able to understand, Darlene couldn't, from the label on the back of the bedside lamp in her room to the notices posted on bulletin boards in the halls. At some point she began to associate French and Quebecois nationality with Marcel's transgenderism; they accepted Marcel, who was becoming transgender, which meant, to her at least, that they accepted everything about his transition, including his worsening descent into violence and sexual sadism.

The windows at the shelter were the same thin glass as any other house, and visitors were forbidden. But to Darlene, those few days were seeming to take weeks, even months to pass; when the sun rose that morning, it seemed to her as though she'd been living in that shelter all her life. The act of having convinced herself that she was alone, even without having said or done anything to bring about that belief, it seemed a self-reinforcing feeling. "He's going to kill me if I go back," said another woman, within earshot of Darlene. "You don't have to go back," said the counselor. If she had been able to speak French, if she had been able to understand what that woman had said, she might've been moved by at least some small empathy, given that Darlene feared Marcel was out there, waiting to beat her or kill her if ever she should've left the shelter. It was a deeply frightening, even psychotic feeling for Darlene, to fear that Marcel might've been there to leap on her and attack her again. No one understood, she thought. It rained that night, a light but long rainfall that reminded Darlene of the rain that fell on Vancouver seemingly every day from October through May. The rain, it was strangely calming to Darlene, the familiar sound of a steady pattering against windows reminding her of every lonely rainy day in Vancouver. Even the rain, though, sometimes sounded a little different, imagining as Darlene was that the rain fell a little heavier in Quebec. The nights seemed a little darker, as well. She took to leaving lights on at night in other parts of the house, even empty rooms, until Marcel began to complain she was wasting energy. Everything in Quebec just seemed *angrier* to Darlene.

As quickly as it'd all started, as quickly as she'd come to have summoned the courage to strike out on her own, Darlene felt as though her courage was evaporating. Even the shelter was eerily quiet most of the time. "I need help," said another woman, speaking with one of the counselors in another room just off one of the common areas. Again, both this woman and the counselor she was speaking with spoke in French, in the kind of rapid, colloquial, Quebecois French unknown and unknowable even to most French speakers around the world, never mind an Anglo like Darlene. After that last Christmas where Darlene hadn't been able to spend any time with her mother, Marilyn, she wound up not seeing her mother again for years. But Darlene's first boyfriend, her only boyfriend before meeting Marcel, was a young man in the grade below she befriended during the last weeks of the eleventh grade. They dated throughout that summer, hanging out together as Darlene managed to get a part-time job at a Tim Hortons. The young man's name was Martin, but he liked to be called Marty by his friends. When the new school year started in the fall, Darlene felt a little more confident, seeking as she was to be seen with her new boyfriend a little more. But then she heard the rumours, the same rumours everyone else had been hearing in the grade below for a long time: Marty was gay. This in turn inspired in her a new self-doubt, the brimming confidence she'd managed over the last summer all done away with in the time it'd taken those rumours to reach her. Still a virgin, she resolved to end this the only way she knew how. When her father was visiting someone out of town, she invited Marty over for the night and had sex with him, her first time, the first and only time they'd sleep together.

The police weren't to come by again, not for a while, apparently finding other things to do with their time besides tend to a bedraggled, forty year-old woman with two young children. This was some small relief to Darlene, worth precious little against the stark terror assaulting her at every moment of every day. There was another woman, a woman younger than Darlene who spoke English, who Darlene only noticed when she came across the woman in one of the common areas after having not seen her before. The young woman's name was Natalie, and she spoke passable English in addition to her native Quebecois French. This Darlene only learned when she walked through one of the common areas with her sons, leading them from their room to the dining room for dinner. Even before Darlene had slept with her first boyfriend, Marty, there were things about him that didn't quite track. She was afraid to ask directly about any of them, presuming as she did that Marty would've reacted as she'd reacted to his having asked about her mother. Sometimes she heard snippets about him in the halls, in class, but no one seemed willing to tell her directly what they were saying about him, and she was too afraid to ask. Regardless, her father, Wayne, took a liking to Marty, happy as he was that she was dating, that she was doing things that he thought normal, healthy girls her age should've been doing. He even said as much once, over dinner, leaving unsaid the implication that he was happy she wasn't turning out like her mother.

Natalie and Darlene were almost exactly alike in many ways. She was fleeing a boyfriend who was addicted to drugs, who had prostituted her out to pay for his drug debts, only to assault her repeatedly over a period of months, each assault coming in a drug-fueled fury. Natalie had arrived in poor shape, bruised and bleeding a little from freshly-inflicted wounds. These things Darlene learned through conversations with Natalie over Darlene's remaining days at the shelter, gradually finding the courage to allow herself to open up to the younger Natalie. It seemed to Darlene as though it was gradual, although in fact there wasn't enough time for anything to take place gradually, despite the seemingly glacial pace at which events were passing. Finally, the social worker came around to see her again. Although the shelter was supposed to have dedicated social workers on staff, it took some time for them to find one who could speak English, given that they were located in the most ardently francophone part of Canada. It was something Darlene hadn't expected, to find someone who was simultaneously uninterested in and devoted to her and her two young sons. There were few legal options for Darlene, the social worker said, unless she could get Marcel to agree to let her take the sons with her. She mentioned that she wanted to leave for British Columbia. But the social worker seemed, to Darlene, unable or unwilling to offer much in the way of help.

She still felt the craving for alcohol, even after she'd spent a day in the hospital sick from drinking hand sanitizer. It was unlike any craving she'd ever had before. It made her feel like there was something inside her that'd expanded to fill every part of her body with a deep-seated *longing* for *something*. It was like a wound inside her that wouldn't heal, that pulsated raw with each heartbeat. After all that'd happened, Darlene had nothing to look forward to, nothing to see in the way of a future, or so she thought. That afternoon, she spoke with Natalie, the two sitting on a couch in one of the shelter's common area. It was too early for Stephen and Stuart to be asleep. As both waited for dinner at the shelter to be served, they took to talking. Not right away; at first, they simply sat in the same area as one another, difficult as it was for Darlene to reach out for anyone, anyone at all. They were both on the wrong side of something sinister.

3

After Darlene had spoken last with her oldest son, Stephen, she had no way of knowing when they'd speak next. It wasn't the first time this had been so, but it was something Darlene had never become used to. There's something about some kind of external trauma that doesn't help those who it's inflicted on to suffer through any easier or any better. Although she tried to call him more than once, each time seemed to be more pointedly ignored than the last. Texts went ignored, as well. She even tried emailing him, but also received no reply. She began to think herself wrong. There was some part of her that began to consider whether she should've said or done something, anything besides what she'd said and done when Stephen had told her he wanted to be known as Stephanie. But she couldn't, she just couldn't have done anything different, couldn't have brought herself to see her son as a daughter. Although she was tired, there were moments when Darlene felt herself on an even keel, moments when it'd seemed like the end of a recent crisis might've broken without a new crisis taking over. She was at home, thinking, thinking, thinking, sitting on the edge of the bed or on the end of the couch. Although she kept on working, kept on persisting, she felt as though she could just sit there with her face in her hands and cry through the day and night if only she would let herself. But she was stronger than that. "How long until you know for sure?" asked Darlene, speaking with Stuart on the phone, asking about his exam results. He was still in the University of British Columbia. He told her. "How are you finding things out there?" she asked. He told her. There was something else that she was too afraid, too nervous to ask. Eventually, she said to Stuart, "I'm sure you'll do very well." She didn't say she loved him; that was She hung up without asking him what she'd called him to ask. She'd wanted to ask him to speak to Stephen, to tell his older brother something for her, but couldn't work up the courage to do it.

But when Stephen had been at school, many years earlier, there came a time when Darlene had no choice but to speak to his teacher in person. As the night came, Darlene looked to the meeting with mounting dread, as if she could've done anything at all to ward off what she knew must've been coming. Even then, she felt as though something was amiss, as though something would surely go wrong when she set foot in that school. As this was more than a decade before Stephen would declare himself Stephanie, Darlene was still skeptical of the notion that anyone who would purport to help, even as she'd relied on help from others to get through some of the worst moments of her life. But she went into the school anyways, trying her best to get through it, to keep an open mind. The school itself was unremarkable, the kind of new school that'd been put up only recently after many years of bureaucratic wrangling and at great expense. It was squeaky clean; the floors squeaked beneath Darlene's shoes after she'd come in out of the rain. Even after she'd wiped her feet on mats laid out in the main hall, still her shoes squeaked with every step forward. It made her feel acutely aware of herself, as though the sound was drawing attention to her, even as no one was looking at her, even as she was sure no one was paying any attention to her at all. Arriving at the classroom where Stephen's teacher waited, she gulped down her fears, reached for the door handle, and twisted it, pulling the door open.

Waiting there was Stephen's teacher, a portly, middle-aged woman with hair an impossibly white shade of blond and lips covered in a bright red lipstick. "I'm glad to finally get the chance to meet you," said Mrs. Howell. Darlene imagined an insult hiding behind the teacher's greeting, but made the effort to make nothing of it. "It's very good to meet you too," said Darlene, sitting in front of the teacher's desk. These schools, they weren't all that much better than what she'd remembered from the time when she'd lived with her father as a young girl. After exchanging these few pleasantries, behind which were hidden a seething invective for one another. "He's having a lot of problems," said Mrs. Howell. But something else was happening, something Darlene couldn't have seen and wouldn't have recognized even if she had. Children are like sponges, absorbing everything they see, everything they see and hear, in the process growing into whatever it is they're to become.

"Yes," Darlene said, "he can be a bit of a handful." She was trying to suppress her disdain for the this Mrs. Howell, knowing as she did that she wouldn't have been doing Stephen any favours if she replied in kind. "Now, I don't want to pry," said Mrs. Howell, "but I can imagine that he has a less than ideal home life." She made as if to say she thought she might've been the first person to ever say this, to ever broach the subject with Darlene, offering a mix of presumptuousness and genuine, good-hearted concern. But this Mrs. Howell wasn't the first person to offer this to Darlene, meaning its effect was neutered by repetition. "There's this counselor," said Mrs. Howell, who offered Darlene a sheet of paper with information and contact numbers printed all up and down both front and back. "Do you think that's necessary?" asked Darlene. She inadvertently thought back to her own limited experience in dealing with counselors, social workers, and the like, recalling them as utterly useless to her. "It could help," said Mrs. Howell, "please think about it." Darlene took the sheet, put it in her purse, and said, "I will." They kept on talking for the remainder of the half-hour, until Darlene's time was up and the next parents' began.

Later that night, after Darlene had made it home, she found both Stephen and Stuart in the living room watching TV. She told them both to turn it off and go upstairs. Stuart complied immediately, hopping off the couch and pausing to ask her what was for dinner before bounding upstairs. But Stephen kept on watching TV, seeming to ignore her request. He was at that age when she couldn't have been sure whether he was deliberately ignoring her or just playing a game. It made little sense to her. Finally she walked over and turned off the TV herself. "Hey, I was watching that," he said. He seemed to be saying things entirely unlike what a boy his age should've been saying, although Darlene couldn't have known this, given that she'd never been a boy his age herself. "And now you're not," she said, "do you know where I've been just now?" He looked away and said, "I don't care." He started across the living room, headed for the stairs, but Darlene kept talking anyways. "You should," she said. "Well I don't," he said, "leave me alone!" He made as if to thump up the stairs, but stopped to turn around and say to her, "I wanna go and live with my dad!" It was clear to her that he was saying this just to provoke her. Ordinarily, she'd let him be. Ordinarily, she'd let him shout whatever he wanted and make whatever noise he wanted before he left the room. This she'd always done preferring to avoid conflict wherever possible, even as sometimes, often, nearly always she did things that wound up fomenting the very conflict she always wanted to avoid. This time, though, she couldn't just let it be. After having worked through an extended shift at the hospital and then gone to see Stephen's teacher at his school while still wearing her scrubs, her fuse was a short. Even as she worked up towards saying something she'd immediately regret, she felt as though she was outside of herself. It was a strange place to be, mentally. It made her feel almost exactly like she'd felt when she would sometimes lose track of time, only this time fully aware and in control of everything she said.

"Well then maybe you should," she said. But she didn't mean it, she didn't mean it, saying it only because she was at the end of her patience for the evening. Stephen said, "maybe I will." And Darlene said, "I'm not stopping you." More was said, contentious words exchanged, Darlene saying things that she regretted immediately before Stephen stormed up the stairs and into his room. If she'd known what she was openly inviting him to do, what she was saying in a moment of weakness, then she'd have been mortified at herself instead of only regretful. But even then she'd had no way of knowing what he'd been through, what he would continue to go through every time she took him and his younger brother to the airport and sent them off down the gate to board a plane all by themselves. If she'd known, if she'd known, she wouldn't have sent them, even it'd meant defying a court order to send them. If she'd known, she might've turned to the police, to those police who'd done nothing to help her when she'd needed help more than any other time in her life. But there was more to it than that, as there always must've been more to it than that. She'd never learn the truth, because he'd never tell her and she'd never ask. It'd never occurred to her to ask. This was the tragic limit of Darlene's own, limited perspective. Even she knew this. Later, she went up to Stephen and apologized for what she'd said. But the damage was done.

After she'd gotten off the phone with Stuart, all those years later, she chided herself for failing to ask him about Stephen. She felt as though every opportunity that came across to do something, to reach out in some way was lost. All this was rapidly coming to a head, she was sure of it. She could only come to grips with the fact that all she could do was let Stephen be Stephen, whether he wanted to be or not. Eventually she'd learn that Stuart was only erratically in touch with Stephen, her two sons having had a falling out of their own. It was over something that'd happened years earlier, or so Stuart said. Over time, Darlene would learn the truth, that issues had been lingering between her sons for a lot longer. Even if she knew the full truth, though, she'd never be able to unpack what'd happened.

Chapter Thirteen

1

Although the end of Darlene's time at the shelter was drawing near, even she felt as though it would never end. The constant state of terror she was in had proven to be absolutely exhausting, along with her lack of sleep the whole experience causing her to enter an almost drug-like trance. She thought she might see and hear things that weren't there. She thought she could've turned around at any moment and come face to face with a Marcel who'd just materialized out of thin air. But most worryingly she thought someone, anyone at all might've come to see her for who she really was, for the frightened and sad woman, for the shiver and shuddering mess she'd become. The young Darlene graduated high school without much fanfare. She went to a community college in Victoria, transferring after two years to the University of British Columbia where she earned a degree in nursing. In the intervening period she heard very little from her mother, Marilyn, but as well had little free time to contemplate all the things she'd been through as a youth. She went home for Christmas and on a few other occasions every year, yes, but only to her father, Wayne's apartment, Marilyn never to be found or heard from. There wasn't any one moment when Marilyn dropped out of Darlene's life, nor any one moment when Darlene might've realized her mother was no longer there. An example of this gradual realization came around her high school graduation, when she

invited family and family friends to the ceremony,
never even thinking to invite her mother. It was
hard and awkward to understand, even for the new
person Darlene had become. By the time she was
to have come into something, adulthood was on
her. And then it happened: her mother showed up
one last time.

But her new friendship—it wasn't really a
friendship—with the younger Natalie at least gave
her something to do during the days, during those
few days left in Darlene's stay at the shelter. It'd
been so long since Darlene had a real friend that
she couldn't remember what it was like, how it was
done, not that Natalie was much of a real friend
anyways. They were two women, one younger, one
older, frightened and vulnerable, Darlene with two
young sons, Natalie without any children at all.
Although Natalie had been prostituted by her
boyfriend to pay his drug debts, she'd only gone
along with it because she'd been well and truly in
love with him, something he'd taken advantage of.
They had this in common; Darlene eventually
managed to explain that was the same reason she
stayed with Marcel for as long as she did, that and
the desire to look out for her two young sons. The
much younger Darlene, though, had to look out for
herself. But her mother Marilyn was the very last
thing Darlene needed at a time in her life when she
was out of high school and trying to make her own
way through life. Darlene returned home to her
father's in Victoria, invited over for dinner. Her
father hadn't told her that her mother was going to
be there. When she walked in through the door of
the townhouse he lived in and saw Marilyn sitting

on the living room couch, it was quite the shock. She felt more than a little betrayed by her own father for not having warned her, for not having given her the chance to prepare for this meeting. It was awkward and uncertain for Darlene to not know what to expect, to have felt as though her father, even her trusted father might not've felt the need to ask her first. Regardless, they talked. They talked all evening. They talked about things Darlene wouldn't have wanted to talk about but felt strangely compelled to stay for. By the time it was over, Darlene felt as though her mother was well and truly dead.

But years later, things were different. Darlene wondered, she wondered what Marcel was doing outside the shelter, wondered what the police were doing. Although she still had some small hope that she'd be able to take the boys and leave for Vancouver soon, as she'd originally planned, it began to seem less and less likely to her that this would happen. It all hinged on Marcel giving his consent, without which she'd be legally considered to be kidnapping her own children if she should've tried to leave. And she knew, she knew in her heart that this was something he'd never agree to, if only out of some sick desire to keep on controlling her, to use the last remaining tool at his disposal to keep her firmly in his clutches. She sometimes, during this time, looked at her abdomen, still badly bruised as it was from that final assault of Marcel's on her body. It was an experience she couldn't exactly remember, for all the pain that'd clouded her memory and overpowered her thoughts. Even below her abdomen, her vagina was still sore; she'd bled from the wounds his assault had caused. It was almost two weeks later, and she was still in some pain. It didn't matter to her, as she was reminded by these wounds and would've been whether they were still there or not. She might've been imagining the extent of her injuries or their longevity, but she might not've. She couldn't tell. The pain was still real. Sometimes her whole body was wracked with pain.

Even already, so recently after Marcel's assault on her, Darlene was already coming to be disgusted by her own body in ways she'd never before been disgusted. It wasn't as though she blamed herself, but felt as though she'd been betrayed by something she couldn't have controlled. It'd be a few more days before these bruises would disappear finally, but she'd never forget the sight of those bruises on her body, nor the feeling of painful sensitivity on her body in every place where he'd struck her. At some point, that evening, she stepped outside of her room and went to speak with Natalie. "Are you lonely?" asked Darlene. "A little," said Natalie. They spoke for a while. "Where do you come from?" asked Darlene. She asked this not because she really wanted to know, but because she felt as though talking about Natalie would take Darlene's attention off her own pain. "I was born in Labrador," said Natalie, referring to the part of Canada. She talked about her own upbringing, slurred as it'd been beneath drugs, booze, and violence. At some point, Darlene started to ask, "are you…" But she couldn't think of the right word. She asked, "…native?" To this Natalie only nodded.

282

Darlene

But then, sitting alone in that little room where she'd come to stay with her two young sons, Darlene thought something else. With the boys sleeping, she rose from her cot and walked out into the hall, taking great care to quietly tip-toe her way across the room and open and shut the door slowly so as not to wake the boys. She tiptoed across the hall, in much the same way she used to tiptoe across the hall in the little house she'd lived in with Marcel and the boys, looking to avoid rousing the attention of someone she knew wasn't even there. That night, Darlene and Natalie had kept talking quietly. "I'm sorry," said Darlene, "I don't know what the right term is." But Natalie shook her head slightly and said, "that's fine." Darlene thought she never would've guessed Natalie was native, given that Natalie was very white, with very pale, white skin that accentuated her bruises and little cuts exposed on her arms, legs, and face, and with her flowing brown hair. "How did you come to be here?" Darlene asked. "I came here from Montreal," said Natalie. The young Natalie went on to explain, in the careful, guarded way she did, that she left her hometown of Labrador with her then-boyfriend for Montreal, where she broke up with him before finding in with another. Although she didn't explain it fully to Darlene, throughout this time Natalie had been using drugs. They were both afraid to admit the full extent of their struggles, of the pain they'd been through to each other. They were both too closed off, too suspicious of each other, too made to be suspicious of each other. "It's hard to sleep here," said Natalie. "I haven't slept much in the past few days," said Darlene.

They spoke a little more, but didn't say much. Darlene was afraid to reach out.

In the hall at night it was never dark, the lights in the common areas of the shelter on all through the day and night. Darlene and Natalie were able to stay up a little while longer, sitting on that same bench in the hall. They were within sight of the office, so that every now and then one of the volunteers would stick her head out to check on them. That she was able to sit out and have this conversation with another woman meant something to her, although she didn't know, couldn't have known what. The following morning, it was time for Darlene to confront the truth. She couldn't live at the shelter forever, and she didn't intend to. Whether she wanted it or not, Marcel controlled her immediate future. All that she'd been through over the past few days, in fleeing Marcel and taking her two young sons to live in this battered women's shelter, it seemed to her as though it'd come from something, from somewhere else. And then there were the cravings, the seemingly random shiverings and shudderings that struck Darlene and brought her to her knees. Sometimes someone was there to help as she struggled back to her feet, shaking off the shiverings and shudderings as she moved forward. They offered her help, but there was little help to be had. She was sure there were some discussions on transferring her to a detox centre, only for her to decide silently she wouldn't take any. Natalie must've known what Darlene was going through in terms of withdrawal, but said nothing about it, seeming to choose instead to let Darlene have the space she needed. After having gone to the hospital and come back in almost exactly twenty-four hours, Darlene only wanted to be anywhere other than where she was.

Even then, she couldn't help herself from momentarily lapsing into flashbacks to the night she'd tried to flee her own home. In particular, she imagined Marcel standing in front of her, blocking her way forward with his hand on the far side of that door's frame. Sometimes, even as she was living in the shelter, she'd go to the door of her little room and open it, only to find Marcel standing there, blocking the way with his hand on the frame, his tall, lanky figure dressed in women's clothes. Sometimes, she'd see him standing there in the darkness, but she'd also smell that pungent, stinging smell of hard liquor on his breath. It wouldn't be as though she could simply *imagine* these things, these sights and smells; she'd well and truly see and smell them. It was all too much for her to bear, every moment she spent in that shelter at the mercy of Marcel another second she was forced to remain in place, frozen in terror, unable to move forward, seemingly forever stuck. But she wouldn't be stuck for much longer.

3

Even after they'd begun their rough and rocky transition to adolescence, Darlene always chose to view Stephen and Stuart as the same small children she'd thought they'd always been. Exactly when this thing had happened to Stephen, even he wouldn't have been able to remember that later in life. Nothing seemed to matter, nothing seemed to help, to Darlene, to anyone else who might've cared to take an interest in young Stephen's life. If anyone should've stepped in and done something, anything at all to help, then Darlene might've been suspicious all the same. In Vancouver, sometimes even in the summer it rained for a couple of days incessantly, just as it rained in the winter, all winter, with a steady thrum that always seemed to linger in the distance but only very rarely to approach. In the middle of the night, some nights, Darlene would be able to listen to the rain as she tried in vain to sleep, thoughts of the very near future and the distant past kept at bay by the relentless drumming of the rain against her bedroom's window. It'd been so long, so long since Darlene had been able to love anyone at all that she thought she might've forgotten even what it meant to love anyone like that.

But all that was in the near future, still the near future as Stephen was in the midst of his own trouble. This all came to a head when he was suspended from school for bringing a weapon onto school grounds. It wasn't a gun; he couldn't have possibly gotten a hold of a gun, not in Vancouver, not in Canada. No, he'd brought a knife, a butterfly knife, illegal in Canada all the same. He wouldn't say where he got it, which meant he was facing arrest. A weapons possession charge would've been the wrong thing to start off his long and awkward transition from child through adolescent and on to adult. Everyone seemed to know that. For once, it seemed to Darlene as though everyone, his teacher, the principal at his school, even the police officer they called in to help, as well as Darlene herself seemed to all be on the same page. For once, it seemed to Darlene as though there might've been someone out there besides her who had Stephen's best interests at heart. As she sat in a meeting with the principal, a counselor, and the school's police liaison officer, her thoughts weren't drawn elsewhere but laser focused on every word that was said. She was mostly silent, though. She was mostly silent because she was acutely aware that her son and his upbringing were being judged, that it wasn't only the things he'd done but everything he'd been through since birth that was being considered by everyone present, whether they said it or not. Even still, the agreement by all that Stephen was on the precipice and needed to be pulled back at any cost was a rare comfort to her.

But even this apparent moment of unity provoked in Darlene a subsequent moment of doubt, provoked the instincts she'd learned over twenty years of hardship and pain. Now, in Canada, no one under the age of twelve can be charged with a crime. At this time, Stephen was barely thirteen, too young to ruin his life over something like that. He wouldn't have known what he was doing, not that he could've. Although Darlene would never know because Stephen would never tell her, he brought the knife to school because he'd been threatened by a group of other students, a smattering of boys from one class or another, no more than two in any one class. He'd started taking the knife with him to school a couple of weeks before he'd been caught; he'd bought it at a pawn shop, after pawning some of the video games he'd had. It didn't really matter, not to Stephen nor even to Darlene had she known, what the threat was over. After the meeting had ended, Darlene was about to leave when Stephen's teacher asked to speak with her privately. As Darlene was putting on her coat, the teacher, a young woman named Miss Leung, asked Darlene to remain behind for a moment. Although Darlene would've normally politely but awkwardly declined, this time she stayed. One of the things Miss Leung, whose first name was Bonnie, said was, "I know it's not your fault." Darlene said, "I'll try to keep that in mind," as she eyed the door and fidgeted a bit with her coat. "I think he's a good kid," said Miss Leung, "he just needs more help." Darlene nodded.

By the time Stephen had grown up, moved out, and later come to the decision that he was really Stephanie, Darlene had gone over every part of their lives in search of the exact moment where it'd all gone wrong. But she couldn't find it. She couldn't find it. Every time she thought she'd found the moment when young Stephen had taken a turn, she always realized some earlier moment, some earlier trauma that might've, that must've caused him to fall apart at exactly the wrong moment. But the weapon he'd brought to school, it was something she couldn't ignore, something she couldn't just grit her teeth and get through. She took Stephen home at the end of the day, driving quietly home. "You can't keep up like this," she said, finally, bravely breaking the silence. "I didn't do anything wrong," he said. "Lots of guys have things like that," he said, "I've known guys who have brought guns to school. They never get in trouble." Darlene wasn't sure whether to believe that. She thought he might've just seen it on TV or read about it on the internet. Even as they were talking in the car, she tasted booze on the back of her tongue, and her mouth began to water in anticipation of the drink she'd have at home. Her hands repeatedly tightened and loosened their grip on the wheel, even without her thinking about it, her body having learned to instinctively tell when booze might've been near.

"You know I'll always love you," she said, "and I'll always take your side. But when we're alone I have to tell you honestly what you're doing. And you're headed down the wrong path." But Stephen didn't say anything. It was one of those times Darlene would later look back on and wish she'd tried harder, as hard as she'd needed to try until she got through to him. "I'm trusting you to stay home on your own all week," she said. By then, they'd made it home, and she'd parked outside in the street, turned the engine off, but then left the keys in the ignition as they talked. He continued to insist he'd done nothing wrong, but became less defensive. She thought he was making some progress, even as he continued to insist he'd done nothing wrong. After a few more minutes, she let him go. They both made it in through the front door. He made for his room, and she made for the kitchen. But she didn't reach for her bottle of vodka. Instead, she had the urge to open the cupboard, reach for the bottle, and then pour out every last drop into the kitchen sink. She didn't do this; she looked at the bottle for a little while, then reached for it and took it in her hand by the neck.

Holding the bottle, she twirled it a bit, watching as the vodka swirled about. But then she put the bottle back in the cupboard.

All this was leading towards something; it had to be, or else Darlene's experiences would've all been meaningless, like dust in the wind. The rain in Vancouver, this time of year it kept on pattering and pittering at a steady thrum, lining the streets with slow-moving currents, filling patches on the road like rivers. When it rained, Stephen and Stuart walked to school in the rain. The best Darlene could manage was giving them good raincoats and shoes, the former of which she'd found at a thrift store just off Cambie street. There were a lot of children their age in Vancouver who wore clothes bought at one thrift store or another, clothes in varying states of wear and tear. When she sent Stephen to school one time in jeans she'd patched up personally, she didn't know he was setting him up to be picked on and bullied. She didn't know jeans with holes in strategic places were at least somewhat more fashionable than patched-up jeans. She didn't know the patched-up jeans were an open admission of struggle and hardship. When he came home after having almost gotten into a fight with some of the other boys, if she'd have been more inquisitive, if she'd have made it her business to know what'd gone wrong those days, she might've been able to intervene then to head off his later struggles. At least, these were the things she'd later come to think, after Stephen had announced himself to be Stephanie. These were the things she'd later come to believe, that it was her

fault her oldest son would succumb to delusional
beliefs in his own femininity.

Even still, there was the years-later when
Stephen had asked—demanded—to be called
Stephanie. She thought it was possible that she
might never speak to Stephen again, something
that broke her heart even as it tortured her.
Although it'd been a while since she'd reached out
to him, she thought to try again, she thought to
keep on trying, thought to do things she never
imagined just to hear his voice again. It was so
deeply heartbreaking to be so cut off from
someone she loved, from someone she'd always
loved so unconditionally, only because some idea
had been put in his head over so many years by
people and forces beyond her control. Like his
father, Stephen had spent so much time on the
internet as an adolescent, something Darlene had
thought was normal for young men. Many years
later, she'd come to wish she'd policed his internet
use, someway, somehow, to have headed off his
delusions. She never knew what he'd done on the
internet, what he'd read. She never knew, and
would never know the websites he'd gone to where
people he'd never met had encouraged him to act
on normal adolescent confusion, where people
who knew nothing about him had planted ideas in
his head that would grow into intricate and
extensive delusions that couldn't have been
unpacked by the odd conversation here or there.
Even earlier, she wished she'd done more.

But she wouldn't, couldn't. With her younger
son, Stuart, having turned out to be halfway decent,
it seemed as though there must've been something

else at work. At least, she thought, Stuart always had his good grades to save him, his studies to sustain him despite the bully he went through as well. Stephen hadn't had anything. Stephen had always been lost, Darlene would later realize. Even during this time, Darlene contemplated telling Stephen that she would accept him as Stephanie, if only to get him back in her life in some small way. Even the thought of this possibility hurt her. She didn't want Stephanie. She didn't want a daughter. She wanted her son back. These days, as she worked through the days at the St. Paul's hospital and then came home to an empty apartment she felt as though her son had died and that he wasn't coming back. It was the same, to her, as though she'd put him in the ground herself. Except she'd had no funeral, no eulogy, and there was no grave for her to go to and pay her respects. Her oldest son had simply disappeared. There were days when she called in sick to work simply because she couldn't stop crying, couldn't manage to pull herself out of bed, couldn't summon the energy to do anything at all after having been brought right to the edge again by the loss of her oldest son. It seemed to her as though there was no way forward.

At some point Stuart had to have found out about Stephen's having decided to become Stephanie. When she asked Stuart if he knew, her younger son said that he'd only found out recently himself, that he and Stephen weren't really on speaking terms. On hearing this Darlene chided herself inwardly, believing as she did that both her sons—and she firmly believed she had two sons, not a son and a daughter—were too young to be caught up in this kind of infighting. But Darlene was only beginning to suspect the truth, that her sons were doing what they'd learned from watching her and their father during the early, formative moments of their lives. Sitting on the end of the couch on a rainy day, nursing a cup of coffee on her own, Darlene thought of some way to get through the days. She went back to the bottle. This time, it was a bottle that'd been there for a few months, where once she'd have reached for a bottle that might've been there for a few days, a week or two at most. She drank some vodka, but only a little, pouring it into a glass rather than taking a swig directly from the bottle. She hated the taste. It made her want to throw up. She didn't pour the bottle out, but on impulse threw it at the floor, causing it to shatter and the vodka to splash at her feet. After cleaning up the mess, Darlene went to look at old pictures of Stephen and Stuart on her phone, and she cried.

2

After Darlene had last angered Marcel by asking to leave their home in Quebec to visit a friend, she began to think of a way out. All this had to lead to somewhere, she thought, had to culminate in something, as if by some higher power's *design*. Her routine became something painless and dull, something she could only force herself through by detaching herself from her own sensory experiences, as if to have a controlled, at-will out of body experience whenever she needed to survive one of Marcel's sick fantasies for her.

293

Although he routinely subjected her to physical torture and pain, she'd still thought him capable of some kind of love. "I don't know why you can't accept me for who I am," said Marcel, one night after he'd come home from a night out on the town. She'd made the mistake of asking where he'd been, something that'd set him off on one of his tirades. He was yelling at her. He was screaming at her. But sometimes he was yelling and screaming past her, seemingly yelling at everything, something, or nothing at all. "I accept you," said Darlene. She thought quickly, as quickly as she could, before adding, "I'll always accept you for who you are." She didn't mean it, but she thought it was what he wanted to hear. She thought it would calm him down at least a little bit. But it didn't. "You don't accept me now," he said, "tell the truth." His face was red, and veins bulged in his forehead, along his temples, and in his neck. He looked at her and she saw the fire in his eyes.

"I'm trying," she said, pleading with him to calm down, only to calm down, always to calm down. "You're not trying at all," he said, before taking a glass that'd been on the table between them and throwing it hard against the wall behind her. She flinched. He looked to breathe fire. "I'm sorry," she said. But this only seemed to enrage him further. He clenched a fist and took a step around the table towards her. "No you're not," he said. She looked away, closing her eyes. It was as though she'd left her body and was looking down on herself, wondering who the person that she saw was, screaming out silently at herself to run away, far, far away and to never look back. "No I'm not," she said. She kept her eyes shut, expecting a blow to come, to her face, to the back of her head, somewhere, anywhere at all. But it didn't come, wouldn't come, not yet. But all this came to a head, one night, when Marcel did something, said something Darlene had been fearing for a long time, that some small part of her had been fearing almost from the very moment he'd first confessed to her beliefs in his own femininity. And so she turned back to the internet, whether on their computer while alone during the day or on her cell phone at other times, turning back to the internet message board where she'd made friends. She felt as though it was pathetic to have an internet message board as her primary social outlet, but feeling isolated as she was in a staunchly-Francophone part of the country she also felt as though she had no choice. She eventually read the private message sent to her on that message board, but wouldn't respond to it, not right away or ever. In the meanwhile, this message board seemed to offer a complementary escape to her reading and drinking, her books seeming to offer less of an escape than before. Even while she kept posting on that internet message board there were always books nearby, on the desk or in a drawer, some to be read, others to be re-read.

"I'm going to live as a woman all the time," said Marcel. She said nothing in response, her whole body having become seized in a still-mounting terror. "I mean, I'll be a woman outside the house as well as in here," he said. Still Darlene said nothing, unable, unwilling to say anything. "You have to support me or else I'll die," he said.

It wasn't the first time he'd said this, wasn't the first time he'd made this threat, only the latest and most melodramatic. Even still, after Marcel calmed down from his tirades, Darlene would turn to the internet for answers. She found communities of women online who were skeptical of the transgender phenomenon; some of them even reported having transgender husbands or ex-husbands, boyfriends or ex-boyfriends. Darlene didn't share with them any account of her own experiences with Marcel, but found in their accounts her own. She wouldn't even participate in discussions, wouldn't join these communities, but followed along as any visitor to those communities might've. Darlene almost always had a drink as she followed along. It was amazing to her that there were these communities of women hiding in open sight, groups of women who had been beaten, abused, coerced, even raped, all seeming to freely share their experiences with each other in places where anyone could find them, where anyone could watch. Even though they were hidden behind the shield of anonymous screen names, Darlene still read a part of herself into each of them.

It was around this time that Marcel told Darlene he'd started seeing a gender therapist—that's exactly what he said it was to her, a 'gender therapist'—through the local health authority. He said he'd been thinking of killing himself for some time, and that the therapist had said thoughts of self-harm were common in cases like his. This was the first time he'd even raised the possibility of harming himself, and it frightened Darlene. It frightened Darlene so much that she felt as though her heart had stopped. It wasn't the thought of him taking his own life that frightened Darlene, but the thought of him taking the lives of her sons and herself before doing so. "If you don't support me as a woman," he said, "then it's the same thing as you killing me yourself." But he said this without the slightest hint of irony or emptiness, as though he was ready and willing to carry out his threats, something which seemed unlikely even as it frightened her. Later, she took to the internet again. She found that message sitting in her inbox on a particular night, a particular night after Marcel had one of his tirades against her. She opened it again, and read through the message, from a fellow user she knew nothing about. Drinking, she read over it again, then again, then again. Suddenly it was later, hours later, her drink empty and tears coming down her face. She shuddered and shivered as she sobbed. It became impossible for Darlene even to pretend, even to convince herself there was something worth pushing through all the pain and suffering for.

That night, things took a turn for the worse. Marcel dressed in one of his women's outfits, this time donning a faux-nurse's outfit stretched to ridiculous proportions, complete with a white cap on his head and black stockings underneath a miniskirt over his legs. Even Marcel, a short and slender man, seemed like a hulking ogre under the makeup and outfit. This night, this night he forced her to lie on her stomach, in a prone position, kneeling in front of the foot of the bed. Once he'd maneuvered her into position, he yanked her pants down, then her panties, then proceeded to whip her bare bottom, ignoring her cries. "Please stop," she said, crying out through tears. "Mistress," he said, "I'm just getting started." He whipped her bottom again, and again, then a few more times while she kept on crying, crying until she had no more tears left to cry. Then, in a moment of clarity, she began to struggle against him. She pulled her arms in, put her palms flat on the bed, and began to push up. "Where do you think you're going, Mistress?" Marcel asked, grabbing first her left hand, then her right, then kneeling on her legs, forcing them into a position painful and awkward for her. "You're hurting me," she said, her voice rasping and croaking. "Shh," he whispered, dropping the whip on the floor, then turning himself until he'd pried her legs apart and had knelt between them. She might've thought to fight back, but she was too beside herself. This time, he seemed to attack her with a viciousness that left her dazed and confused. She found herself reduced to the pain she was experiencing, a pain that'd expanded to occupy every part of her body all at once.

He pulled her head back and whispered something indistinctly into her ear. "This is what it feels like to be a real woman," he said, before letting go. Her whole head fell forward, "I love you," she said, unsure what else to say. He was, seemingly, on the verge of becoming something other than what he'd been for almost as long as Darlene had known him, even for longer than Darlene had known him. It was all coming to be too much for her to bear. It'd long been too much for her to bear. She was rapidly approaching the end of her rope. Later that night, as Marcel slept Darlene lay awake in bed, on her side, staring at the far wall, looking right through it, imagining herself far away, anywhere but there. Even through all that'd happened, her breaking point had not yet been reached. It wasn't to have been the last time he'd subject her to violent sex, wasn't to have been the last time he'd push her that much closer to the edge. Although she was trapped, there was something inside her that kept her going, some hidden reserve of strength that kept her alive. The next day she'd stay in bed, pretending to still be asleep when Marcel got up for work. She'd still be in bed, still be pretending to sleep when he left with their sons. When she saw Stuart and Stephen home from school, she'd only barely managed to pull herself out from under the covers. She greeted them while she was still in a robe, a robe and some hastily-applied concealer to cover her scratches and bruises. Even to her sons, she felt, she was lying. But it wouldn't be this way much longer.

Some time passed, not much time, a few days at most. Even for Darlene it was hard to keep track of all the time that was passing, her days slurring into nothing. Over the next several days, Marcel more or less left her alone. But then he didn't.

Chapter Fourteen

1

That night when she'd tried to leave Marcel once and for all, its events continued to dominate Darlene's thoughts even as she'd come to live for a few days in the shelter. Somehow the flashing of all the red and blue lights that'd cast eerie glows on the ground, on the façade of their little house, even on the street, it created a surreal look, as if the world had been preserved in a sea of amber and gold. Although Darlene had been allowed to keep Stephen and Stuart with her at the shelter, she still feared they'd be taken from her at any moment, as if the police could've come in and whisked them away. Except for her midnight talks with Natalie, Darlene never left her sons, never let them go more than a few feet from her. She remembered her time in university, a time which some people enjoy for parties, drinking, and late nights spent talking about nothing at all. As Darlene was in a practical nursing program, she had to work a lot harder than most. Still, she always counted her blessings back then; she knew of students who took science courses and had a full-time lab schedule. Even at university she felt out of place, always too awkward and uncertain of herself to strike out and make new friends in a new city. The peak of this came one night when she was in her dorm room, alone as her roommate had gone out for the evening, and she found herself sipping on a bottle of vodka her roommate had left. She began to get a little tipsy, and posted a few telling things on a certain social media site. Someone saw the things she'd posted. In short order two young police officers were at her dorm, there to take her to the hospital, something she reluctantly agreed to. Spending the night in the hospital, just one night before her release the next day, it was a revealing experience, only one of many she'd had over the years.

The police who responded to the initial call of a domestic disturbance never said who made the call, nor would anyone afterwards. In the weeks and months to come, Darlene would suppose it was one of their neighbours, but she'd never know which one. She'd never known any of their neighbours, never had so much as a casual conversation with almost anyone else living in the neighbourhood; this was down to three factors. First, she spoke only English. Even after having lived there she'd only acquired a few words and phrases of Quebecois French. Second, she'd had no job in Quebec, and was never able to find employment, in no small part due to her lack of Quebecois French. And third, Marcel had done his best to make sure she'd made no friends, keeping her isolated at home, punishing her for any acting out, for even the most modest of attempts to do anything by herself. That night, that night, it was a night like any other in the world at large, but for Darlene it was another night of unrelenting terror, a night with that familiar wick of fear rising from some unknown spot deep in the pit of her stomach. It was the same wick of fear she'd felt throughout her encounter with Marcel that night, that particular night, out of the darkness and the light something frightening and enlightening compelling her to fill her mind with thoughts she'd have never wanted. But after having spent that one night, that solitary night on the psychiatric ward at Vancouver General Hospital, she redoubled her efforts, managing to set aside her own problems for at least the few years it took to get through university. She saw a psychiatrist for a brief time, but didn't wind up taking any medication. Those years in university continued to be lonely, but she never again fell to the depths that she'd fallen that night. It all seemed to be working out, to her at least. She thought she was on the right track for the first time in her life.

But the police who responded to that initial call of a domestic disturbance would never have imagined, could never have known what she'd been through, even if they'd have been willing to listen. When she was younger, she'd worked in a restaurant as a waitress. After working there for only a few months, she saw one of the other waitresses, a woman in her forties with two children to feed, taking home leftovers for them. It was food that would've wound up in the trash anyways, but the manager found out and fired her for stealing. At the time, Darlene would've blamed the manager himself, even though she couldn't have afforded to quit the job herself. But Darlene said nothing, at the time only hearing of it after the fact, even then keeping her opinions to herself. After having been through so much, after having survived more than fifteen years with Marcel, Darlene came to believe, in retrospect, that the manager himself wasn't to blame, but the world which would show no kindness or mercy to people like her old co-worker, her old friend, to people like her. As she'd sat off to the side, waiting for the police to do something, anything at all on that night in question, it might've occurred to her that this was another powerful lesson, one she couldn't have appreciated or even understood at the time but only has after many, many years of reflection. It was only after her sons had both left home that Darlene had finally found the peace and quiet to hear herself think. But even then it was too quiet to think. Even then, she was to have found she'd come to crave the crisis.

Even Darlene herself, as she spent those few days with her sons at the shelter, never expected anything good to have come from it, anything to have turned out the way it'd turned out. That night outside her own home, that night when the police had shown up and intervened in her abortive escape, Darlene wasn't sure what she'd have done if the police hadn't shown up. Her plan—to leave with Marcel's reluctant, grudging consent—had fallen apart in the time it'd taken him to lapse into his masculine self. She sat on the side of the road, at the side of the road, in their neighbourhood the sidewalk consisting only of a rough gravel strip that provided traction to vehicles and the sound of crunching underneath every footstep. Even as she sat, the police were expediting her transfer to the shelter, by radio contacting someone who picked up the phone and arranged an immediate intake, the whole sequence of events that saw her arrive at the shelter taking an hour or two but seeming at the time to Darlene to take much, much longer.

Darlene

Eventually, long after she'd left the shelter and escaped to Vancouver with her sons, she'd realize the full extent of what happened that night, of what the police and the counselors managed to pull off. At the time, though, all she could think about was the fear that she might've been made to return home, and the fear that she might've been persuaded to do just that. At the time, for want of even the flimsiest grasp on the French language, Darlene couldn't appreciate all that was going on around her. She felt so alone, so isolated, so unaware of all the things that were being done on her behalf, all the while afraid, still afraid Marcel would somehow find the shelter and enter it, to kill her and her boys.

But Darlene and Natalie, almost-friends in the three days they'd be in the shelter together had learned so little about each other that they'd remember over the coming years. At night, on the second last night she'd spend in the shelter, something happened. "I'm so lonely here," said Darlene, speaking with Natalie that night. "Me too," said Natalie, nervously looking herself over before smiling weakly at Darlene. "I need a drink," said Darlene. "Me too," said Natalie. Inside the shelter, they both tried to cover their bruises and cuts, Darlene wearing her hair long overtop scarves to conceal injuries to her neck. She could only guess what Natalie's wounds were. But she saw needle marks tracking up Natalie's arms, as well as patches skin darkened slightly. Suddenly she realized herself and looked away; Natalie turned her arms to hide the needle marks, but couldn't hide the bruises. "I'm sorry," said Darlene. "It's okay," said Natalie. They talked for a little while longer, a little while that turned into hours. Darlene shared secrets she hadn't shared with anyone before, secrets she wouldn't share with anyone after. And Natalie, Natalie shared secrets she hadn't shared either. Natalie spoke of having run away from home when she was only thirteen, having fled a step-father who'd sexually abused her since she was much younger and a mother who was in and out of jail. Natalie spoke of having been taken in by a much-older predator who sent him around to all his friends in exchange for drugs. She never mentioned exactly when she started using drugs, and Darlene never asked. Eventually she shacked up with one particular man, a man a few years younger than her, and this was okay for a while. But then he started beating her too. Even throughout these years she kept on using drugs. She was still using drugs until just before she came into the shelter. It wasn't clear to Darlene exactly when Natalie had last used drugs. Darlene didn't ask.

That night, that second last night saw the power fail in the midst of one of the worst heat waves in years. Darlene was reluctant to open the windows in her room, fearing she'd open a path through which Marcel could've attacked her at any time. But it quickly became far too hot and stuffy for her or her sons to tolerate, their shirts soaking with sweat and their brows needing to be mopped, their hair turning into a matted mess. When Stephen complained, Darlene summoned the courage, standing up and reaching for the window, sliding it open a little bit, no more than a couple of inches. When Stephen complained again, she opened it another couple of inches. After Stephen complained a third time, she looked at him and saw the confusion and frustration in his eyes. She slid the window open as far as it would go, then after watching the boys fall asleep she went to the common room and looked for Natalie. She went to see Natalie, only to find Natalie gone. Darlene checked inside Natalie's room, and found her friend wasn't there either. Later, much later, Darlene would learn that while she was recovering from her seizure, days had passed and Natalie had left the shelter. By the time Darlene returned to the shelter, she found staff and volunteers wouldn't tell her where Natalie had gone, as a matter of policy. Darlene would think about Natalie on many occasions throughout the years to come, wondering where she went, wondering whether she was all right. Even as she struggled through continued withdrawal, she continued to wish Natalie was still there with her, still there to provide at least one friend for her during the loneliest time in her life, as well that she was still there to do the same thing for Natalie.

Things were coming to a head, even as Darlene thought her whole life was slowing to a crawl. Although Darlene had only spent a few nights at the shelter, less than a week, she felt as though she'd been there for years. It was as though time had slowed, any given moment from her point of view passing as quickly as any other, yet between moments there something that hadn't been there before. But something was coming, Marcel soon to interject into their lives again, lives that he'd never left. Darlene needed his consent to take their sons away from Quebec, to take them back to Vancouver, something she thought she'd never get. But she'd be wrong.

2

Even after telling her he was thinking of living full-time as a woman Marcel hadn't mentioned the possibility of surgeries or hormones, but Darlene had discovered on the family's computer searches to that effect. She wondered what the effect of these procedures and treatments might be on a an already unstable man, on a man who was already prone to fits of violence, whose fantasies always seemed to centre on imagining himself as a woman, doing things no woman would ever do. Even though she'd seen him spend much time over the years on the computer, or on his phone, and even though he'd openly told her that's where he found most of his ideas for things he wanted her to do in bed, his announcement of wanting to live full time as a woman had struck her hard. Even back then, even as this was happening, it was hard for Darlene even to imagine these were the sorts of things that were lingering in the world, waiting for damaged, impressionable, or deranged people to find them and incorporate them into their lives. As she made the effort to go about her life as best she could, the unrelenting pain and suffering seemed sure only to get worse. Soon, Marcel was giving her detailed, point by point instructions on what she was to do with her days, even on days when he was off work. He'd spend those days mostly on the computer at home, Darlene thought probably adjusting his plans for what she was to do that night in helping him act out his then-current fantasy. It all seemed like a drunken haze to Darlene, who'd taken to drinking almost daily to cope with the constant fear of when Marcel's next assault might take place. She could never predict it.

One day she came home from running her prescribed errands, her errands having been prescribed by Marcel. She came home to find him still sitting at his desk, as he'd been sitting when she'd left. It was the little details she noticed, the little details she'd learned to notice. The same can of beer sat in the same spot next to his keyboard, on the same coaster. "I love you," she said, hoping to elicit some kind of a reaction, hoping to spark some kind of resurgence in him of the man he used to be. Instead of saying nothing, Marcel looked up at her and said, "I doubt that." Then, he looked away, back to his computer. That night, Marcel put her through the act of his latest fantasy. It was like all the others in that it made Darlene deeply uncomfortable, in that it caused her pain, but like all the others she went along with it anyways. She complained very little as he put her through the act of playing the dominant role to his submissive, only to switch roles for a final climax in which he struck her hard, again and again. She drank before, enough to dull the pain of Marcel's strikes against her body. But she found that no amount of booze could dull the pain she felt inside. She was dying. She was dying. The light inside her was dimming, the flame inside her soon to be snuffed out. By the time this act was finished, she was hardly able to breathe. His blows against her with a small paddle had cut her, leaving wounds on her bare bottom. The following day, she couldn't bring herself to wash the sheets that'd been stained with bits of her blood, so she waited until Marcel left the house, then put spare sheets on the bed and burned the old, stained sheets. As the sheets burned, she drank wine from the bottle, crying softly. At some point, she noticed both her sons watching, both Stuart and Stephen peeking from around the corner. Normally she might've said something, anything at all to them, but this time she couldn't find the energy to say anything at all.

Soon, it was Darlene's birthday, her thirty-eighth. She felt much older. Although Darlene was used to doing nothing for her birthday, one of Marcel's sisters unexpectedly insisted on taking her out for a little party. Darlene didn't want to go, not right away, but Marcel's sister wouldn't take no for an answer. Marcel tried to stop her from going, but she got his friends involved in planning it, until it would've been too conspicuous for him not to allow Darlene to go. Darlene would wind paying for it, in repeated sexual humiliations and degradations for weeks afterwards, but for one night, one precious night she was glad to have at least one friend in the world. Even still, as the day had drawn nearer Darlene came to feel more nervous than ever. When Marcel came home and found her on the phone with his sister, he became angry and demanded she get off the phone right away. Darlene obliged, but later that night withstood the most violent and dangerous sexual fantasies Marcel had yet conceived. As the day had drawn nearer and nearer, these acts repeated, with Marcel catching Darlene doing one thing or another that he didn't want her to do, only to punish her by subjecting her to steadily more humiliating and painful sexual acts each night. But she wouldn't relent. She couldn't relent. There was a part of her that refused to be beaten down, refused to be cowed, even as she couldn't help but comply with Marcel's every request. By the time the night of her birthday came she'd already endured so much torture there was little left for Marcel to threaten her with, or so she might've thought.

The bar was crowded and noisy. It was a typical sports bar, but for the dominance of the French language almost identical to the bar in Darlene's memory where once she'd first met Marcel. But this, this bar was to be a place where Darlene would meet her one and only true friend in all the time she'd spend living in Quebec. This friend was an anonymous woman, a random woman she'd never have met before and wasn't to have met again, a woman named Sophie who'd looked on Darlene from across the bar and seen a broken, haggard-looking Darlene in desperate need of a good friend, if only for an evening. Darlene was sitting with her group, surrounded by people but somehow feeling as alone as ever. Sophie must've seen this, and approached Darlene to ask, "are you okay?" At first, Darlene tried to play dumb. Darlene asked, "what do you mean?" She fumbled for her drink, taking the slightest of sips, before Sophie stopped her. Sophie said, "you seem like you're really sad about something." Darlene took a moment to think of her response, to carefully consider each word, as though Marcel was watching and would've harshened his punishment with each word she misspoke. "I might be," said Darlene, some part of her wanting, so sorely wanting to connect with this woman. Sophie persisted. Marcel wasn't there. He'd determined to stay home and wait for her to come back at the end of the night. She believed, then, that he'd have been waiting for her. She spoke with Sophie for a while, sometimes interrupted by others in her party; most of them left one by one, until Sophie had to go. The last thing Sophie said to Darlene before leaving was, "try and stay safe." And to this Darlene said, "I'll try."

Darlene went home that night and drank heavily to numb herself, to numb herself against the pain she was certain to be coming. After having taken to drinking so often, she thought it wouldn't have surprised or angered Marcel to find her slumped over the dining room table in a drunken stupor. But Marcel didn't come home that night. He came home the following night. He came home as Darlene was in the midst of another night of heavy drinking, Darlene finding him staggering through the front door while she and the boys watched. "You stupid bitch," he said, before asking, "you really are a cruel person aren't you?" This time, she wouldn't pretend she didn't know what he was talking about. This time, she said, "I wasn't trying to hurt you." He took one more swig from the bottle before throwing it at the floor. It shattered, causing Darlene to flinch. "You're lying," he said, "you're always lying. Why do you lie to me?" When she didn't answer right away, he said, "everyone is a liar except me." He took a few moments, as if to consider his thoughts, what thoughts he could consider in his drunken state. During these few moments, Darlene was still seized in a fear. "I work so hard for you," he said, "I work so hard for you. I make all the money and I pay for everything we have. And still you try to hurt me like this." She said nothing, falling back on her hard-learned habit of leaving her body and imagining herself somewhere else, far away from there. But even this hard-learned habit couldn't help her much, like a drug against which she'd developed a tolerance the power of her own imagination unable to take her away. "You're going to have to make up for this betrayal," he said. She'd closed her eyes, and she knew right away what he meant by this. He begun to smile, the thin beginnings of a smile, when Darlene opened her eyes to look at him through her own tears.

That night, that night, after having led her into the bedroom and pushed her down onto the bed, he changed into one of his woman's outfits, Marcel seemed to relish in the pain he caused her. He struck her again, and again, and again, then turned and demanded she strike him again, and again, and again. He bullied her into squeezing into an ill-fitting vinyl dress and then insisted she penetrate him with the largest strap-on she'd seen. Even as he knelt on the bed and urged her on, he hurled slurs at her. "Come on," he said, "treat me like the stupid cunt I am." She thrust into him as vigorously and forcefully as she could, eliciting moans and gasps from him in time with each thrust. "That's right," he said, "I'm such a fucking worthless cunt." The things that he said cut through Darlene, even after she'd endured so much already. "You don't know what it's like," he said, as he urged her to take him faster and harder. When she complied, he only said, "yes, yes, yes," while seeming to shiver and shudder. At some point he reached between his legs and began to manipulate himself. As he did this, Darlene began to become detached from herself, began to feel as though she was immersed in a warm haze that kept her from feeling everything she was feeling.

She was dying, slowly but surely. As soon as he was near his climax, he turned to face her, pushed her aside, and then violently wrestled her to the mattress, striking her with the back of his hand as ripped the strap-on off her and forced himself inside her. "You stupid cunt," he said. He pushed her face down into the sheets until she struggled to breathe. "You're such a fucking worthless cunt," he said. He struck her again, and again while he took her from behind. Then he clutched at her throat and pulled her upright, choking her as he came, she reaching with both hands to claw at his. But he only clutched tighter, tighter, choking her until she felt as though she might pass out. Then he released her. They both fell on the bed, gasping for breath. He'd torture her some more the following night, then the night after that, then the night after that, each successive act becoming more violent and inflicting more pain on her. Although she was near her breaking point, there was still one thing left to happen, one violent act yet to be inflicted on her before she realized her need to break free.

Darlene

3

There were a lot of things Darlene would never learn about what her sons had been through when she hadn't been around. The boys' visits to spend time with their father in Quebec, although not specifically mandated by any court but by mutual agreement between Marcel and Darlene after she'd left him and taken the boys with him, had come only after Marcel had taken nearly everything else from her. In the divorce agreement, drawn up and finalized only after she'd left, had been It was on one of the boys' first visits back to Marcel in Quebec that Marcel began to sexually abuse Stephen. The sexual abuse was never out in the open, never spoken of, as it'd been when Darlene had been subject to Marcel's increasingly violent and deranged sexual fantasies. It wasn't enough that Darlene was *there* for Stephen. Even this she'd never come to terms with, never come to understand. That year, that year was unusually hot and dry across the country, from Vancouver Island to St. John's, as Darlene saw Stephen and Stuart off to visit their father in Quebec a heat wave pushing temperatures to record highs. Without air conditioning at home, Darlene had taken to leaving their apartment's windows open all hours of the day and night, only closing them when no one was home. Sometimes Stephen and even Stuart complained it was too hot to sleep, but Darlene could do nothing to help them except offer them maybe an extra fan or a glass of ice water. In truth, it wasn't all that hot very much in Vancouver. The peaks of the heat waves lasted a few days at most.

Darlene never had much trouble sleeping, not for the heat at least. But when her sons went over to spend some weeks she couldn't sleep at all, not without drinking. She drank herself to sleep some nights. At some point while her sons were away, though, she saw a psychiatrist for the first time.

Why Marcel chose Stephen and not Stuart was something even Marcel probably wouldn't have been able to explain, if asked. Stuart and Stephen kept on going to Marcel's during Christmas and Spring breaks, as well as for a few weeks during summer vacation between grades. Every time, Darlene took them to the airport, helping them carry their bags to the check in counter, then seeing them off to the gates. While Stuart always seemed sad to go, Stephen always kept quiet, cooperating, but never looking up from the patch of floor in front of him. Darlene knew something was wrong, but felt powerless to do anything about it. That year, that year that was unusually hot and dry across the country, it saw Darlene spend the whole six weeks her sons were away in a kind of excruciating paralysis. The psychiatrist she saw, she saw him only once; she didn't go to a follow-up appointment, not even cancelling but simply not showing up. It might've been bad form, but she supposed psychiatrists from the local mental health unit were used to flaky patients, and she didn't feel bad about it. After her sons had gone off to spend some weeks that summer with their father in Quebec, Darlene tried to rededicate herself to work, volunteering for overtime whenever it was offered, sometimes even working six or seven days in a week. It was hard, it'd become hard for her to make it through the days only to come home to an empty apartment, to an apartment that seemed to threaten her with its emptiness. She left lights on so she wouldn't come home to a dark apartment. She sometimes even left the television on while she went to work, so she might've been able to trick herself into thinking there was someone there when she came home at the end of the day. It was so curious and unsettling to Darlene, to come home to an empty home for the first time in more than fifteen years; one night, one night not long before the boys were to come back she set down on the couch with all the lights on and the TV turned to the news, only to suddenly find herself sitting in the dark, hours later. Even while this was happening, though, Stephen was enduring something infinitely worse.

The exact moment it started was something even Stephen probably wouldn't know, even years later. It wasn't as though Stephen had spent much time over there; a couple of months out of the year in total. Even things other people might've been unable or unwilling to understand, Stephen knew from first hand experience, the kind of first hand experience that can only come from pain. Even after Marcel had picked the boys up at the airport in Quebec City, to drive them all the way back to the old family home in the Saguenay region. Marcel had kept on living in that home after Darlene had left and taken the boys with her. During their stays, both Stephen and Stuart slept in their old bedrooms, on their old beds, everything as it'd been the last time they'd lived in that very house. But that year, that year that was unusually hot and dry across the country, it was the one year when Darlene might've been tempted to splurge on an air conditioner for the apartment. It would've cost several hundred dollars, and would've gone right on a credit card. And the boys, for the boys she thought it would've been a nice surprise when they came home. She found a particular model of air conditioner on an online retailer's website while on the computer, a model she could've easily mounted to the outside of the sliding window on he main floor patio. She almost bought it; she was about to submit the order when she hurriedly closed the browser window. For the next several days she received emails from the retailer inviting her to continue and finish her order, invitations she promptly deleted each time, her anxiety mounting each time. Even while she worked through her time alone, across the country her oldest son was in bed with her ex-husband, going through something horrible.

It'd started like this. From the first time the boys flew over to visit him for holidays, Marcel invited Stephen into his bed at night, sometimes three or four nights in a row. The first night, nothing happened. The second night, nothing happened. The third night, the third night saw Marcel touch Stephen for the first time, only touch him, Marcel putting his hands in places his hands shouldn't have been put, leaving sometimes one, sometimes both hands to touch. But then, he'd stop, as though he was aware of what he was doing. Every morning this happened, Stephen would get up before his father and go into the kitchen, quietly getting something to eat and drink.

Darlene

One morning, one morning while Marcel was still sleeping off a hanger Stephen found the place where Marcel kept his booze. Before Marcel woke up, Stephen poured out the booze, then when Marcel finally woke up and made it into the kitchen and found the bottles empty. But Marcel just went out and bought more. All day that day Stephen would wonder what'd happened the night before, and on into the next night, and the night after that. It wasn't until it happened again that Stephen began to fearfully anticipate it happening again. Even still, Stephen was too confused, scared, and young to understand what was happening to him, or way. He'd seen his father wearing women's clothes so many times over the years, just as he'd seen his father screaming at his mother, threatening this or that, demanding this or that, and yet still he couldn't process what was happening. He wouldn't sleep in the same bed as his father every night that summer, only about a third of the nights, the uncertainty making him feel a terror very few children ever feel. Even this was impossible for someone so young as Stephen to process, the whole thing becoming a blur that he'd decide to try and forget about as soon as he was old enough to understand it.

After Darlene had left Quebec and taken Stephen and Stuart with her back to Vancouver, Marcel had reconsidered his intentions to live as a woman. He kept on seeing the same gender therapist at the local mental health unit, who kept on reassuring him that to assert his own gender identity was a bold and brave move, something he shouldn't fear to embrace but should turn towards.

All this was unknown to Darlene, who preferred to try and use the time she had with the boys away to recuperate from the previous school year. All throughout their nearly-twenty years together, Marcel had never displayed the slightest inclination towards abusing children, save the general neglect that went along with his escalating obsession with his fetishes as their marriage went along. He stopped dressing as a woman when the boys were around, at least at first. He put off his plans to transition fully into a woman, which would've involved various surgeries and hormone therapies. He kept on seeing the same gender therapist, though, who kept on advising him that he should transition from man to woman as soon as he felt ready, who kept on reassuring him that it'd all be paid for by the public health authority. He kept on acquiring new sets of women's clothes as well as makeup and jewellery, mostly buying them off the internet. A lot of sources told Darlene that she should've just accepted her ex-husband for who he was. Even though she'd only recently succeeded in breaking free herself, Darlene still entertained at least the notion of acting as though everything had been forgotten, as though the things he'd done to her were all in the past for the sake of spare their sons the greatest possible hardship moving forward, for the sake of giving them the closest thing possible to a normal life.

Even still, she never could, she never could. The whole point of having sent her sons back into the home in which she'd been subject to such horrific torture and abuse, it never sat well with her. It was court-ordered, agreed to by Darlene and

Marcel. But Darlene's guilt could've never escaped her if she'd have ever learned what was happening. It was while Stephen and Stuart were away at their father's that Darlene kept on meeting with her friend Cherise, still the only real friend she had in the world. "Can you come over?" Darlene asked. Instead, they met at a 24-hour restaurant just off East Hastings, not far from the old Pacific Coliseum. The restaurant might've been there longer than the Coliseum. After ordering their coffees and dishes, they began to talk. "I feel so alone without them here," said Darlene. "That's normal," said Cherise. "I just wonder what they're up to," said Darlene, "the Marcel I knew wasn't even…" But she couldn't even finish her thought, couldn't even bring herself to put into words the vague but impossibly powerful intuition she had that something was *wrong*. The diner was mostly empty, and outside a low ebb of traffic glid along the street. Even at night, every so often a bus would go by, trundling one way or the other, sometimes stopping to pick up or drop off passengers but mostly just rolling past. Darlene took a sip of coffee, then another, then another, until her cup was empty, a waitress who looked much older than her seeming to appear at exactly the right moment to offer her a refill which she gratefully accepted. It was only a week until her sons were to come home from Quebec, and already Darlene was wondering how she'd make it through that week without sleep. "You can't control everything they do," said Cherise. "I know I can't," said Darlene, "and I just, I just don't feel good about letting them go off into that place

321

again. I can't tell them everything they saw was normal, but I don't know if I can stand to ask them what they're going through." But Cherise said, "they'll be back soon."

That night, that very night, as Darlene spoke with Cherise over coffee, over four thousand kilometres and three time zones away Stephen was in his father Marcel's bed, clutching at the covers as he lay on his side at the very edge of the bed. It was just as Darlene had once laid on the edge of the very same bed, clutching those same covers, looking off into the same darkness imagining herself somewhere, anywhere but there. What happened next even Stephen wouldn't know, wouldn't remember exactly. It all turned into a blur for him. He didn't exteriorize, didn't leave his body and look down on himself; even as he remained fully aware of everything that was happening to him, every sensation he was experiencing still the whole night turned blank. He was too afraid to do much of anything but bear it. He was too young to know anything at all. In the darkness of the night, in the bedroom that Marcel had once shared with Darlene, the only thing that could've been heard above the sound of ragged breathing was the circling of a ceiling fan above the bed. Stephen still felt the scrape of his father's stubble on the back of his neck, even hours later. All the music had stopped, and all the gold had faded into a dull rust. When Marcel raped Stephen for the first time, even Marcel didn't know what he was doing, or why. That didn't matter to either of them. Marcel was the most confused of all.

Darlene

But Cherise wasn't all there herself. "There's something else," said Darlene, "something I can't quite figure out." Cherise took a sip of coffee, and then said, "you'll never figure out everything." A lot more was said between them, some of it about Stephen and Stuart, some not. "It's totally fine for you to worry," said Cherise, "it'd be more alarming if you didn't." Darlene said, "but I'm totally powerless to do anything." She paused to take a sip of coffee, then said, "even after they come back I know I'll still feel powerless to help them." Even at night, in the middle of the summer it was hot and humid outside, the cool, dry air conditioning of the diner offering a welcome respite from the stuffy heat in Darlene's apartment. "My boys are the only good thing he gave me," said Darlene. "I can see that," said Cherise. Darlene fidgeted a bit with her coffee, nearly empty as it was. She hoped the waitress would be along to pour her more coffee. "I want him to just disappear from my life," said Darlene, closing her eyes and shaking her head slightly as she spoke. Cherise said nothing, only listening. "I wish I'd never gotten together with him," said Darlene, "but then I'd never have had my boys. And I love them more than anything in the world." Still Cherise only listened. "I can't wait until I get them back," Darlene said. Finally the waitress appeared to pour her another cup of coffee. It was a new waitress; the other's shift had ended. Darlene was grateful. The conversation shifted. "I've met someone," said Cherise, "and we might be getting married. If it happens, I'd like you to be there." Quickly, Darlene agreed. Even as Darlene had been struggling through her recovery

323

from years of abuse, Cherise had been struggling on her own, struggling with the perils of loneliness, of watching her friends all find families while she spent the prime years of her own life alone.

That night, that very night, as Darlene spoke with Cherise over coffee and doughnuts, her oldest son Stephen summoned the courage to get out of Marcel's bed. He made it to the bedroom door, quietly twisting the knob, pulling it open, then leaving it a crack open behind him. Uncertain exactly what to do, too scared and still in physical pain, from what'd happened just a few hours earlier, Stephen walked through the darkness to Stuart's room. After gently knocking on the door and getting no reply, Stephen opened it slightly and called out to Stuart, as quietly as he could manage. When Stuart complained, Stephen asked if he thought it was a good idea to go back to his own room. Stephen was afraid their father would wake up in the morning and realize he wasn't there. That'd make Stephen angry, and he'd come after him. It was hard even for Stephen to explain, not that he could've at so young an age. They said something to each other. they were just a couple of kids. Reluctantly, Stephen returned to his father's bedroom and quietly climbed back into his father's bed. There came a time when he'd look over his own body and feel disgust at what he saw, even if he couldn't understand the compulsion to hate himself. Whatever happened over the last week both Stephen and Stuart were to be back in Quebec, neither Stephen nor Stuart were capable of understanding it. Had Darlene known about it, she might not've understood it either. Even after all she'd been through, after all the torture and abuse she'd endured, she might not've been able to comprehend such a horror as that inflicted on her oldest son.

Chapter Fifteen

2

After Darlene had been taken out for her birthday, sure enough her predictions that she'd pay for it proved true. She went home that night to find Marcel waiting, already dressed in the outfit he'd chosen for that night's fantasy. He insisted she drop what she was doing and get herself into the bedroom, to which she reluctantly complied. That night he struck her again and again, seeming to take particularly sadistic pleasure in watching her cry into the sheets. A slur of pain and sadness seemed to wrack her whole body, coming in waves as she tried to withstand this latest assault. But over the next few days, something clicked in Darlene. Even she didn't know what it was. Even she couldn't have known what it was. As she counted one day after the other of ritual torment and sexual abuse, there was something else coming. That summer, that summer it'd been unusually hot and dry throughout the province, saw new highs give way to new lows. They were at home, all of them. Darlene was in the kitchen, while the boys sat at the table. Marcel came storming out of the bedroom. He yelled and he screamed and he threatened this and that. "You think you know what you're doing," he said, "but you don't know shit." And to this Darlene only said nothing, looking away, thinking, thinking, thinking about something, anything at all. "Fucking look at me when I'm talking to you," said Marcel. She looked back over. She saw the rage in his eyes, the seething rage. His whole face was flush red, and veins bulged on his temples and neck. The smell, the familiar sting of vodka on his breath filled the air. He reached for her and grabbed her roughly by the neck. "Fucking look at me," he said. She looked him right in the eye. But this only made him angrier. "I'm looking at you," she said.

The community she'd become a part of on the internet, it continued to offer her something vaguely resembling a social life. She kept on drinking as she spent more and more time sequestered in a world away from the pain and suffering of her home life. She never responded, she hadn't yet responded to that message from a concerned fellow user of that particular community, and the concerned fellow user hadn't sent another. Even the posts she continued to make on the publicly-viewable parts of the community, they hardly changed. His posts—she soon discovered the other user was a man—made no mention of anything he'd seen or heard. It made her feel welcomed. It made her feel as though there was someone out there watching and waiting, there should she ever need a shoulder to lean on or someone who would listen to her complaints. But she never took it. She never took advantage of it. She hadn't taken advantage of it, not yet. For his part, Marcel didn't come after her right away. It seemed to Darlene as though he was biding his time. He found something she'd written on the computer. That must've been it. "Then fucking tell me what you're doing," he said. "Let me go," she said. "What did you fucking say to me?" he asked. "I said let me go." She looked right at him. he looked right at him and managed courage for the first time in as long as she could remember. "You're fucking asking for it aren't you?" he asked. For a moment, only for a moment, her courage disappeared, replaced by the familiar feeling of self-loathing and doubt. "Fucking you don't know what you want," he said. "You don't know what you want either," she said, her courage reappearing as she went on to say, "you never knew."

As she kept posting on the internet when Marcel and the boys weren't around, Darlene began to wonder, began to fear. Actually, she'd always been afraid, always worried Marcel would find the things she'd been reading, the things she'd been writing online. But now she began to wonder whether any of this would come of it, whether she'd ever do anything useful with all the time spent drinking and reading, drinking and surfing, drinking and chatting with people she'd never met. Even as the community of almost-friends online offered her an escape, it posed a challenge, something she became increasingly aware of even as she took no steps to protect herself from the inevitable. And it was inevitable that Marcel should discover her internet use. At some point, she just stopped caring. Even more time was yet to pass, in that time Marcel seeming to relish in the waiting, as though there was something he was waiting for, something he knew about, something she didn't know he knew about. But she didn't care, she didn't care. "This has gone on long enough," said Marcel, "I've let you fucking do whatever you want and it fucking ends." She looked past him, into the living room, looking for Stephen and Stuart.

"Don't fucking look away," he said. "What do you want from me?" she asked. "What did you fucking say to me?" he asked. There was a moment of quiet. "Why have you become this way?" she asked. It was as though she'd left her own body, and she felt a dawning horror as the words escaped her lips and floated up into the air. She was watching everything that happened on a delay. "You don't get to speak like that to me," he said, "this is all about who I am." Without skipping a beat, Darlene said, "of course it is." It was the first time she'd really argued with him, the first time she'd offered any resistance in all the years since they'd met. "You fucking cunt," he said, "you don't know how hard it is to live like this. You cis-women don't know anything about what we have to go through." And then he lapsed into French, Darlene's mastery of the language still too primitive to pick out anything for the rapidity of Marcel's speech.

But Darlene would eventually respond to the message sent by that poster, expressing gratitude for the offer of support. It was a small moment, one unbefitting the gravity of the situation, but one she'd never forget. Then the night came. Marcel seemed to have saved up all his aggression and rage for one night, coming for Darlene at exactly the right moment. As always, she'd finished seeing the boys to bed, first Stuart, then Stephen, and closed the door to Stephen's room when Marcel came for her. He made no effort to lure her into their master bedroom, instead coming out to intercept her as she made for the kitchen. "I don't know what the fuck you think you've been doing," he said, "but you're mine now and you better not fucking forget it." "What makes you think I won't do it?" he asked, "what makes you think I won't do it all?" To Darlene he seemed to make a point of referring to something as vaguely as possible. "I found what you're doing," he said, "I found it on the computer." Her insides turned to ice as she listened, and time seemed to slow, slowing until it finally stopped. "Did you think you could hide from me?" he asked. "I don't know what you're talking about," she said. "You fucking liar," he said. "I'm not lying," she said, "I've got a right to—" His hand came at her. He slapped her hard. Her whole face stung, then felt warm. She looked at nothing. He grabbed her. "Don't fucking lie to me," he said. She smelled the booze on his breath. Suddenly, in a surge of strength she brought her hands up and pushed him back, then broke free from his grasp. She started towards the living room, started towards Stuart and Stephen who were both watching silently. But a hand gripped her shoulder, and spun her around. She came face to face with Marcel again. She put her hands up to protect her, but it was no use.

He balled up one fist and punched her in the stomach. The wind knocked out of her, Darlene dropped to her knees, only for Marcel to grab her by the hair and pull her into the bedroom, slamming the door behind her before dropping her on the floor next to the bed. Gasping and wheezing, she could only lie in a heap, tears streaming down her face. There was the sound of Marcel's shoes kicking off against the far wall, then the unbuckling of his belt. He pulled his pants down, then stepped out of them. "Please," she said, still struggling for breath. He picked her up roughly by her shoulders, then threw her on the bed. She struggled to turn over, to crawl away, but his hands found her shoulders again and he roughly held her in place. She kicked about, trying to kick him off her, but he fell between her legs. "Don't," she said, "please don't." Her voice was desperate, but still quiet. "Shut the fuck up," he said, "and learn your fucking place for once." This was something unusual for him to say, even in the heat of the moment. "Please," she said. Still she struggled under his weight. Then, suddenly, he was inside her. At that moment, for Darlene everything seemed to slur into nothing. The searing pain followed by the lessening of her own body's resistance to a violent invasion made Darlene acutely aware of herself. She cried, but not quietly, sobbing loudly as she feebly tried to push him away. Everything about that moment, that one, extended moment would later be drawn out a thousand times, relived whenever time seemed to slow to a crawl and filled with her thoughts whenever she found herself lost in the span of one moment. He forced her head down into the sheets. He gripped her by the shoulder and held her down with his weight. He forced himself against her, thrusting violently into her until reaching his climax, holding himself against her as he seethed and shuddered, then stilled.

Afterwards, Marcel had rolled off her, and seemed to have fallen asleep on the other side of the bed. For a while—and even she couldn't have known how long this was—Darlene stared at the ceiling, clutching at herself, gasping and gulping down air, her whole body shaking and shuddering. She felt paralyzed. The places where he'd touched her, the places where he'd roughly held her down, the places where he'd roughly entered her all seemed to burn hotly, seared into her as if she'd been branded his. She felt betrayed by her own body, by her own thoughts and feelings. The pain that seemed to writhe throughout her whole body, it coursed through every vein and pulsed along every nerve, even as there was a part of her that sought to compel her to return to the man who'd caused her that pain, the worst pain of her life. After some time had passed, she was still hardly able to move. But there was something, in the darkness of the night, that made itself abundantly clear to her, even in her detached state. It was the vague sensibility that came from the negative space, from the darkness pierced by the light slanting through the blinds to the smell of human sweat lingering in the air along with the stinging scent of vodka, always the vodka. Although both her sons had heard what'd happened, had seen at least part of what'd been done to her, she'd never ask them anything about it. There was a small part of her that still loved him, even then. She'd never admit it to anyone, but there was a small of her that'd love him, that'd love him for the rest of her life. It'd be that part of her that she'd come to hate more than any other.

It wasn't immediately but some time after that she'd make the decision to leave her husband and take her two young sons with her. It took her some time to come up with a plan, even after she'd made that all-important decision. It'd be a few months before she'd finally break free, before she'd take into that shelter for a few days before moving back to Vancouver. In that time, he'd rape her again, and again, and again. He'd beat her again, and again, and again. By the time she made the decision to break free, little would've changed. But that wasn't the point of it, not to Darlene. The exact moment she'd made the decision to leave him came when he took the little porcelain heart she treasured and threw it hard against the bedroom wall, shattering it into a hundred little pieces. They were in the middle of another fight, and he went on to punch her and kick her, before raping her more viciously than he'd ever raped her before. The next day, she acted on plans she'd been working out in her mind for a few weeks. The next night, she announced she was leaving him, and the rest of it followed, in ways she hadn't expected but could've easily foreseen if only she wasn't so overwhelmed with pain. But she pushed through it. She wouldn't have done anything else, no matter how much pain and suffering it'd have meant.

1

It came quickly, as such things tend to. After meeting with Marcel quickly, he agreed to let her take the two sons and move to Vancouver. The details were to be worked out at a later date. She'd never learn why he seemed to so quickly change his position, seemed suddenly so willing to let her take the boys and leave him, only that she was happy to have finally achieved this. It'd only been about a week—a little less than a week, actually—since she'd tried to strike out on her own, since she'd told him she was intending to leave him, and in that time she'd learned to connect with someone else for the first time in years. The last night Darlene spent in that shelter, the last night there she spent restlessly tossing and turning, hardly able to sleep except in fits and bursts. The boys both slept soundly. It was unusually hot that night, with the power never failing but the air conditioning throughout the building seeming to struggle, finally failing sometime after midnight. She felt as though she had no friends. She felt as though the sudden departure of the young woman Natalie had deprived of something, somehow, in ways even she couldn't have explained. Everything was falling into place, though; everything that'd been arranged for her, by people working out of sight. Travel back to Vancouver had been secured, by way of an order from a local judge. It was all very confusing and disorienting to Darlene, who could only agree to be helped by others. But after meeting a few more times with the social worker, with that one social worker who spoke passable English, Darlene came to the belief that she had to leave. She'd always intended to leave, but when she sat in that little room with the social worker, she somehow realized it was time to go.

Finally, she left. It was the logical culmination of her days at the shelter, at the only battered women's shelter in that small provincial centre in the Saguenay region of Quebec. Taking her sons Stuart and Stephen with her, she took a bus directly to Montreal where she used what little money she had to buy one-way tickets for the three of them back to Vancouver. After all she'd been through, after all they'd been through, it felt to Darlene decidedly anti-climactic to simply pick up and leave, something she wished she'd have been able to do in the first place. She'd left, but had only begun the long and difficult journey of recovery from fifteen years of horrific torture and abuse at the hands of a monster. Whether or not Marcel was to follow she never knew. The help that'd been offered her—mostly unseen even by her—had enabled her to break free. Her leaving that shelter and moving back to Vancouver was only the beginning, of course, of an entirely new struggle, unlike anything she'd ever been through before. It was to be one of the most difficult times in her life, difficult as the others but for entirely different reasons. Regardless of the challenges ahead, it made her feel grateful to once again live among people more or less like her, among people who spoke the same language she did.

He wound up taking everything. The terms of the divorce they'd wind up settling would heavily favour him, giving him full ownership of the home they retained in Quebec, as well as both cars, leaving her only a monthly sum in child support payments. But that didn't matter to Darlene. None of it mattered, save the fact that she kept full custody of Stephen and Stuart. They'd have continued on the path they were on, and she'd have been powerless to help them if she hadn't kept them. She wanted to keep her boys out of the house of horror she'd fled, and she gave Marcel whatever he wanted to make that happen. By the time the divorce was finalized, she'd already made something vaguely resembling a life for herself and her sons back in Vancouver, having found work as a transcriptionist at a clinic not far from the old hospital where she'd worked before moving to Quebec. It was difficult at first to adjust to life back on the job after having been out of work for so long, but she became fortunate enough to have co-workers and a manager who were supportive. The times when she had to leave in the middle of her shift to tend to one crisis or another or the times when she needed a moment, only a moment, always a moment, to head to the break room or outside to keep herself composed. Even still, throughout those times she'd never forget about that young woman Natalie, wondering what became of her, as well as the others she saw or spoke to in the shelter. There were a lot of people she wondered about, a lot of people she wasn't to have heard in all the years she struggled to raise two boys on her own, two young men who took such radically diverging paths. Eventually, Stuart would graduate from university and go on to get his master's degree in psychology, then enrolled to earn his doctorate at the Memorial University of Newfoundland. But Stephen, Stephen would wind up confused and disoriented, each step he took only making more disoriented and confused.

In a lot of ways, the city she returned to hadn't changed a bit from the city she'd left. But that became less important, as she put together the very beginnings of a life for herself and her two sons. Finding an apartment and a job, those were the most essential but in many ways the easiest things for her to accomplish. That first night after she and the boys had gotten off the plane in Vancouver was spent sleeping at a motel. Soon after, Darlene reconnected with Cherise, then moved out of the motel and into Cherise's place. Her long-time friend lived a little further out, driven out of the city of Vancouver itself by sky-high rents and horrible traffic, but was still close enough to offer that critical support she needed. She had no one else. She had no one else anywhere near the city, no one else anywhere in the world. But after her time in the shelter, after her sudden and unceremonious escape from a life of sadistic torture and sexual abuse, she somehow found herself able to recommit to something she'd never have expected, never have seen coming. At night, some nights, she bolted upright, still asleep as she fought for her life against something that wasn't there. Sometimes, every now and then she woke up one or both of the boys. It rapidly became impossible for her to imagine anything other than an evil lurking in the darkness, even the darkness of her own home, stalking her, waiting for the perfect moment to strike.

Even still, the terror and the horror of those nights spent in that shelter restlessly wondering her future would continue to shape her thoughts and feelings for many more years, for the rest of her life, recovery never to come quite the way she might've hoped. It was in this frame of mind that the young Darlene would come to strike out on her own, graduating from university and taking up work at Vancouver General Hospital as a nurse. The shifts were long and arduous, and required frequent overtime. Even still, she felt as though she'd made progress, even in her early twenties still having become something better than nothing at all. But there was something missing from her life, she thought. There was something missing. The first time her father, Wayne, came to visit her in Vancouver after she'd graduated from university, he'd been more casual. This time, he seemed to be preoccupied with something from the moment Darlene met him at the ferry terminal. He said, "I don't regret anything I did with your mother, because she gave me you." And all she could say to her father was, "I promise I won't end up like her." But this prompted her father to say, "that's good to hear, but sometimes these things can be hard to predict." He stopped, seeming to think, before continuing to say, "no matter what happens with your mother, she's still your mother. I don't know where she is, but wherever she is, I hope she's getting better." She didn't tell him about all the loneliness and insecurity she was facing, hoping instead to convince him that she was well. Although this wouldn't be the last time they'd speak before he died—he was still some years before the end of his life—Darlene would always look back on this particular moment as one of the last real opportunities to confess her insecurities to the one person she'd always been able to rely on.

"I have something for you," said Wayne. He gave her a small gift. She unwrapped it to find a porcelain heart. It was to be the last gift her father would give her before he died. When he died, he left her all but alone in the world, with only one real friend in Cherise. When he died, she felt compelled to try and force herself to reach out any a connection, any connection at all. It was under these circumstances that she started going to bars and clubs, with co-workers or with anyone she could reach out to. It was under these circumstances that she met Marcel. What followed after that would dominate her life for as long as she lived. Even by the time she made it out of that shelter and found her way back across the country, she could only make it belatedly to her father's grave for the first time since his death. He'd died just after Darlene had moved with Marcel and the boys to Quebec, and Marcel hadn't let her go to the funeral. He hadn't let her go. Even at the time she was aware of how horrible it was for him to deny her attendance to her own father's funeral, but she couldn't have done anything about, so afraid as she was of angering him. This would haunt her for the rest of her life. She'd go to her father's grave at least once a year after moving back to Vancouver, sometimes with their sons at first but increasingly alone as they got older. Sometimes she'd lay flowers, but mostly she'd just sit and talk to him. It became stronger than any therapy or medication she could've ever imagined, standing in the rain in front of her father's grave asking only for him to listen. And she thought he always seemed to listen, somehow.

3

The truth was that Stephen, for his part, had anguished for many years over the lasting effect of his father's abuse, privately attributing nearly everything that went wrong in his life to the abuse. By the time he announced to Darlene that he was really to become a woman, there'd been no turning back, nothing to help repair him into a healthy and functional member of society. Although Darlene would never give up on him, there'd come a point when she'd eventually have to accept that she couldn't do anything more, and that point came not long after he'd made his announcement to her. It was an afternoon, a moment on one rainy Vancouver afternoon when Darlene had been invited to a late lunch with some friends. Having recently started making the effort to connect with people, Darlene had found it difficult but rewarding when she'd worked her way into a couple of different, partially overlapping circles. Eventually, like many of his peers Stephen would find himself in a dark, dark place, in this dark, dark place Stephen would come to the determination that he was, in fact, Stephanie, that he'd been Stephanie all along. Darlene knew this wasn't the case; she knew her son. But she also knew he was suffering, that she was at least partly responsible for his suffering. She felt trapped by decades of terror and sexual assault. She felt frozen, unable to move forward, condemned always to look back and relive every moment of everything she'd endured. But at one point or another—and she didn't know when that point came—she could only make the conscious decision to press forward, always to keep moving forward, towards something she couldn't see.

No matter what happens, Darlene resolved, she'll be there should Stephen realize the mistake he's made, the mistakes he's made. She wouldn't hear from him for a very long time; she still hasn't heard from him. Every now and then she reaches out to him, somehow, someway, never hearing back but always trying anyways. From time to time she asked Stuart whether he'd heard anything, whether he knew anything about where Stephen lived, what he was doing, whether he was still managing to survive. But Stuart never knew either. Like Marcel, Stephen seemed to simply disappear. Unlike Marcel, she always wanted to have Stephen back in her life, even if he insisted on living a lie, on referring to himself as something other than what he was, something other than what she knew him to be. It hurt her more than she thought it possible to hurt, to be cut off from one of her children, to be so completely incapable of just reaching out and touching him at any given moment. She'd never know what Stephen had been through at his father's; Stuart would never say anything. Even if asked, Stuart would probably say that it never occurred to him to say anything. It was just the sort of thing that happened when they were younger, and that he never thought anything of his older brother being invited to share a bed with their father, with their sexually confused, mentally deranged father, with their father who'd totally allowed a fetish to take over every aspect of his life. None of that would've mattered to anyone, least of all to Darlene. She couldn't have changed the past, even if she'd known all about it.

Although Darlene had succeeded in breaking away from Marcel, she'll probably never be able to completely overcome the lasting effects of the years of sexual torture and abuse. This is something she's come to accept after so much difficulty and soul searching. Last she'd heard, Marcel moved from Quebec to someplace in Southeast Asia; either Thailand or Cambodia. She imagined he'd chosen to do so in order to gain easier access to a sexual culture where he could do what he wanted with young boys or girls. But she had no way of knowing this. And she certainly had no way of seeking justice for everything that'd been done to her. Justice wasn't even a part of it, in anyone's mind. Justice simply didn't figure into it at all. She could only put her head down, turn into the wind, and put one foot in front of the other to pull herself through each and every day. As she'd watched her boys get older and follow dramatically diverging paths, she came to the firm belief that she'd done everything she could even as she knew that couldn't have been true. The city, meanwhile, seemed to grow in parallel with her boys, seeming steadily more assured of itself even as it grew more and more confused. Sometimes Darlene saw expensive cars cruising through their neighbourhood; this took place around the time that a variety of new condo developments were begun. Sometimes they took only months to complete from the time when construction fences went up and crews began spending hours each doing as little work as possible. Then the buildings opened and the expensive cars started parking immediately outside the little townhouse she now came to live in all alone.

Finally, she went to Cherise's wedding, held at a church in a city outlying Vancouver. It was a small wedding, with around fifty guests. Darlene was offered the chance to be one of Cherise's maids of honour, but politely declined, citing her own difficulties in handling such a responsibility. This wedding came only some months after Stephen had told her he intended to become a woman, and all she wanted to do by this time was find some way to break through to him, even after she'd all but given up on finding him again. The wedding was small and simple, attended by around a hundred people, not unlike the small and simple wedding Darlene once had. Although Cherise was Darlene's only friend, Darlene wasn't Cherise's only friend. It was a little awkward and uncertain for Darlene to go to a place filled with people she didn't know, and she became acutely aware of her own discomfort even as she drove up to the church and saw the parking lot filled with cars. But she managed to put aside her own fears and anxieties to be there for one of her closest friends.

At the reception after the wedding, a young woman Darlene didn't know went up on stage and sang with the band. Darlene thought the young woman looked to be eighteen or nineteen, not much younger than she'd been when she'd first struck out on her own. Although Darlene knew nothing about the young woman, still she imagined what the young woman might've been like, what the young woman might've had in store for her. (She'd later learn the young woman's name was Maxine). In her mind, Darlene analyzed the possibly similarities of young Maxine's life to her own, all the things the young Maxine might had yet to go through. It never occurred to her that the

344

Darlene

young Maxine was on a different path than the path she'd been on. The young Maxine seemed full of hope and promise. Darlene thought she might've been destined for something vaguely resembling the terror and the horror she'd been through, and wanted to warn her, somehow, someway. But it was all imaginary, all futile. Even Darlene could appreciate that she knew nothing of the young Maxine. She saw only herself in the young Maxine's place. As she watched Maxine sing, a part of her wanted to warn the young woman about the world she was coming of age in, the world that seemed to care so little about people like them.

At the end, Darlene went to go get a drink from the open bar. The bartender asked what she'd like, and she almost asked for a straight shot of vodka. But she wound up taking a glass of coke, walking back to her table. She stayed a while longer, pausing occasionally to chat with one person or another. It made her feel awkward and uncertain to be surrounded by such a crowd of people she didn't know. But she hung in there. "How long have you known the couple?" asked Martin. Darlene paused for a moment, but only for a moment. In that moment, there were a lot of different, contradictory feelings she had to deal with. "I've known Cherise for many years," she said. He seemed nice enough, smiling and relaxed as he contented himself to talk with her from a few feet away, never trying to get too close, never seeming to try and cross any personal boundaries. They chatted for a little while, then a little while longer, Darlene managing to relax a little as the

345

afternoon went on. Before the reception was over, they exchanged phone numbers. She found herself able to look beyond the moment and imagine something besides the unrelenting terror and horror she'd been through nearly every day of her life since she was so young. And to Darlene, that was enough.

The End

Darlene

A Note From the Author

Thank you for reading this novel. You can follow me on my website, jtmarshauthor.com, where you can find updates on current books, as well as essays and other content.

If you enjoyed reading this book, please consider leaving a review on the website of the retailer where you purchased it.

CPSIA information can be obtained
at www.ICGtesting.com
Printed in the USA
LVHW050248161121
703455LV00009B/731

9 781989 559260